SILVER BATAL

RACE FOR THE DRAGON HEARTSTONE

K. D. HALBROOK

HENRY HOLT AND COMPANY

NEW YORK

FLOATILLIAN

Henry Holt and Company, *Publishers since 1866*
Henry Holt® is a registered trademark of Macmillan Publishing Group, LLC
120 Broadway, New York, NY 10271 • mackids.com

Library of Congress Control Number: 2019949484
ISBN 978-1-250-18109-1

Our books may be purchased in bulk for promotional, educational, or business
use. Please contact your local bookseller or the Macmillan Corporate and
Premium Sales Department at (800) 221-7945 ext. 5442 or by email at
MacmillanSpecialMarkets@macmillan.com.

First edition, 2020 / Designed by Liz Dresner
Printed in the United States of America by LSC Communications,
Harrisonburg, Virginia
10 9 8 7 6 5 4 3 2 1

SILVER BATAL
RACE FOR THE DRAGON HEARTSTONE

GLITHERN

DECODRO

ONE

Silver Batal, World Water Dragon Racing semifinalist, dug her fists into her water dragon's snow-white mane, set her jaw, and narrowed her eyes at the smooth, glistening slide of ice before her.

Ready? Silver thought to her beloved Hiyyan, communicating mentally with the Aquinder through their special bond. In response, the water dragon let out a roar and launched bellyfirst onto the icy slide. The fur collar on Silver's cloak whipped against her ears and neck as the landscape around them blurred into a single shade of pale green. Hiyyan kept his head low and his limbs splayed out to the sides so that nothing slowed his speed as they raced over the ice on his smooth stomach.

"You'll never catch us!" Silver yelled, knowing the words would carry over her shoulder to Mele, once a cleaning girl at an inn in the royal city of Calidia, but now a friend and companion-in-hiding. Mele replied with a wordless battle cry as her own bonded water dragon, a Shorsa named Luap, slithered down the slide, almost completely flat against the surface.

Silver laughed as Hiyyan added a triumphant cry of his own: "*Huuunnnnrrrrgggghhh!*"

It was a moment to relish: Girl hearts sprinted in time with water dragon hearts; their breaths came fast, shrouding their faces in soft veils of mist.

Faster, Hiyyan, Silver urged her water dragon. *We're winners!*

Hiyyan grunted in agreement, flattened his stomach harder against the slick surface, and lowered his nose even closer to the ice.

"Not too close. Your mane is sticking . . . slowing us down." Silver glanced behind her. Mele and Luap were gaining on them. This was the first time Silver had raced against Mele, since the Shorsa had only just been freed from Calidia's royal kennel, but everyone knew Shorsas were the fastest breed in racing. And even though they struggled to walk on dry land, Luap's long, narrow body was aerodynamically suited for zooming through the water and, as Silver was now discovering, sliding across ice.

"Ha-ha!" Mele's triumphant laugh echoed off stone walls. A flash of multihued, pastel dragon hit Silver's peripheral vision. They were neck and neck.

Silver laughed back. "I've beat better racers than you before!"

"*Kwonk!*" Luap snorted indignantly and glared at Silver.

Hiyyan chuckled at the Shorsa and sent a happy wave of warmth to Silver.

"You won't this time!" Mele waved her fist in the air.

The girls dissolved into giggles that bubbled up from their bellies.

Let's finish this, Hiyyan bond-said to Silver, pressing his wings more tightly to his side to minimize wind resistance. Silver grinned, even though the cold hurt her teeth. Hiyyan's limbs were healthy and strong, well-healed after all the run-ins with cave monsters and enemy water dragons, and after the exhausting races of their last adventure. That was thanks to Nebekker—the old woman was a master of the curative arts.

Yes! We are champions, my Hiyyan. No matter where we race.

The winter world they'd called home for the past weeks sped by, so unlike Silver's desert city of Jaspaton. A wind so cold it froze Silver's hair to her temples sliced across their skin. Sharp, cool light bounced off the snow, searing their pupils. And the dark, moody mountains rose into the sky on every side of the valley they raced through. There had been many downhearted moments of late: of wishing to build warm fires but fearing the smoke would give away their position; of worrying their toes would turn blue in their soft boots that were meant for scorching sand, not snow; of a darkness at night so pure and black that Silver marveled she was even still alive at all.

But none of those things mattered now. Today, the race thrilled Silver to her core, heating her belly like the great ceramic ovens Aunt Yidla baked bread in back in Jaspaton. The memory stabbed Silver with a pang of homesickness, but she quickly shook it off.

"Watch out!" Silver and Hiyyan caught sight of a rock bursting through the ice at the same time and, together, banked to the left, swerving majestically.

Scrisshhh. Silver's heel grazed the solid surface of the icy river.

"Argh!" Silver heard Mele call out.

Mele and Luap weren't so fortunate. Hiyyan's large body blocked the rock from view until the last second, and the Shorsa didn't see it. Luap bumped against the edge of the rock and ricocheted across the flow of the ice-stream toward the riverbank before finally righting herself once more.

When one quick look assured Silver that her friends were all right, she faced forward again and pumped her fist in the air. "This race is *ours*."

They were almost to the marker they'd set as the finish line: an evergreen tree so harassed by wind that it leaned all the way across the frozen stream like an arch.

"Go, go, g—aaahhh!" Silver lurched out of her seat as Hiyyan hit a rough patch in the ice, his belly sticking long enough to pull down his head and send them both sideways. One dragon wing pitched skyward as Hiyyan scrambled to regain balance. Silver slammed into the ice as Hiyyan's weight dragged her across the frozen river.

"Unnggghhhh!" The ice scraped painfully along her thigh, but Silver held on tightly. She would not give up so easily, not even during an unsanctioned race between friends in the hinterlands.

"Let go!" Mele shouted.

"Never!"

Using all her strength, Silver clawed her way up Hiyyan's mane. *His* claws, in the meantime, scraped against the ice, emitting a screech that sent shivers up Silver's spine. She didn't know which was worse: that sound or the way the sharp ice continued to slice away at her upper leg.

"*Knawwwnk.*" Luap reached Silver and honked at her. Mele and her water dragon scowled at Silver.

4

"I'm not letting go!"

From Luap's back, Mele leaned over, her hair whipping behind her, the strands nearly frozen together. "Silver, stop!"

Silver gritted her teeth even harder. Mele could be more stubborn than a lazy herd animal, but when it came to racing, no one was more motivated than Silver. After all, hadn't it been Silver's love of racing that had gotten them into this mess—hiding in the mountains from Queen Imea with a supposedly extinct breed of water dragon plus one stolen Shorsa?

Despite living in fear of being found, Silver had been watching this particular spot in the mountain-valley wilderness for the last two weeks, ever since the first thin slivers of ice appeared at the edges of the narrow, steeply south-running stream that was an offshoot of the main river. As winter marched on, those icy ribbons had widened until Silver could walk across the frozen water one bank to the other. On this day, though, clouds had rolled in, bringing a slight warmth, along with a brief drizzle that had slickened the ice until it looked like hard candy. They'd never get another chance like this to race.

"No way! This isn't over until the finish line."

"You're being ridiculous."

"Keep racing!"

Mele's eyes flashed, but with anger or mirth, Silver couldn't tell. "Suit yourself. Enjoy losing!"

The Shorsa and her rider sank low to the ice again and sped forward, leaving Silver and Hiyyan behind in their mound of ice shavings.

"Grrruuullll," Hiyyan growled after them. As Mele and Luap slid past the finish line, Silver finally released her hold on her Aquinder and flopped onto the ice, breathless.

"Some champions we are." A shadow fell over Silver as Mele returned. "Go ahead, gloat all you want."

Mele shook her head. "You are so competitive. Here, let me see your leg."

"It's fine." But now that the thrill of the race was over, the sting of scraped and frozen skin was settling in. Silver gnawed on her bottom lip, and Mele winced as she peered at the raw spots through torn cloth.

"Let's get back to Nebekker so that she can tend to this."

Silver scrambled to her feet. "No, let's go back up. I want a do-over. We would have won if not for that rough patch."

"Obstacles are part of racing." Mele shrugged.

"I know we can beat you!"

"You lost, Silver. I guess a desert fox like you isn't suited to these frozen lands." Mele raised an eyebrow loftily and turned away. She and Luap continued down the ice stream toward the mountain caves the renegades had been hiding in.

"Rude!" Silver scooped up a handful of snow from the stream bank and tossed it in Mele's direction. The wind, with its own infuriating little laugh, blew the snow back into Silver's face.

Even Hiyyan had to chuckle at that.

"Thanks, you overgrown lizard," Silver muttered.

Two

Two days after her ice-race loss, Silver stood at the edge of a mountain cliff and shaded her eyes against the reflection of light off the low-lying clouds. Hiyyan's mother, Kirja, with her bold blue and white markings, should be easy to see against the monotony of gray that surrounded the mountains, but there was no sign of the rare Aquinder dragon on the horizon. Silver turned in one last circle, but still no Kirja. No *anything*, and for a band on the run from the Desert Nations queen and her ilk, that wasn't a terrible thing.

It had begun snowing again. Between that and the many feet of packed ice beneath her boots, Silver's toes were going numb. She scrunched her shoulders around her ears as a wind whipped through. Silver was still wearing her riding suit even though there was no chance of joining a race anytime soon. The material, woven from Kirja's lush underbelly fur, staved off some of the cold of the harsh mountain climate. Silver had begun collecting Kirja's shed fur when she started the journey into the mountains nearly a month ago, and she had just enough to make herself a pair of warm socks, too. If only her restless fingers would calm long enough to work the fibers.

For now, though, the throbbing in Silver's feet meant it was time to seek shelter again. Kirja would be back soon. It was only another trip to Herd Valley, just outside Jaspaton, to gather supplies and news. She'd done it before and would be all right. She just *had* to be.

"Can we start a fire *now*?" Huddled under a blanket in the back corner of the mountain cave, Mele huffed at Silver. After all the trudging Mele had done through the cold, her wide-set eyes were no longer glinting with laughter. Now they narrowed crankily at everyone.

"Not until we get word from Kirja," Nebekker said from the opposite side of the cave.

The old woman Silver had befriended in Jaspaton, before she'd even met Hiyyan, relaxed beside the Aquinder, sharing the warmth his body threw off. Nebekker was wrapped in the furs of the mountain animals Kirja and Hiyyan had hunted in the first two weeks of their hiding from Queen Imea and her trackers. Silver wrinkled her nose, recalling how Nebekker had smoothly cleaned the hides, covered them with the salt Kirja had fetched, and then left them to cure for days, the smell finally dissipating after about a week. The warmth was worth it. And the water dragons had enjoyed the fresh meat, but without a fire, the humans were stuck nibbling on crackers and ice-burnt dried vegetables.

"I wish I'd never come with you," Mele snapped, digging even deeper into her blanket. The days when Kirja went scouting for signs of trackers, or hunting for what little edible animal life roamed the harsh landscape, always made Mele snippy. They were hungry, they were bored, and they questioned all the choices that had led them to the northern mountains. "Luap and I were fine in Calidia."

Luap tipped her chin up and down in snappy agreement with her bonded human.

"You weren't together in Calidia," Silver reminded her. "The queen had Luap trapped."

"We should have gone straight to King A-Malusni," Mele said. For the thousandth time.

"We aren't guaranteed his protection," Silver replied. For the thousandth time. Until they had the protection of the Island Nation's king, they were waiting it out in the mountains. Silver and Hiyyan were wanted: she, for using camouin, an illegal substance that camouflaged anything it touched, and he for being an Aquinder, a banned breed of water dragon.

But as soon as Ferdi sent word to her cousin Brajon that the coast was clear, Brajon would relay that message to Silver and they'd head east, where a king just as powerful as Queen Imea could help them out.

Mele glared at Hiyyan for a moment, then turned her attention back to Silver. "*You* aren't."

Anger warmed Silver's belly the way a fire never could have, and she clenched her fists. A few feet to her right, Hiyyan stood, his body warming, too. Silver felt a flush of gratitude that she and her water dragon were of the same mind, always prepared to defend each other.

"Things are changing," Nebekker said, cutting in just as Silver opened her mouth to shout at Mele. "Especially for those with water dragon bonds. You may not be wanted the same way Silver and Hiyyan are, but for the moment, you are safer here than under Queen Imea's nose, Mele."

Mele turned her face away. "Freezing to death doesn't sound safer to me."

Silver slowly relaxed her fists and tried to keep her voice even. Fighting with her friend never got them anywhere. Besides, Mele had given up just as much as anyone else to be with her water dragon. Maybe more. All because of Silver. "Kirja will return soon, and she should have word from Brajon. The bundle we sent down will have bought us some time."

A week ago, the travelers had stumbled across a smattering of still-fresh bones in the snow. Human or animal, they couldn't quite tell—nor did they want to try to guess—but Silver had the idea to bundle a few up with fabric torn from their clothes, and even some bits of Aquinder fur. Kirja had flown it all down to Herd Valley with a note: *This is us.*

Would Brajon understand that, after he secretly assured the Batals that she was all right, he was supposed to spread word that Silver and her companions had perished at the hands of some carnivorous mountain beast? Had he even managed to arrange a mock funeral? That would be the kind of theatrical event Brajon loved. Most important, would it convince anyone looking for them that Silver and Hiyyan had perished in the mountains?

Silver was doubtful, but the bundle was only one part of their attempts to hide. Nebekker had been working on animal hide costumes so they'd look like a herd of goats climbing, but what Silver wouldn't do for a bagful of camouin! It wasn't like she could get into even more trouble using it. And Mele, former inn-cleaner, was doing a great job of covering their tracks when they moved.

But Silver knew it wasn't enough. Now that Queen Imea was aware of the existence of living Aquinder, long thought to be hunted to extinction, she was surely searching for them. Sagittaria Wonder, the greatest water dragon racer of all time, might even now be on the hunt in the mountain caves. Silver gritted her teeth and huffed her frustration. They had to get to King A-Malusni as soon as possible. Hiyyan sat again and pressed his big head into Silver's side, nearly knocking her over. She exhaled and wrapped her arm around his mane, the touch calming her.

"Here." With one gravelly word, Nebekker tossed a balled-up object to Silver.

"Socks!"

"You and your excellent fiber working skills weren't making progress with them, so I thought I'd finish them up for you."

Silver smiled and squished the fabric between her fingers, delighting in the luxuriousness. She'd never known a fiber as soft and insulating as Aquinder fur.

"And for you," Nebekker continued, sliding an even larger bundle to Mele.

Mele squealed. "Socks *and* mittens!"

Luap stuck her snout into the bundle, as though hoping for something, too.

"Sorry, Luap. I'll make something for you and Hiyyan next," Nebekker said.

"You are full of secrets, Nebekker." Silver tugged her boots off and exchanged her old socks for the new, wiggling her toes and grinning. "They're perfect."

"I could explore a whole world of ice now," Mele agreed, pulling the mittens on and pressing the palms against her cheeks.

"Let's—"

"—*not*, though," Mele finished for Silver.

Silver laughed and looked back to the cave entrance, lifting her feet in the air. She felt light and eager for adventure. Hiyyan forced his head under Silver's arm and gazed up at her with a glint in his eyes. They both wanted to get out of the cave. "The more we know about the world around us, the better off we'll be once we get word from Kirja."

"True," Nebekker said cautiously. She reached into a basket, frowning at what little food she brought forth in her hand. A bit of dried meat, a jar of pickled sea vegetables, some grains and bread crumbs.

Silver looked away, guilt springing into her chest. It was a good thing the water dragons could hunt for their meals. Hiyyan had even begun carefully bringing fish up through the river hole they'd drilled with Silver's jeweler's tool. He'd flip them onto the ice for the humans to eat, but nearly as many flopped back into the hole before Silver could wrap her half-frozen hands around their slick bodies. Besides, Silver craved pillowy bread, juicy fruits, sweet cakes. What she wouldn't do for a steaming bowl of chicken in sour cherry and pine nut yogurt sauce! *Anything* other than partially frozen, tiny nibbles of bony, raw fish and a spoonful of cold, soaked grain.

"What more do we need to know?" Mele asked. "We already know where the river is, which way is east, once we're cleared to go that direction, and that all the smart mountain creatures are hunkered down for the season. Unlike us."

Silver would not be convinced. Every day she ducked out into the ice-and-granite world to explore a little more, a little farther, a slightly different area. She was eager to return to one spot in particular: a dark hole in the ground on the edge of a glacier field. Where did that hole lead? She hoped it might be an escape route if Queen Imea ever found them. Even with the promise of King A-Malusni's protection, the path to the Island Nations would be dangerous, leaving them exposed for long stretches. If she hadn't been alone, Silver would have entered, but the moment she'd crept up to the edge of the hole, she heard Brajon's voice in her head: *Only you would slip into an ice world of the unknown. Be sensible, Silver!*

But Brajon wasn't here. Her cousin was back in Jaspaton, and Silver had to figure things out on her own. She was determined to persuade Mele to come with her. Surely *two* explorers, plus Hiyyan, were safe enough for even Brajon's approval.

Silver plucked an errant bit of fur out of one sock. "What if we found a new place to hide . . . one where we could safely have a fire?"

Silver could almost see the way Mele's ears pricked up. "Fires are too dangerous."

"But if we found a place that hid the smoke?"

A shrewd expression played across Mele's face. "Would it hide, say, the smell of hot food?"

"It might."

"There is no such place," Nebekker said. "We are safest right here. I feel Kirja . . . She is well. Tending to the task we set for her. She'll be back soon, and this is where we'll wait."

As if to emphasize her point, Nebekker replaced the meager supplies, pulled a blanket to her chin, and slumped so deeply into the side of Hiyyan that she practically disappeared into his sky-blue scales.

Silver hid a smile as she pulled her boots back on. "You stay. I'm going out there. Hiyyan?"

Let's adventure! Hiyyan got to his feet so quickly that Nebekker went sideways. She grunted and glared.

"Mele?"

Silver's Calidian friend paused, working her fingers in her new mittens. Silver watched doubt spread across Luap's face. If Mele went, her Shorsa would remain behind. Luap may have been as fast on ice as Brajon's hand reaching for sweets, but she struggled through snow. The possibility of a hot meal was too great a lure, though, and Mele finally nodded. "I'm coming."

Nebekker had never been one to keep Silver from going off, so the old woman merely said, "Be back before nightfall."

THREE

Luap took Hiyyan's place, wrapping herself around Nebekker for warmth, as Silver, Hiyyan, and Mele faced the winter world once more.

"When Hiyyan and I were exploring, we found a hole on the far side of the glacier field. I'm hoping it's a cave entrance. A safer hiding space, or maybe even part of an underground network that could get us off this mountain without being seen." Silver said, leading the party down the sloping rocks from their cave, through the river valley, and north to where dirty ice met the last of the tundra soil. The girls worked their way slowly up the glacier, steadying themselves on Hiyyan, who could dig his claws into the ice. After every few steps, they paused so Mele could sweep away their tracks with evergreen boughs.

Silver shaded her eyes against the sunlight that bounced off the ice and blinded her momentarily. Hiyyan sniffed, sussing out the trail they'd taken days before. *That way.*

Silver had never known a quiet like the one in the mountains north of her desert home. Jaspaton and Calidia were loud, bustling cities, and even her solitary moments on the dunes outside Jaspaton were met with a gentle symphony of wind, desert beetles, and shifting sand.

But snow had a way of absorbing sound, even muffling the exhale of Silver's breath. The only thing reaching her ears was the crunching of their boots and paws as the three approached the spot where Silver had seen the dark hole.

A snowflake landed on Hiyyan's nose, and he paused, lifting his face to the sky. *Smell . . . people.*

Silver stopped. *People that aren't me and Mele?*

Strangers, he responded.

The hairs on Silver's neck rose. She turned a slow circle. Objects were easy to spot in the world of white, but she didn't see anything out of the ordinary. Should they go back to the cave? The glacier hole wasn't much farther.

Close by?

"Mrrooungh." Hiyyan shrugged.

For all the beauty of the still and silent mountain air, it held challenges, too. Silver suspected that Hiyyan's senses were altered, the cold dulling his receptors, the thin air throwing off his judgment of time and space.

"We're almost to the hole," Silver said aloud, as much for Hiyyan's benefit as for Mele's.

"These are amazing." Mele was occupied with nuzzling her face into her mittens. "I could be out here all day."

Silver's heart swelled at her friend's delighted tone. "Let's find you a place to make a fire instead."

With another step, Silver felt her skin tingle. She squinted across the bleak landscape. No one was there, but it *felt* like there was. Should she call out and ask them to show themselves? Did she want to face whatever was out there? If it was nothing, would Mele think Silver had one too many frozen brain cells?

She kept her lips closed tight against the cold and marched on. When they reached the hole, Silver said with relief, "The entrance has grown. You'll fit now, Hiyyan."

"It's dark." Mele scrunched her cheeks doubtfully.

"That's good for hiding. Careful, the floor of the ice cave is a tiny jump down. Come on." Silver pushed through the opening. Her feet landed on slippery ground and shot out from under her so quickly that she ended up on her backside despite throwing her arms out to catch herself.

Hiyyan pinched his eyes closed as he snorted a laugh at Silver, sprawled in the snow. *"Hyuunkkaa!"*

"Always so graceful," Mele teased, entering behind Silver. She had no trouble staying on her feet.

Hiyyan followed last, his wings just scraping through the hole.

Above Silver, early afternoon spilled a thin line of yellow sun rays through the hole. A muted blue glow came through the ice field ceiling. There was enough light to see that they'd entered a wide space with tunnels branching out, but not enough to see where those tunnels led. The farther into the tunnel, the deeper the blue color, from pale cerulean to startlingly vibrant turquoise to deep, rich navy. All around, sharply cut edges of ice and slowly dripping icicles glittered.

"Beautiful," Mele breathed.

"And big enough for smoke," Silver added. "But we'll still want to move in farther, away from the entrance. Let's explore."

Without Silver's needing to ask, Hiyyan crouched so that Silver and Mele could climb aboard his back.

See, things, high, the Aquinder bond-said.

Yes, the view from eight feet in the sky was encompassing, but even more than that, Silver was glad for a rest. Her stomach rumbled.

"Smell any food close by?" she asked Hiyyan hopefully.

The Aquinder shook his big mane free of icicle droplets and raised his nose high, sniffing the air. Then he swiveled his neck to face Silver.

"Well?" she asked hopefully.

Hiyyan sneezed.

Silver flinched against the snot that flicked across her face. Hiyyan shook with laughter.

"Hiyyan!" Mele protested, even though she'd ducked behind Silver and barely got hit.

"Gross." It was so cold in the cave that Hiyyan's snot froze on Silver's skin and fell off in flakes.

"*Caar-shaar-shaar!*" Hiyyan laughed again, tucking his wings close to his sides to cover Silver's and Mele's legs for extra warmth.

"I don't think there's any food down here," Silver said, "but I did pick up the scent of one promising thing: salt."

"You think these tunnels lead to the sea?" Mele asked.

"Either that or there are salt deposits down here. I'm hoping for the first option, though, because that means we could travel all the way to the coast without being seen if we need to."

"Fire *and* safe travels? I feel like I'm floating on a happy cloud."

"Nah, just on a lumpy Aquinder back."

"*Harrrmph!*" Hiyyan shook his head.

After their laughter faded, Hiyyan moved into the tunnel with the highest ceiling. The way was open and clear, each dark section lasting only seconds before the ceiling thinned out again, letting enough light through that they could see a good ways ahead of them. At one point, the tunnel began sloping downward, and rock replaced as much as half of the glacial ice.

"I think we're getting closer to a space that would be safe for a fire," Silver said. She dismounted and ran her hands along the smooth, cold walls. The ceiling was mostly stone, too. "Not much chance of melting the cave in around us here. And far enough in that we could fan the smoke into the tunnels so it won't go out the main entrance hole."

"It won't be easy getting Luap down here," Mele said.

"We'll manage it together. Let's go back and tell Nebekker."

Silver pressed her cheek to Hiyyan's shoulder. Was there anything as miserable as cold food in a frozen landscape? The promise of fish roasted over a fire made her head dizzy and her mouth water.

Hiyyan turned to face the way they'd come, but he stopped halfway, his head snapping up and his muscles tensing. A low growl rumbled in his belly. Silver sat up, on alert, but it was Mele who saw it first.

"We're not the only living things down here," she whispered, pointing urgently at something over her shoulder.

FOUR

A huge, gray-furred mass slid into the chamber on its belly, just as Silver and Mele had slid down the frozen stream days before. It was twice as large as Hiyyan, but with a similarly shaped head, the scaled face clean of fur. Its mouth slowly opened to reveal a row of wide, flat teeth.

Is that a water dragon? Silver bond-asked Hiyyan. Other than its size, it didn't look particularly intimidating.

Ice. Screw. Claw.

That's when the dragon grinned its curious smile and spread its paw meaningfully. The digits were webbed, like any water dragon's, but the claws were viciously long, dagger-tipped, and cut in a swirl like one of Rami Batal's jeweling screws. Saliva gathered at the edges of its mouth.

Silver gulped. To the Screw-Claw, there was *plenty* of food in the ice caves.

"Those claws are *green*," Mele said. "Do you think—"

The Screw-Claw curled its finger joints and stiffened, ready to attack.

"I think we should run!" Silver cried. "Go, Hiyyan!"

Silver gripped Hiyyan's mane tightly, and Mele flung her arms around Silver's waist as the Aquinder bounded back through the tunnel from where they'd come.

"*Vvoooorrrrhh!*" The Screw-Claw wasn't pleased with their departure. Its deep rumble shook the very foundations of the ice cave, loosening a shower of icicles. One sliced across Silver's forearm. Three tiny blood drops appeared on her skin and immediately froze in place.

"It's gaining!" Mele shouted.

Silver glanced back, and her heart leaped into her throat. The Screw-Claw was shooting forward on its oily belly, using its claws to propel itself. It was moving much faster than Hiyyan, whose claws slipped against the icy ground as he ran.

"Why . . . can't cave beasts . . . ever be friendly?" Silver's blood pumped hotly in her ears as she struggled to keep upright on Hiyyan's bouncing back.

"Why . . . are you always running . . . into cave beasts . . . in the first place?" Mele shot back.

"We all have talents! Just a bit farther, Hiyyan," Silver panted, her voice growing thin with panic. "There's room in the first cavern to spread your wings and fly us out—aggh!"

The Screw-Claw clipped Hiyyan's rear leg with one swipe of its paw, sending the trio careening to the side. Hiyyan slid and rolled, throwing Silver and Mele off to slide across the chamber.

"Duck!" Silver screamed.

The girls flattened themselves on the ice just as the Screw-Claw swiped where their heads were a second ago. The iridescent green in the claws glowed as the dragon raised its paw again, ready to strike.

Hiyyan snarled and rushed the Screw-Claw, ramming his head against a furry flank. The Screw-Claw tumbled back but didn't lose its footing.

"*GnnAAAArrrrllll,*" the Screw-Claw roared.

"It's too big!" Mele said.

"And too agile and too *hungry*." Silver patted herself all over, but the dagger Nebekker had given her more than a month ago, before her quest to Calidia, was back in the mountain cave. *Daft as a desert beetle.*

Her eyes swept the cavern, desperately searching for some weapon or tool that could help them. Icicles glinted menacingly above, but how to reach that high? "We have to distract it."

She scrambled to her feet, sending a message to Hiyyan as she ran: *Icicles. Fall.*

Silver didn't know if Mele followed her or not; she only pressed her boots into each step she took, pumped her arms, and with a breathless movement that swept all thought of danger or terror from her mind, flung herself at the belly of the Screw-Claw.

A desert fox would have had an easier time knocking down a full-grown Jaspatonian. Silver got a face full of rancid-smelling gray fur before bouncing off the side of the Screw-Claw and landing hard on her shoulder with a crack of pain.

"Owww!" she howled. Her voice echoed back at her a hundred times. Silver raised her hands to cover her ears, but she could move only one arm. The other was twisted under her shoulder, popped out of place.

With his wings outstretched, Hiyyan roared, and a shower of icicles fell around them. Silver rolled onto her side and blocked her face, letting the ice bounce off her cloak.

Hiyyan shook his mane angrily, and the Screw-Claw shook its fur, too. It hollowed its chest and screeched over Silver, dripping saliva onto her face. With one sure motion, the Screw-Claw kicked Silver across the floor and into a frozen cavern wall.

"Ungh," Silver moaned, curling up.

Through slatted eyes, Silver watched Mele snatch up one of the fallen icicles and charge the Screw-Claw. Instead of sinking in, the tip merely bounced off the ice dragon's arm. With another screech and swipe, Mele also went sliding across the cavern to land in a heap next to a rock. She did not move; her eyes remained closed.

When Silver tried to push herself up to help Mele, pain sluiced through her ribs and into her shoulders. She collapsed, useless.

The Screw-Claw advanced on Hiyyan. The beautiful Aquinder erratically took flight, ramming his head against the cavern ceiling and releasing more icicles, but that did little to stop the Screw-Claw. It skulked toward Hiyyan, glossy black eyes flicking from Mele to Silver.

Warm. Food. That wasn't Hiyyan's thought reaching Silver's mind. It was an altogether different-feeling voice. The Screw-Claw.

"We're not your dinner," Silver yelled.

Hiyyan's ramming became more desperate. His wings slashed the cold air, his jaw clenched, his body shuddered as he hurled himself against the ceiling. On his next pass, he hit the ceiling so hard that it cracked; a thin-but-widening black line snaked greedily across the aquamarine glow of ice. The splintering sound echoed through the cavern, but it couldn't drown out Hiyyan's distressed mewl as he fell to the ground and shook his head, disoriented. Silver's vision went cloudy, as she knew Hiyyan's was at that moment.

The Screw-Claw loomed over Hiyyan. It raised its front leg. The sickly green claw flashed before it cut quickly downward and sank into Hiyyan's wing joint. The nasty talon turned once, then twice, before ripping free.

"Noooo!" Silver screamed. "Hiyyan!" Her shoulder pain intensified until fireworks dotted her vision. The Screw-Claw became a shadowy form that then started toward limp Mele.

"No," Silver said again, weakly this time. She stretched her good arm out blindly, fingers grappling for something, anything, that would slow the salivating beast. She found a large pebble, barely lifted it off the ground, and tossed it pathetically in the direction of the hulk.

Hiyyan lashed out with his hind legs, which slowed the Screw-Claw slightly, but the beast kept going. Silver let out a cry of frustration and prepared to launch herself in front of Mele . . .

Until a grand crash sent heavy, jagged blocks of ice plunging down into the cave, followed by an extraordinary burst of white sunlight. Outlined in the light was another winged beast, roaring with its mouth open to the sky, rows of razor-sharp teeth blazing.

Kirja was back!

She shook her mighty head and screamed defiantly, a battle-ready glint in her onyx-black eyes.

"HuuuGGGHHAAARRRR!"

You may not have them!

No dancing festival scarves or flapping racing banner could ever raise Silver's spirits like the majestic fluttering of Kirja's wings.

Hiyyan, too, was buoyed. He got to his feet with a snarl, dragging the injured wing to his side, ready to join his mother in battle with whatever energy he had left.

Kirja didn't wait for the Screw-Claw to react. Like a sand hawk with prey in sight, she tucked her wings close and dove. Her jaws clamped onto the Screw-Claw's shoulder, and the two tumbled to the ground, bouncing over rocks and rolling into one of the tunnel entrances as a tangle of screams and growls.

Silver had never seen Kirja fight. When Sagittaria Wonder had come for Kirja in the deep desert, Kirja was forced to stand down. Sagittaria threatened to harm Nebekker, and Kirja wouldn't risk the life of her beloved bond-human.

Now, though, Kirja had a son to fight for and nothing to hold her back. And as even Silver knew, you don't mess with mothers.

"Ffhhwwooooo!"

The Screw-Claw shot back into the entrance cavern, tumbling head over feet. Kirja strode in after. She raised herself a few feet off the ground, then dove again, this time rear talons first, heaving the Screw-Claw back toward the tunnels with a strength that belied her size.

"HiiirrRAW!"

Each time Kirja tossed her dragon opponent to and fro, more of the cave ceiling fell, slowly filling in the entrances to the other tunnels. Silver saw the Aquinder's plan clearly and was awed by her cleverness. Hiyyan, too, understood what his mother was trying to achieve and began pushing rocks and ceiling chunks to block the smallest of the entrances.

The Screw-Claw rose and shook its head, dazed and furious. Its limbs swiped the air frantically. Kirja deftly sidestepped its attacks, looking for a way to get one last grip and send the Screw-Claw into the tunnel where it belonged.

But one green claw caught Kirja, slashing her belly and coloring her silver fur red and green. Kirja grunted, slowed.

"HAccccKKK!" From the side, Hiyyan chomped on the Screw-Claw's hind leg and then got one more good bite on its front shoulder joint.

Kirja took that opportunity to wrangle the Screw-Claw's head between her back feet, whip him in a circle over the ice, and fling him for the last time back into the tunnel. Before the Screw-Claw could make its way back out, Kirja rammed the icy ceiling until enough of it had fallen to block the Screw-Claw from reentering the cavern.

Through the sliver of space at the top of the rock, Silver watched the Screw-Claw roar and bat at its frozen prison, but pain and weariness had made the ice dragon weak for the moment. This meal was not worth the effort.

Silver let out a shaky breath. "Kirja. Hiyyan."

Both Aquinder breathed heavily, their eyes piercing the Screw-Claw. A warning: *Stay where you are if you know what's good for you.*

"That won't contain it forever. We have to get out of here."

Silver sat up, her body throbbing. Her left shoulder was a tangle of unfamiliar, white-hot pain. But she'd felt the pain in her right shoulder before, back when it had popped out of its socket during their escape from Calidia. Then, she'd had Brajon with her to help ease it. Now, with Mele prone on the ground, Silver had no one.

She shook her head. No, she had *Hiyyan*. Who else did Silver need?

"I need your help to put my shoulder back into place,

26

please," she said through gritted teeth. She sent Hiyyan an image of how she remembered Brajon doing it.

"Hrumn?"

"I know, your paws are different from hands. But if you push against me and I push against you . . . maybe we can maneuver just right . . ." Silver and Hiyyan moved at the same time, thoughts connected. He braced his leg against Silver's back and pressed his chin to the front of her shoulder. Silver took a deep breath and, as she let it out, she let her body relax. Hiyyan squeezed. There was a crunch, a new burst of pain, then a rush of relief. "Ahhh. That's better. As much as better can be right now. I don't think that shoulder will ever be the same again."

Silver got to her feet and walked toward Mele, but the ground seemed to tremble. The world shifted. A swirl of dizziness hit Silver hard.

Silver lowered her head between her knees to catch her breath. Shades of blue like the seas of Calidia swam in her vision. Silver swallowed back bile and breathed slowly until the dizziness passed. "Kirja, can you carry Mele out? Good. And . . ." Silver eyed the oozing mess of Hiyyan's wing joint. "I'll have to ride you, too. Hiyyan, can you get out like that?"

Hiyyan lifted his chin determinedly, and Silver gingerly climbed onto Kirja's back.

The quartet exited, Kirja taking flight right through the opening in the ceiling, and Hiyyan carefully picking his way up a staircase of ice blocks and rocks. It was slow going back to the cave where Nebekker was waiting, and even through her pain, Silver felt over and over again the sensation that someone was following them. But each glance back revealed an unbroken ice plain. No Screw-Claw on their tail.

"Where am I?"

Silver glanced up to see Mele easing into consciousness just before they reached the cave.

"Are you all right?" Silver asked.

"I'm a bit banged up, and my head's pounding," Mele said, rubbing her temple. "But I'm okay."

Silver's relief was short-lived. As soon as they reached the opening, Nebekker burst out of the cave, her face stormy.

FIVE

Even as Nebekker ushered them inside, she lit into all of them, her concern transformed into anger.

"Of *course* you would be dragged back here like half-eaten prey! Look at these beautiful Aquinder! They're . . ."

"Healable?" Silver said hopefully.

Nebekker pressed her lips into a tight line. "Possibly. Here. You do something with this while I work on the dragons."

In spite of her fury, Nebekker flashed Silver a mischievous look and pulled a paper and a string-wrapped assortment of parcels from the large pack on the ground next to her. Silver's favorite scents filled her nose. She closed her eyes and inhaled deeply. Her stomach twisted like a wrung-out scarf.

"Fresh bread and meat pies," she whispered. "And golden cakes!" Silver unwrapped one of the packages. Inside, a sticky cake—full of the saffron, dried apricots, figs, and almonds grown in Herd Valley, just north of Jaspaton—glistened with its honey glaze. Silver took an eager bite. Tears pricked the corners of her eyes and she forgot all about her aches for a moment.

"Good food does that to me, too," Mele said, eyeing the sticky cake.

But it wasn't just the food. It was thinking about Aunt Yidla's hands, which had made the pastries, about the last time Silver had eaten one, seated between her mother and father after a large family meal. They hadn't been celebrating anything more than being together at that time, but now Silver's pang of homesickness was greater than any other ache in her body.

She broke off half the cake and passed it to Mele. The Calidian girl, too, became emotional as she dove into the delicious food.

"Brajon . . . ?" Silver asked between mouthfuls.

"Yes. Sent by way of Kirja," Nebekker said as she studied Kirja's wounds. "She'd stopped here first. But then took off almost immediately. Sensed something was wrong."

"She came just in time," Silver mumbled. She could tell Nebekker wanted to hear more, but Silver was too busy stuffing her mouth. Warm food!

"Someday, I will reward him tenfold for this," Mele mumbled, licking every crumb and sticky remnant from her fingers.

"I'm sure he'll hold you to that. It's a burden keeping up with all the trouble you two get into."

"It's good to keep him on his toes!" Silver chuckled. She dug into the pack to see what else Brajon had sent from home. Another thin but tightly woven blanket that must be from her mother, lots of dried and preserved food, paper and ink, a compass, candies, a little pouch of coins, and even a small bar of soap and a comb—Silver couldn't hold back a laugh at that; Brajon was always so concerned about hygiene.

"I love all the things Brajon sent," Silver said, "but I was hoping for some *particular* news."

"*Good* news," Mele emphasized, taking a hard candy from the pile and sucking on it.

"I have the letter here, and there's news aplenty." Nebekker nodded to a spot on the ground next to her furs. "I have to warn you: It's mostly bad."

"King A-Malusni?" Silver asked, alarmed. *Had he denied their request for protection?*

"No word at all on that, yet. But there are people out there looking for something. They're moving closer to the foothills."

Silver cringed as a sharp pain dashed up her arm. "Is it Hiyyan's turn for healing yet?"

"Almost," Nebekker muttered.

"People are coming? What kind of people?" Silver passed a cake to Hiyyan, pressing her nose to his for a moment, and gave an extra treat to Mele for Luap before taking up the parchment.

They're not wearing signs, Brajon had written, *but I'm pretty sure they're Q. I.'s people.*

A tiny smile broke through Silver's discomfort. It was a valiant attempt at secrecy, but anyone who might have intercepted the missive would have immediately known Q. I. stood for Queen Imea.

"Mercenary trackers," Mele said. Silver raised her eyebrows, and Mele shrugged. "They stayed at Mr. Homm's inn often enough. There's good money in tracking."

Mr. Homm's was one of the busiest inns in Calidia. It was also one of the closest guesthouses to the royal palace, and Mele had learned to keep her ears open and file away interesting tidbits spoken by people who didn't think much of a cleaning girl hanging around. Her encyclopedia of knowledge was random and surprising, but often useful.

"If they're trackers, that means they're better prepared and more experienced in this terrain than we are," Nebekker said. "We can't stay here much longer."

"Brajon agrees with you." Another bit of parchment, torn as though from a school essay assignment, accompanied the main letter.

> In Jaspaton, gold is common enough. And silver is even more common, plain, boring, and completely, entirely uninteresting. So what is an adventurous miner to do (besides stay HOME where it's nice and safe)?

Silver sighed when she saw that Brajon had underlined "silver" several times. Stealthy, her cousin was not.

> A legendary material might draw a miner's attention. Camouin, a fluid metal that solidifies under heat, is rumored to create invisibility, though it's more likely to use some kind of light reflection to create enhanced camouflage. According to stories, this material was used in the brutal Land and Sea Wars and is a banned substance. Those who hold it face death.
> Of course, no one has seen it in hundreds of years, and anyone with an ounce of sense knows it doesn't really exist. If they saw it, they would run.

If they touched it, they would RUN EVEN MORE from those who would track them. Even if they were presumed ALREADY DEAD.

Silver frowned. The bundle of bones hadn't worked.

"He wrote that for school?" Mele peered over Silver's shoulder, and Luap peered over Mele's. "Look at his handwriting! What a mess."

"What's a miner need great handwriting for?" Silver shot back defensively.

"Not like our ele-jeweler over here," Nebekker added.

Silver grunted. It seemed a whole lifetime ago that she was training to follow in her father's footsteps as the greatest jeweler in all the desert.

"It's good enough," Mele conceded, "to tell us it's time to move. The trackers must have just left Jaspaton. We have to take advantage of our head start. But without King A-Malusni's protection, where do we go?"

Silver said, "I still think our best move is to follow the river all the way to the summit and—"

"No," Nebekker interrupted. The old woman looked up from the salves and poultices she was mixing. "That way leads to the Watchers' Keep."

"Exactly," Silver said. "And why don't you want us to go there?"

Luap sent a tragic wail through the cave.

"Quiet," Nebekker muttered. "I need to concentrate."

In anticipation of the healing, Silver's arm thudded with a last burst of pain as Nebekker pulled out a violet pendant on a chain from beneath her cloak.

"Thank the sands Nebekker has a dragon heartstone," Silver said to Hiyyan. The Aquinder nodded in agreement, shifting his own painful shoulder to try to find a moment's comfort.

Silver watched Nebekker press the heartstone to Kirja's belly and closed her eyes. A warm breeze brushed strands of hair across Silver's forehead, and the sweet scent of a meadow filled her nostrils. Through the soft, glowing amethyst-cream light that grew out of the heartstone, Silver saw the green poison from the Screw-Claw drain down Kirja's scales and to the ground. Nebekker studied the wound, her eyebrows knitted together.

"Hmm. Too much to heal at once? I think it's clean. That's something, at least." Nebekker applied medicinal goop and a bandage, and when she was finished, Kirja tested the healing by stretching one way, then the other, and finally nuzzling her cheek to Nebekker's.

"You look like a brand-new dragon," Mele said.

"Please," Silver whispered. "Heal Hiyyan now."

Silver crouched next to Hiyyan. They locked glances, eyes mirroring pain. But there was a softness, too. A gentle love born of their bond. Silver would do anything to help Hiyyan get better. She ran her hand over his smooth snout and caught her fingers in his white mane. Hiyyan began a song of friendship in his mind and silently sent it to Silver.

It was a melody like rolling rainbow hills of wildflowers framed by a clear blue sky. In her mind, a sparkling blue stream cut through the scene, nourishing the flowers. The breeze that made the petals dance was gentle and tickling, and it bore whispers of her and Hiyyan's own friendship: how they met, how loyal they've been.

Ever since they were in Calidia, Hiyyan and Silver had been eager to learn the songs that water dragons sang to one another. Unlike her language, where Silver could simply point to an object and tell Hiyyan the word for it, water dragon language was complex. Each tune expressed a different emotion, told a unique story. Silver had learned a song of pain, a song of cold, a song of fear, a song of love, and a song of family.

All the time stuck in the mountain cave with Kirja had been well-used; Hiyyan and Silver could express themselves through the dozens of songs she'd taught them, short and long.

Hiyyan's love warmed her through, and Silver snuggled closer to him, taking care not to jostle his shoulder. Even Nebekker's rattling on as she examined the Aquinder couldn't break their spell.

"This is a terrible wound. How you manage to meet every fierce creature in existence . . ." Nebekker shook her head. "I'll heal Hiyyan, and then we'll discuss going east to the Island Nations, even if we don't have King A-Malusni's promise of help."

Silver felt in her own shoulder every poke and prod Nebekker gave Hiyyan. Girl and water dragon winced and gritted their teeth in unison. But when the light of the dragon heartstone began to fill Silver's vision, she took a deep breath, ready to be free from the poison.

Nebekker pressed the heartstone to Hiyyan's scales. The soft glow began. Silver felt the poison shift as though it were blood beneath her own skin.

Nebekker closed her eyes.

And then the heartstone light went out. Mele gasped.

"What's happening?" Silver asked.

Nebekker didn't answer. She frowned, pressed her forehead to Hiyyan's scales, and focused, her wrinkled skin flushing burgundy with effort. There was the soft violet light . . . More poison shifted, with even a dribble running down Hiyyan's side, and there was the tiniest bit of relief from the pain, but the wound refused to respond. The light went out again.

"Nebekker?"

The old woman shook her head, sitting back on her heels. Silver's breath came fast, as though knowing what terrible news Nebekker was about to deliver.

"My dragon heartstone doesn't work on your bonded dragon."

◊ ◊ ◊

SILVER CLUTCHED AT her short hair. "It should have worked. Why didn't it *work*?"

Nebekker wordlessly went to her dwindling supply of healing herbs and tonics, opening a bag and sniffing, or holding a vial of potion up to the light to study its contents. There wasn't much left of her supplies.

"But before . . ." Silver paced, stopped, put her hand on Hiyyan's side to calm herself. "After Calidia, the dragon heartstone worked on Hiyyan."

"He is young," Nebekker interrupted sternly. "His wounds weren't as—" The old woman bit off her words and snuck a glance at Silver before looking at her medicines again. "Cuts and scrapes, bruises and bone aches. That's all they were . . ."

A shadow crossed over Nebekker's face. That was all Silver

needed for her heart to fly into her throat, as though she were duneboarding from the moon itself.

"Don't worry. Nebekker is a great healer." Mele pressed her fingers to Silver's wrist. "She'll fix him up the old-fashioned way."

Silver nodded, but her heart squeezed like a gem in a vice. This was different. Cuts and scrapes . . . no. This was *poison*.

Silver ran her hand over the back of her neck. "You've seen this poison, and you know how to counteract it? Will you have enough for a dragon Hiyyan's size?"

Nebekker sighed impatiently. "Your energy is distracting. I need water. Go get some."

"But I—"

"Go!"

Silver trekked back outside, glad for the cold to numb her thoughts. Mele's boots crunched after her.

"She'll heal him," Mele repeated.

"He's suffering," Silver said. "I can't stand that he's hurt."

"What about your pain?"

Silver shrugged, but that shot sparks down her arm. Mele gave her a knowing look.

They walked the rest of the way to the river in silence, but after Silver had hacked away enough ice to fill the jug, she whispered, "Do you think Screw-Claw poison kills?"

"It looks pretty bad."

Mele could have said a lot of things to reassure Silver, but instead she went with brutal honesty. Silver appreciated that.

"I can't imagine a world without Hiyyan. And with our bond . . ."

Such was the power of a bond: that a dragon and a human

could not long exist without the other. A world without Hiyyan meant a world without Silver.

Mele set her mouth into a firm line. "Stop thinking that way! Of *course* Nebekker will heal Hiyyan. Her talent is without measure. And he has youth, strength. Just as Nebekker said."

Silver nodded, a flicker of hope erupting into a flame. "You're right. He might even be healed by the time we get back!"

But when Silver and Mele reentered the cave, the silence that blanketed its inhabitants was thick with worry. Nearly all of Nebekker's bottles and bags were empty. Kirja was arranging a blanket over Hiyyan. And Luap was sniffling as though death was imminent.

Silver set the water jug at Nebekker's feet. "Please tell me he's better."

"Healing takes time," Nebekker snapped. She closed her eyes, weary. "I have done what I can. We will know more in the morning. Now, sleep is the road to health for us all."

Silver shared a look with Mele. They had been dismissed, and all that was left to do was follow in Nebekker's footsteps, wrap their furs and blankets tightly, and sleep off their wounds.

◊ ◊ ◊

IN THE MORNING, Hiyyan was worse.

"We have to do something, Nebekker!" Silver patted over Hiyyan's scales, feeling the feverish heat of him. His wound oozed more than before, and his pain was greater. Silver knew this because her pain had increased, too.

Her mind worked frantically. If Nebekker's heartstone

couldn't heal Hiyyan, and Nebekker's tinctures couldn't heal Hiyyan, and strength and youth couldn't heal Hiyyan, then what?

"For Kirja, the heartstone is an antidote," Silver said frantically, pacing the cave. Mele followed after her, trying to calm her down.

Nebekker shared a look with Kirja, who was patiently sniffing Hiyyan's wounds, performing her own health check.

Nebekker grunted. "That's a special case, and you know it."

"But then why can't we just find a heartstone for Hiyyan?" Mele asked.

Silver whirled around. "Mele, you're a genius!"

Nebekker scowled at Mele. "It's not so easy just to find one. I've had mine for years, and even I'm not entirely sure about the nature of the stone or what it's capable of."

Silver paused next to Hiyyan, frowning, her palms hovering over his wound. She knew dragon heartstones were mysterious objects. Little understood. Nebekker had said before that she couldn't really even remember how she'd obtained hers. But Silver knew one thing for certain.

"At this point, even if we got word from Ferdi, Hiyyan could never make it to the Island Nations. No. We're going north," Silver declared firmly. Hiyyan nodded in agreement. "For two reasons: If there's an antidote in nature, the Watchers will know about it. They're the closest human settlement to the Screw-Claw. Also, they're bastions of sharing information. They'll tell me everything they know about heartstones and how I can get one of my own."

Schoolchildren in the Desert Nations learned a few facts about the Watchers to go along with the strange rumors: how they were the keepers of knowledge and history, charged with sharing that knowledge freely; how they were responsible for choosing the ruler of the deserts when needed; how their Keep in the vast northern reaches was a place of political neutrality and welcomed all.

"But what if our enemies are waiting for us there?" Mele asked.

Silver drew her eyebrows together. No one had ever referred to Sagittaria Wonder or Queen Imea as her enemy. She didn't like the sound of it. She hated even more the whimper of pain Hiyyan was trying to hold back, but couldn't.

Kirja shuffled closer, letting Hiyyan lean against her. Guilt rose in Silver's chest. Not just her own for getting everyone into so much trouble, but a wave of emotion from . . . Kirja? Silver caught the mother Aquinder's eye, but Kirja looked away quickly. She seemed to feel some responsibility for Hiyyan's injury, as though she should have gotten to the ice cave sooner.

"It's a risk we have to take. Either way, the Watchers won't turn us over to the queen. We could find shelter there while we plan our next move."

Mele went over to Luap, putting her arms gently around the Shorsa's neck. "Some of us could find shelter there even longer than that. Or did you forget that I'm wanted by the queen, too?"

The Shorsa caught Silver's eye and raised her chin regally in the air. Even though Mele was, like Silver and Nebekker, bonded to her water dragon, Luap legally belonged to Queen Imea. When Mele decided to flee from Calidia with Silver, she became a thief.

Silver had promised Mele freedom and safety, but she hadn't delivered on that promise. Yet. Silver didn't like what

Mele was hinting at: that Mele and Luap would stay at the Keep even if Silver moved on.

"We'll have to wait," Nebekker said, standing near the cave entrance. "An unexpected southerly wind is picking up, and it's bringing sleet this way."

"Which means the path will be even more treacherous than usual," Mele said.

"That's true for everyone else, too," Silver said.

Nebekker clicked her tongue against the roof of her mouth.

"We must go. Or we must resign Hi—*ourselves*—to dying here." Silver jammed every possession—double-checking for her dagger—into her weather-worn leather bag, then rolled her blankets and buckled them to the harness Kirja would wear. She massaged her shoulder but couldn't shake off the pain.

Nebekker marched over, her long gray hair swaying, and kicked the harness across the cave floor. "Kirja and I are not going to the Keep. She's wounded, too."

A quiet growl rolled from Kirja and Silver felt another wave from her, this time cold and angry. Anger toward Silver? Mele cleared her throat, looking at Kirja's belly pointedly. The mother Aquinder's wound had closed in the night, the long split in her skin sealed by new scales.

Silver narrowed her eyes. "You'd leave us here to die on this mountain, just like you did your friend Arkilah?"

In any other circumstance, Silver would have bitten her tongue until it bled before speaking to an elder with such a tone. She knew Nebekker's abandonment of her old friend was painful history. But this was life or death, and Nebekker was simply being stubborn.

Silver rushed on. "We have more supplies now. With

trackers crawling over the mountains, which is the better option: wait to be found, or see if the Keep holds an antidote to Screw-Claw poison?"

Nebekker cleared her throat, ready for her next argument, but she paused when Kirja craned her neck around to glare at the old woman. Hope rushed into Silver's heart. Kirja was on her side! The two bonded elders stared each other down for several seconds. Kirja's nostrils flared while Nebekker's wrinkles slowly smoothed as she sat back in resignation. Kirja was, after all, Hiyyan's mother. Silver fetched the harness and held it out to Nebekker.

Nebekker sighed deeply, finished gathering her items, took the harness from Silver, and attached it to Kirja. "We'll take the river up. It goes nearly as high as the Keep. Silver, you ride with Mele to alleviate the strain on Hiyyan. It's a lot of weight for Luap, but we'll be carrying the supplies, as well as assisting Hiyyan."

"As long as we'll be back in the water," Mele said happily.

Nebekker took Silver's bag and attached it to Kirja. "The freezing water."

"A temporary condition," Mele said loftily. "But then, warmth! Hot food, fires, snuggling into thick blankets. Do you think there will be tea at the Watchers' Keep? I have missed tea."

Nebekker hesitated. "It's no Calidian Inn, but it's surprisingly well-stocked."

Silver joined Mele at the cave entrance, pressing her shoulder against her friend's. "Thank you, Mele. I hope there is more tea than you could drink in a lifetime."

Mele rewarded Silver with a smile. "How far do you think they are?"

"The mercenaries?" Silver frowned. "It depends. We have no way of knowing when Brajon wrote his letter. They could still be at the base of the mountain or moments away."

"So it's a race to the Keep," Mele said. "Your favorite thing, Desert Fox."

Silver smiled at her friend. "And I race to win."

Six

As the band of six reached the riverbank, the humans climbed on the healthy water dragons and dipped into the current. The frozen layer of ice at the edge of the river crackled beneath their feet.

Silver tucked her feet high and held onto Luap as best as she could, but two riders on the small Shorsa was awkward. She and Mele were just barely able to stay out of the water, even with Luap's swimming as upright as she possibly could. It wouldn't be long before they were soaked through and half-frozen. But it didn't matter. Getting Hiyyan to the Keep as quickly as possible was what mattered. Silver beckoned for him to stay close to her.

The Aquinder tucked his sore wing into his body and settled into the water. Just the little bit of movement from the cave down the slope to the river made his vision—and by extension Silver's—blur around the edges.

Silver sent him all the feelings of warmth and comfort she could muster. *Soon, my Hiyyan.*

Traveling upriver was slow and strenuous. The current

wasn't as fast as it would be in the spring, but the water still rushed downhill to meet the lush greenery of Herd Valley before diving underground through the desert, meeting the seas past Calidia on the far end.

Kirja looked over regularly, assessing her son's ability to keep up. The water dragon caught Silver's eye with a look of a shared mission.

Must. Heal.

Silver gritted her teeth and tried to drive her thoughts elsewhere.

How long would it take to get to the Keep? Silver spared Nebekker a frustrated glance. She would ask the old woman, but Nebekker kept her secrets. Nebekker's time at the Keep was shrouded in mystery, but then most everything about the Watchers was.

Beyond that, nobody knew what else the Watchers did, how they were picked, why they didn't also choose rulers in other regions—the Island Nations, for example, was a monarchy—and whether they really could do any number of rumored tricks: read minds, stop time, even communicate with the ancient goddesses. That last bit was something Silver had heard from a trader passing through Jaspaton years ago, but nobody believed it to be true.

Then again, nobody had believed Aquinder existed, either.

Silver nibbled the inside of her mouth as the roar of the river grew.

The river banked sharply to the left, around a field of tall boulders. Luap's muscles went taut.

"*Kccclut!*" she called out.

A barrage of white water met the group, pounding against their sides and sending them spinning.

"Turn, Luap!" Mele yelled. She struggled to keep hold of her water dragon, and Silver struggled even harder to keep her arms around Mele. Waves leaped over boulders and slammed back into the river.

The Shorsha waged a losing battle against the mighty flow of what Silver now realized was the main conduit down the mountain.

"No," Silver groaned. They'd only been on a tributary. The going would get even more strenuous from now on. Silver and Mele both leaned their bodies up-mountain, hoping their shifting weight would help Luap face the right direction once more.

"We're losing ground! *Swim*, Luap!" Mele clenched her jaw. Silver turned her face from the frigid spray that stung her eyes and lips. The river churned and forced them backward.

"Gah!" Suddenly, Silver's stomach rushed to her throat, and the world fell away beneath them.

"Waaah!" Mele yelled, pointing wildly. "We're going over a waterfall!"

"AAIIEEE!" Silver shrieked. She caught a glimpse of Kirja rising into the air. As they were swept helplessly over the waterfall, Silver's arms clenched around Mele, and Mele's arms clenched around Luap's neck. The Calidian girl's scream was cast away into the thin mountain air.

"Hiyyan!" Silver flung her arm out toward the Aquinder, as if she could catch him midfall.

"Wwrraaahhrr!" Hiyyan roared as he instinctively flapped his wings, only to tip sideways when only one wing responded properly.

Time seemed to slow, the flinging water like flashing crystals tossed into the sky, the pressure of dropping like a murderous hand pressing the life out of Silver's chest, the battling roars—Hiyyan's, the river's, the air's—exploding in Silver's ears. And then Luap, too, tilted sideways. The last Silver saw of Hiyyan was his head hitting the swirling vortex below, followed by the rest of his body.

"Hiyy—!" Silver's scream was cut off as she, too, was plunged into the river.

Silver slid down Luap's back as the Shorsa unraveled her tail to push to the surface. Silver clung to Mele's tunic, hoping it didn't tear and leave her to flounder in the frigid water. She couldn't feel her feet, her nose, the tips of her fingers. But still she held tight as Luap brought them back to the surface.

"Help," Silver moaned as they crested.

"I . . . can't . . . get hold." Mele's teeth chattered, and her hands slipped and slid over the makeshift reins crisscrossing Luap's neck.

Silver's body quaked with cold, but she dug her hands into Luap's side and held on. Where was Hiyyan?

The river water was white and angry, racing over and around rapids created by boulders and downed trees.

"Hang on!" Mele shouted.

"I'm trying!"

"Wrraahhrr!"

It took a moment for Silver to realize that the next roar she heard wasn't water, but Kirja overhead. The Aquinder's talons hovered close to Silver in an attempt to pluck her out of the river, but Silver shook her head, droplets flinging from her hair. "Find Hiyyan!"

"Let go, Silver!" Nebekker shouted.

Silver flung her head back and gritted her teeth. "Hiyyan first!"

Another drop in the river yanked Silver forward again. Pain

seared across her upper shoulders, but Silver redoubled the tightness of her grip on Mele and pulled herself up Luap's tail. The river's pace would let up soon, wouldn't it?

Silver's ankle banged against a rock, and she sucked in a breath. Her leg pulled up instinctively, tipping the weight on Luap.

"Aaaghhh!" Mele screamed, her hands scrambling for purchase.

"Kccclut, Kccclut," Luap clicked. Her feet and tail circled madly to regain balance, but Silver and Mele went straight into another rock, swirled twice around a small whirlpool, and, finally, were thrown from the Shorsa's back toward the riverbank.

"Oomph!" Silver landed on her shoulder, crushing through a layer of thin ice. Mele tumbled farther down, her body rolling several times, before being spit out into the snow. She pushed herself up to all fours before coughing up the little food she'd eaten that morning.

"Mele?" Silver asked weakly. Then she raised her head and sent her thoughts in another direction, scanning the river for emotion and warmth. "Hiyyan?"

Mrraw.

It was a delicate sound, coming from across the river, right into Silver's heart, warming her from head to toe. Hiyyan was all right.

"Good," Silver croaked before letting her head hit a pillow of snow once more.

◊ ♡ ◊

STAY AWAKE, SILVER.

"Mom?"

Get the furs around her—hurry!

How many times did I say we shouldn't come here?

About as many times as I said we shouldn't be in these horrible mountains at all.

Quiet. Silver. Talk.

"Hiyyan?" Silver mumbled.

"Hiyyan's fine. As fine as he can be. But your fingers are gray." That was Mele, her voice thick with worry.

"Silver," Silver replied. "I'm Silver all over."

"This is no time for jokes." She heard Mele sigh.

A warm, velvety object nudged Silver's cheek, and her lashes finally fluttered open. Hiyyan's big eyes looked down at her.

"Hello, friend," Silver whispered, reaching up to rub his mane. Then, she glared at Nebekker. "Why didn't you warn us about the waterfall? We weren't even on the main river!"

"I haven't taken this route in many years. Landscapes shift on the mountain quicker than even desert dunes."

"The boulders that divided the river in two were probably part of a landslide," Mele added. As if to prove her point, a smattering of pebbles tumbled raucously down the mountain to their left.

Silver's frown deepened, but she said no more.

"You'll ride with me," Nebekker told Silver. "Sorry to saddle you with more weight, Kirja, but we have to keep moving. They're here."

"Who?" Silver said, trying to sit up.

"The mercenaries." Mele pushed Silver's body onto a fur and rolled it around her.

"So quickly?" Silver remembered the feeling of being followed from the day before. Her glance shifted left to right across the silvery forests beyond the riverbanks as Mele helped Silver to her feet and deposited her on Kirja's back. She'd assumed it had been the Screw-Claw waiting for dinner, but now it seemed more likely it was the trackers, close enough to reach out and snatch them up for Queen Imea.

"Don't fall off," Mele said.

Silver caught Hiyyan's eye again and probed his senses. He was picking up all kinds of unfamiliar smells in the forest, but the familiarity of human scent hit her hard. They would be found soon.

"Can you go on?" Silver asked Hiyyan, as though he had a choice.

The Aquinder raised himself to full height, shaking his thick mane to throw off crystalline droplets of water. His muscles were taut and ready, but Silver frowned when he tried to tuck his wounded wing into his side only to have it droop uselessly, the tip dragging in the snow.

Soon, Silver told her Aquinder. Her favorite word to him.

Nebekker mounted behind Silver, and they pushed on, this time with all of them in the river, Kirja leading with a determination cultivated through age and endurance.

Mele fretted over Luap. "She's a tropical dweller. She's not meant for these temperatures."

Silver overheard Mele making promises to spur her Shorsa on: *roaring fireplaces, cozy blankets, dryness.* They were always making promises to their water dragons, Silver and Mele and Nebekker. If only they could keep them.

Hiyyan continued on bravely, and when he fell behind, Silver closed her eyes and, in her mind, sang to him the lullabies her mother sang to her when she was little. She sang until his body relaxed and his legs swam in a gentle but consistent rhythm.

"Do you think they've been able to track us up the river?"

Silver asked at one point, breaking a silence that had endured for an hour at least.

"It's the most difficult way to track," Nebekker said. "But they'll also know it's the most likely way for us to travel."

"Since it's the most direct route," Mele said, gripping onto Luap as the Shorsa half leaped, half swam against the cruel current. "Though not the fastest."

Silver probed Hiyyan's senses again, but this time the sharpness of cold air was all she picked up. "What do we do once we've reached the Keep? Any hope that we'll be the only ones there is gone."

"Let's figure that out once we've arrived. I can't think. My brain is frozen," Mele said.

A litany of jokes about Mele's frozen brain sat on the tip of Silver's tongue, but she was too exhausted to banter. Instead, she faced forward again and searched the rising mountain for any sign of buildings or paths.

As the sun fell, the light in the river canyon took on a sapphire-and-amethyst splendor.

"Look," Silver said, pointing above their heads.

Icicles sparkled like gemstones, and the canyon walls twinkled with tiny, embedded crystals. The world felt like a fabled nighttime mystery.

"It's beautiful." Mele nodded appreciatively. "Like nothing I've ever seen before."

"I've never seen *those* before," Silver added.

She gazed upon a group of creatures at the riverbank stopping for a sip of water. They were furred, like the Screw-Claw, but spotted white and blue and about the size of the Abruq water dragons Silver saw in Calidia. Small enough to carry in her arms, but big enough to be a nuisance. Instead of trumpeting horn snouts like the Abruq, these creatures—water dragons, Silver was certain, judging by their webbed feet and long tails—had snub noses and tall ears that turned to and fro to take in all the sounds in the river canyon. Now, they listened as Silver and her friends paddled past.

"Cute!" Mele said.

"They're Snuckers," Nebekker said from her perch. She rubbed her hands together for warmth as she eyed the dragons. "I've seen a herd of them take down healthy adult moose with ease. Let's move faster."

On cue, each of the dozen or so Snuckers on the riverbank grinned at Silver, baring a row of v-shaped teeth, their eyes flashing orange in the dying light. Silver shuddered, especially when they turned their gazes to Hiyyan, who continued to bring up the rear of the group. One Snucker licked its maw.

"Don't even think about it," Silver yelled. She clenched all her muscles, trying to send Hiyyan some strength. She wasn't sure if it worked, or if it was those Snuckers pawing the ground restlessly, but Hiyyan put the last reserves of his energy into his swimming, catching up to and bypassing Mele's Shorsa.

"Hey!" Mele frowned and glanced over her shoulder.

Silver pulled out her dagger, her senses on alert. "You stay in the middle, Hiyyan. Nebekker and I will bring up the rear."

Nebekker grunted her displeasure but nodded. "Pick up the speed, everyone. If we're still in the canyon when night falls, the Snuckers *and* the mercenaries will be the least of our worries."

Just then, some high-mountain creature sent a howl into the thin evening air. All the hairs on Silver's body stood on end. Her eyes scanned the cliff tops, but every tree loomed, hiding secrets under its branches, and every shadow creeped in the dying light. Anything could be up there.

"When will we get to the Keep?" Silver asked.

"By tomorrow afternoon, if all goes well."

"We should move through the night," Mele said. "If it's so terrible here, why stop?"

"Did you bring skate bones to tie to your boots and a sled for Luap? The river freezes at night. See?" Nebekker pointed at the ice that was spreading from the riverbank into the center of the river. "We have little time left to travel tonight."

Mele made a low sound in her throat. "And Shorsas aren't made for walking on land."

"*And* Hiyyan needs rest," Silver added.

Mele hitched her bag higher on her shoulder and sighed. "Why do I have the feeling I'm never going to get to the Keep?"

SEVEN

Silver remembered the distinct feeling of being stalked from a couple of months ago. Then, it had been a rattling white cave monster following Brajon and her through the river caves, wanting to make them its next meal. Now, though, she didn't know if it was the Snuckers keeping a close eye on Silver and her friends, the trackers hot on their trail, or that thing that howled in the night and made her nose wrinkle with metallic smells laced with danger.

"This way," Nebekker said, holding her lantern higher and waving everyone forward. The light created deep shadows on her face and glinted off her pupils, dilated with determination.

When it had gotten too dark and icy to continue swimming upriver, the party had tiptoed over the growing edges of crackling frozen water, testing each plane before putting their weight fully into their feet. Once on the riverbank, they searched for a place to rest until the river again melted enough for them to continue their journey.

The snow was deep, and Silver pressed her hand against Hiyyan's flank as he faltered into a drift. "Steady-yyy!"

With the next step, Silver plunged into the very next drift. For the first time that day, Hiyyan let loose a belly-deep, snorting laugh at her face full of snow.

"Thanks, you big lizard," Silver grumbled, but she would perform an entire comedy of trips and falls if it meant he'd forget about his pain for a little while.

Hiyyan took Silver's thick cloak in his teeth and helped haul her out. Silver paused on her knees to wrap her arms around Hiyyan's neck and steal a flicker of time for just the two of them to listen to each other's hearts beat hard and fast. Their warm breaths clouded the frosty air.

"I'll be so glad when you're all healed," Silver whispered.

Hiyyan agreed by pressing his muzzle against her cheek.

Nebekker's shadow cut across them. "We have to keep moving," the old woman said as she walked, dragging her long furs across the surface of the snow.

Mele's Shorsa had even more trouble moving through the winter wonderland, her tiny feet struggling to propel her forward. Mele helped her along the path Kirja and Nebekker plowed through the snow.

"How much farther?" Mele called, shaking a lump of snow off her boot.

Nebekker looked up and around, clutching her walking stick with blue-white knuckles. After peering in the direction of the river, which had dropped lower as the terrain began changing into cliffs on their side of the water, she nodded.

"Here," Nebekker said. She moved under the measly shelter of a round of evergreen trees, then proceeded to lay out her furs. "Gather in close. We'll need to share body warmth."

Silver didn't think she'd ever fall asleep in the bone-deep cold, but as she settled in next to Mele, her body thawed slightly. To her right, Hiyyan pressed his back against her and curled up with Kirja and Luap. Their combined heat caused a thin layer of steam to rise into the night. Silver looked around warily. She hated how the glow of the lantern hid anything outside its small radius. Even though she slapped her palm against her skin, the prickles on the back of her neck wouldn't go away.

Still, she forced herself to relax against Hiyyan's mane of fur and breathe out a gossamer cloud of mist.

Tomorrow, we reach the Watchers' Keep. Then once you're healed, we go to King A–Malusni. I know we haven't heard from Ferdi yet, but he just has to help us with the treaty. With everything.

Not sure, Hiyyan bond-said.

But I saved Ferdi's Glithern from being kidnapped! We're friends now, and that has to mean something.

Means not king friend.

Silver shook her head. *Remember how King A–Malusni stood up for me in the palace when Queen Imea wanted to take you away? When she wanted to . . .*

Silver couldn't say the words. Instead, she sent an image to Hiyyan: her coffin, floating out to sea. Hiyyan shuddered.

Something's held Ferdi up, Silver said. *He wouldn't just leave us out here to freeze to death. If his message won't come to us, we'll go to him.*

No more choices, Hiyyan said. A snatch of a sad water dragon song floated through Silver's mind. It was the sun setting on the ocean horizon.

"No," Silver said aloud. "There's no other choice."

Especially since her lifelong water dragon racing hero, Sagittaria Wonder, had turned out to be more confusing than splendid. After trying to help Silver escape arrest, Sagittaria had turned around and battled Silver for possession of Kirja, whom she'd kidnapped for the queen. Silver couldn't figure Sagittaria out: friend or foe?

As for Nebekker's old friend Arkilah, she was definitely a foe. Silver glanced at Nebekker, whose back rose and fell in a steady rhythm even as her hands fussed with the hood of her cloak, pulling it closer around her face.

Sometimes, Silver couldn't help but wonder if Nebekker had known the person Arkilah had become—and had sent Silver looking for her anyway. Arkilah might have been a good companion to Nebekker when they were young, but she had shown Silver that she would do anything to increase her knowledge of the world's mystic secrets, including imprison Silver. And given that she earned a place as the right-hand woman of the queen, she was even more dangerous than when Nebekker had known her in their youth.

When it came to allies, that left only the people Silver was with now and her family back home in Jaspaton. Brajon and her mother at least. Silver closed her eyes. She wasn't sure how her father felt about her. She and Rami Batal, great jeweler of the desert, had not been on good terms the last time they were together.

Still, Silver longed to be with her family again, to sit on cushions around their table and enjoy the delicacies of Jaspaton, to see the jeweled lanterns of the cliffside city slowly come to life as the sun settled beneath the far desert horizon with a sigh. To laugh, to tease, to dream, to rest.

Would she ever be able to go home again?

Beneath her mittens, Silver worried her fingers. Hiyyan pulled his head around and nudged her.

"I'm all right," she told him.

Mele and her Shorsa snored gently, and even Nebekker seemed to have fallen asleep, her body crumpled in on itself like a gnarled desert tree. But every time Silver tried to follow suit, a painful throbbing began in her shoulders and neck.

Soon, soon.

Hiyyan released a low sound of hope along with his breath.

Mele stirred and peered up at Silver. "How close do you think they are now, the mercenaries?" she whispered.

"They'd have to fly on the backs of hawks to catch up with us. Or on Aquinder."

"Let's be grateful we're with the only two in known existence, then."

Silver's toes began to seize up with cold. She wiggled her feet to encourage blood flow, but the restless feeling spread up her legs. She stood and grabbed her pack.

"Just to the river for a drink," she told Hiyyan when he gave her a questioning look. The Aquinder raised his body slowly, intending to follow. "Stay here. You need to rest."

Hiyyan narrowed his eyes and stood fully, shaking his mane free of snow.

"Where are you going now?" Mele pulled a blanket closer around her body in the absence of Silver's warmth.

"We'll be gone just a moment," Silver told her. "Getting water."

"From a frozen river?"

"I'll hack into it."

"Humph. When you die," Mele mumbled as she rolled

over, "I'm going to have them carve 'She was always walking off into danger' on your tombstone."

Silver rolled her eyes. "It's a few steps to the river, then right back here."

Silver and Hiyyan followed the narrow, plowed path back to the river. Neither of them was thirsty, really, but they broke off small pieces of ice and let them melt against their tongues. Silver squinted upriver, hoping to see a light from the Watchers' Keep; the cliffs loomed on either side of the water, creating an ominous channel to the summit of the mountain. But all was dark.

Still. "We're close," she told Hiyyan. "I can feel it. When you're healed, no one will be able to catch you, not the mercenaries, not the queen, not even those Snuckers. And once we petition the Island Nations, we'll be free."

Silver knelt to break off another piece of ice, but she paused, ears pricked. Hiyyan's ears flicked left and right. It was the sounds he heard that were coming to Silver. A shuffling in the snow, a series of low growls.

"Snuckers," Silver whispered. She pulled her dagger out, looking left to right, echoing Hiyyan's movements. "Surely you're too big for them to bother?"

She recalled the twilight flashing against their razor teeth and second-guessed herself. A few could hardly do much to Hiyyan, but how big did their herds get? Twenty or more would be a challenge, especially in a landscape that was treacherous for her and Hiyyan but home to the Snuckers.

Mountain moose. Hiyyan sent an image of the furry, antlered beasts to soothe Silver, and she nodded, remembering what Nebekker had said. Hiyyan was larger than a mountain moose.

A new smell reached Silver through Hiyyan's senses, and she wrinkled her nose. It came from across the river. Mountain moose needed a bath. When she squinted, she could just make out a shadow darker than the surrounding night. The creature made a sound low in its throat.

Did moose *growl*?

"That's no moose." Silver backed away from the ice. Behind her, Hiyyan let loose his own growl. A warning to stay back.

Silver put her hand on Hiyyan's flank. His muscles were just as taut as hers, despite the ability to control his left wing having faded into almost nothing. Silver shifted her dagger to her right hand. She, too, was losing strength in her left arm.

"The ice is too thin. Unless that creature likes swimming, we'll be safe over here."

Her thoughts went to Mele and the rest of her travel companions, sleeping in the copse of evergreens. If the creature did try to come closer, she and Hiyyan were the only things between it and her unsuspecting friends.

A brisk wind blew through the river canyon, bringing swirls of snow and dropping the temperature.

With a defiant crackle, the river finished freezing over in one fell swoop. Clouds split, letting a sliver of moonlight bathe the mountain. Silver could finally make out the distinct shape of a mountain lion. A flash of triumph lit up the creature's eyes.

"I was wrong," Silver said. She licked her lips, the moisture freezing painfully against her thin skin.

The mountain lion remained on its side of the river, but she didn't know how long that would last. Hiyyan backed to the plowed path, with Silver pressing against him. Still, the creature waited, snorting into the chill.

The rustling sound came to Silver again, and she stopped moving. The creature was still as well. Something else was out there.

"But I was right about the Snuckers." When Silver looked over her shoulder, she glimpsed four of the menacing water dragons hovering among a stand of trees. Half were watching her and Hiyyan, while the others looked across the river. The mountain lion stepped onto the frosted ice.

"You should go after that for dinner," Silver said to the Snuckers, pointing across the ice with her chin. Her voice held steady, even though her heart raced. She threw her shoulders back and narrowed her eyes. *Stand tall, look fierce, make the Snuckers think you're too much effort to be worth a meager dinner.*

Kriiiick-WOMP. A tree branch cracked under the weight of snow, then fell from the sky with a mighty crash. It was impossible to see anything in the white cloud of snow that the branch threw up, but Silver heard the clack of the creature running across the river and the shuffle of the Snuckers behind them. Her pulse pounded in her ears.

Now she and Hiyyan were trapped in the middle.

"Run!" Silver cried. She darted downriver along the bank, Hiyyan on her heels. She would not lead any of those night creatures back to the group, and she knew she wouldn't get lost if she followed the river.

But instead of attacking each other, the growling mountain lion and the Snuckers both pivoted to follow her and Hiyyan. They sensed injury and weakness.

The Aquinder, even injured, was faster on his four legs than Silver was on two. Despite his hurt wing, Hiyyan scooped Silver up with his tail and deposited her on his back. Silver looked down, and her temples broke out in a sweat.

A Snucker's jaws snapped at the air right where she had been running. She'd almost been dinner.

As they passed another stand of trees, Silver reached for branches, shaking heavy, wet lumps of snow onto the ground behind them. Her breathing came fast and her arms ached, but she kept at it, each snow plunk slowing their pursuers.

"Aim for that tree," Silver said, sheathing her dagger. Ahead, a branch dangled from its trunk, ready to snap off. It would make a decent weapon with a long reach. When Hiyyan approached the spot, Silver reached up, wrapped her fists around the branch, and pulled.

But instead of the branch coming off the tree, Silver came off Hiyyan. "Oof!"

"Mrawr?" Hiyyan skidded to a stop.

"Keep running!" Silver shouted at him, dangling from the branch that stubbornly held on to its tree.

Hiyyan growled and crouched in a defensive stance. Running wouldn't stop the Snuckers and the mountain lion. The carnivorous cat bypassed the dangling girl in favor of Hiyyan, but the Snuckers paused below Silver, leaping and snapping with their little razor teeth. When they realized she was too high for them to reach, they sat on their haunches, waiting patiently for their meal to fall.

Silver narrowed her eyes at them. "I'm not letting go. Try me."

As the branch snapped and creaked, the Snuckers grinned, their red eyes flashing with delight.

The sweat on Silver's temples moved to her palms. As her grip became clammy, Silver realized how the Snuckers got their name: They began making an excited snuffle-snort through their noses.

"You're not getting me," Silver said, but her voice was a little weaker this time.

Another fierce wind blew through the stand of trees, and the branches swayed. Frozen rain stung Silver's cheeks, and her fingers lost feeling. In that moment, the mountain cat jumped at Hiyyan.

"No!"

Hiyyan reared back and then lashed out. His paws were the size of the cat's entire head, with claws bigger than the cat's teeth, but the cat was stealthy and seemed to have excellent night vision. The cat dashed around Hiyyan's first swipe and ducked under the second. It snapped its teeth close enough to Hiyyan's injured wing to make Silver cry out in fear.

"Hiyyan!"

But Hiyyan could dodge an attack, too. He slid to the left, letting the slick riverbank snow carry his bulk, then he dug his claws into the ground to stop and leaned back just as the mountain lion leaped for his throat. Missing its mark wide, the cat soared into a drift.

The Snuckers snuffled and danced. Silver pulled her knife from her belt and closed her eyes.

"You want something injured?" she said. She opened her eyes and raised her right arm. The branch slowly slipped out of her weak left hand. She had one shot. After that, she would fall.

Silver narrowed her gaze to the mountain cat, waiting until it was out of the drift, head shaken free of snow, hunched down, waiting to spring again. Then Silver flicked her wrist.

The knife sliced through the thin winter air and found its target. The mountain cat yowled, and the Snuckers silenced, raising their snouts in the air at the scent of fresh blood.

"Go," Silver whispered as she dangled for one last second. But it was long enough for the Snuckers to leap away to the cat.

As Silver landed on the ground in a heap, the mountain creatures commenced a new battle. Silver and Hiyyan didn't stay long enough to see the outcome. They rushed into the dark winter night beyond the trees and away from the riverbank. And, after countless minutes of running, Silver paused to look around and figure out where they were: far away from their friends.

EIGHT

Keep walking. Keep walking.

Silver repeated the mantra in her head as much for her own sake as for Hiyyan's, the beat of the words matching each heavy and tired step she took. They couldn't stop to rest. The Snuckers might be following them. More mountain cats could be stalking them from perches in the river canyon. And their blood would slow, thicken, and freeze if they didn't keep moving.

Silver's body shuddered against another gust of frigid wind.

"I only wanted water!" she shouted into the desolate white world.

A wild bubble of laughter rose in her throat. This was not the first time she'd been caught in an unfriendly landscape, woefully unprepared. Mele was right: She was always walking into danger. Would she ever learn?

Hiyyan laughed as a sign of solidarity and then sighed. His poisoned wing dragged in the snow at an unnatural angle, leaving a trail of greenish ooze behind him. It felt as if knitting needles were playing over the right side of her body, her fingers turning a dangerous shade of blue. Without their own dragon heartstone, Hiyyan's blood was filling with death.

And so was hers.

"Nebekker said we'd reach the Keep sometime in the afternoon," Silver said aloud. She was so cold she kept clenching her jaw, and her cheeks were a hot kiln of pain. Talking helped relax her muscles. "B-b-but that was with a few hours of rest overnight. We might reach the Keep by midday if we avoid any more obstacles. I only h-h-hope the rest of them keep moving upriver and don't go looking for us. Kirja should be able to t-t-track us well enough."

Hiyyan grunted his agreement.

"But that m-m-means others will be able t-t-to as well."

Hiyyan shook his head and sent her an image of a warm room, fireplace roaring with heat and thick blankets draped over them. Silver responded by sending him an image of his wing healed.

"I'm r-r-ready for all that," she said.

The drifts of snow began to get shallower, and then they disappeared. Silver's boots crunched and Hiyyan's claws clattered on the new surface. It took a few steps for Silver to notice the changed scenery.

Over her shoulder, she could just make out the reflection of the slender moon on the frozen landscape. They'd long ago left the protection and guidance of the river, but the way was still obvious: As long as they kept increasing elevation, they should reach the Watchers' Keep somewhere high up the mountain. The trouble was, climbing was getting harder with every step. Instead of the fluffy snowdrifts near the river, what stretched out before them now was a barren sheet of silvery-blue ice, glinting under a stark sky of stars. The wind ate away at the surface, revealing cracks and crevasses, and licked the back of Silver's and Hiyyan's necks painfully.

They were on a glacier field once more.

"Here's h-h-hoping this one doesn't h-h-harbor its own Screw-Claw."

Silver took another step and threw out her arms to catch her balance as she slid backward and landed on her rear.

The laugh Hiyyan gave her was so tired that Silver's heart broke.

"Easy enough f-f-for you, with your claws to d-d-dig in," she said.

Silver pressed her lips together and eyed the ice field ahead of them.

"We n-n-need to climb it."

Hiyyan sent Silver an image of walking sticks, then he turned and melted into the darkness they'd emerged from. Silver crouched as she waited, pulling her body into as small a ball as she could to conserve warmth. She rubbed her cheek on the inside of her cloak to make sure she could still feel the soft and silky fur lining.

A few minutes later, Hiyyan returned, a long branch caught between his teeth. He dumped it at Silver's feet. She held the stick between her knees and began stripping it. Her fingers struggled to rip the smaller twigs, but she gave a frustrated snarl and forced them to move. When her hands gave out she used her teeth. Once finished, she had a somewhat crooked but strong stick to help her up the glacier—and a small pile of flexible branches.

Silver dug out a thin blanket partially woven with Kirja's shed belly fur and draped it over Hiyyan's shoulders. At his throat, she threaded the thinnest of the branches through two corners of the blanket. The makeshift cloak didn't even reach Hiyyan's rear haunches, but it was the best she could do. Hiyyan pressed his nose against her neck in thanks.

Silver shivered, her laugh cut off sharply. How was it possible for his nose to be even colder than the rest of her body?

"L-l-let's go."

The chill cut through Silver's layers of clothing, freezing her to her core. She shivered uncontrollably as she walked, and even Hiyyan's jaw rattled with the cold. Silver had her hair shorn off in Calidia, but now she wished she still looked like her mother, like the beautiful and well-kept yarnsladies in Jaspaton, with their thick hair covering their ears and necks, spilling down their backs to their waists. Anything for a touch more warmth.

More than that, she wished she could *be* with her mother.

Tears froze before they could make it past Silver's eyelids. She hastily wiped her face and licked her lips. The wind dried the moisture before it had a chance to settle, cracking her lips painfully. A low rumbling from above made Silver pause. She threw her arm out to stop Hiyyan.

"What was that?"

Hiyyan's ears twitched, his nose sniffed, his eyes narrowed. Then he heaved his entire body into Silver's side and sent her flying.

"Hiyyan!"

Silver landed on her back but didn't have time to take a breath before Hiyyan covered her. The rumbling grew louder. Silver curled up as objects pummeled Hiyyan's sides. He grunted and whimpered, but he held steady. Pebbles and tiny bits of frozen ice skittered beneath Hiyyan's belly to sting

Silver's head, but Hiyyan protected her from the larger pieces of the landslide.

When the world quieted again, Hiyyan gingerly moved aside and sat back, breathing heavily.

"Oh, Hiyyan," Silver whispered. Her Aquinder shook; all along his right side, his skin darkened as bruises formed. Silver ran her palm over his scales, checking for broken skin, but Hiyyan had been spared that, at least.

Silver blinked back tears. "Nebekker always said you should have bonded to someone more capable."

No, Hiyyan said.

Silver frowned and looked away. "What do you know about it, anyway?" He had never been safe and comfortable. All because of her.

In response, Hiyyan used water dragon language, singing the notes that had come to mean more to Silver than anything. It was the water dragon song of love.

Silver closed her eyes and sniffed. Was any force as compelling as love? She stood, and together they walked, Hiyyan waiting for Silver as she struggled beside him with her walking stick. Soon their feet burned with cold.

Silver pulled her furs closer. *Ice. Snow.*

Ice. Snow, Hiyyan thought back to her.

Stick. Silver waved her branch in the air. *Slip,* she thought as she fumbled backward.

Stick. Slip. Claw. Water dragon. Silver. Bond. Mountain.

Silver's breath came as a cloud, and she nodded. What had begun as a game to pass the time in the mountain cave had become a habit. She was teaching Hiyyan her language and, in return, he was teaching her his. As they climbed, trading the dark night skies for the hint of citrine morning reflected on the ice field, Silver switched tactics and began singing under her breath.

The song of cold came to her first, but she shook her head and instead repeated what Hiyyan had only moments before sung to her. She formed the notes of the song of love. Despite the terrain, warmth filled her belly, and hope filled her heart.

With renewed determination, Silver plunged her stick into the glacier. A flash of sunlight stung her eyes, and the crack of ice splintering found her ears. Silver put her arm out as a dark line zigzagged down the ice field toward her. Fear froze her in place, but just when she thought the glacier would open up and swallow her into its depths, the crack stopped. Right at the toe of her boot.

Silver breathed out hard. Looked up the mountain. It was too dark to see anything. How much farther? Could they possibly hope to make it all the way to the Keep?

Fly.

Silver frowned. Hiyyan wasn't making a suggestion; he was reminding her of what he could do if his wing functioned properly. He felt guilty that he couldn't get them out of danger.

"It's my fault that your wing's hurt. I'll get us out of here." Silver set her jaw, but a wave of dizziness hit her. "We have to keep moving."

Hiyyan lifted a trembling leg, prepared to trudge forward, but then his body paused, tipped to the left, then back to the right. *"Hhhrrggg,"* he growled.

"Or maybe we'll sit for a moment. Just until there's a little bit of light."

Hiyyan let his chin rest on the ground, and Silver curled

into his neck. Her arms prickled with the sense that they weren't alone, but soon numbness seeped in and cloaked them in drowsiness. They nodded off, and when they woke, the world dripped at them, a sharp, reflective sun blasting across the mountain above them.

Silver was surprised she'd managed to wake at all and wasn't entirely glad of it. Her lips were crackled, dry, and burnt when she opened her mouth. Her brain throbbed with sounds. But one voice rose above them all to reach her.

"It *is* them! Land here!"

Silver's heart leaped. Mele! *That* was who had been out there.

"Me—urmph." Silver tried to get up but succeeded in only tipping herself over to her side. Hiyyan whimpered once, then raised his head and let loose a grand roar.

"Huuuuurrrooowwww!"

The ground trembled, but neither of them cared. Mele was here, Kirja was here, and they were going to get off the glacier!

Mele jumped from Kirja's back and lifted Silver in a tight hug. "Oof! How can you be so little and so heavy at the same time?"

"Probably all the good food I've been eating."

"Hurmp, hurmp." Hiyyan laughed.

As Mele supported her, Silver gritted her teeth and forced her fingers and toes to curl and uncurl. She looked down at the dull tin-gray color in her fingers and frowned. "Where's Luap?"

Mele nodded across the edge of the glacier. "Waiting with Nebekker at the river. Do you realize you're only a few steps away from it?"

"I had no idea where we were."

"Kirja sensed you, didn't you, you good ol' lady?" Mele patted Kirja's flank. Kirja's teeth flashed in the blinding morning light as she grinned. "As soon as we woke and realized you were still gone, we came. I'm sorry it wasn't sooner."

"It's s-s-so good to see you, my *c*-old friend," Silver said. "*Snow* face is m-m-more welcome than yours."

Mele grimaced. "Are you making up puns? Silver, I think you're delirious."

"Oh, let's n-n-not drag-on our conversation. Ice-ee we all want to g-g-get to the Keep and be warm. I must cre-vass-k: How l-l-long until we get there?"

"Silver, I swear I'll leave you here—" But Mele's words cut off as Hiyyan whipped his head over his shoulder with a growl.

He stiffened and sniffed the air. *Danger.*

Silver nodded. "H-h-hide!"

There was a shuffle, then a crunch of glacial ice, before the big voice boomed out over the ice field.

"Hide? What good will that do? All that hollering makes you impossible to miss."

Three figures emerged from a dip in the ice field, their bodies swathed in puffy, down-filled coats and their faces wrapped snugly so that only slits remained for their eyes. Their packs were full, and mountain tools hung from their belts. Silver spotted the sharp ice picks and swallowed hard.

Kirja drew herself up to her tallest height and loomed over Hiyyan protectively. It didn't matter now if the mercenaries heard her; she let loose a tree-trembling roar, but the trackers weren't fazed.

"Oh, we've heard about you," one of the mercenaries said, her voice muffled but still able to ring out across the glacier.

"That's why we grabbed her first," said another mercenary, dragging a human beside him.

"Nebekker!" Silver cried out.

The man held a knife near Nebekker's temple. Her cheeks radiated bright red, and her eyes flicked side to side, wide and wild. "We heard there's an easy way to get that big dragon to do what we want."

Unable to bear the threat to her human, Kirja sat back on her haunches, waiting and watching.

"We also heard you were a squirrelly, difficult thing to catch," the woman said, nodding at Silver. "But tracking you couldn't have been easier, could it, Jasser?"

A third mercenary, Jasser, was a man taller than the others by two heads and nearly double as wide. He dragged a large litter across the snow with ease, but when his opinion was solicited by the woman, he said nothing, preferring to simply glare at them all.

"Grab Silver Batal. I'll get the other girl," the woman directed, and the trackers moved quickly.

"Silver?" Nebekker's voice had never sounded so weak and confused.

Silver turned to run, but at the sound of her name, she froze. She couldn't leave Nebekker to the trackers.

"Easier and easier," the woman said. It was the last thing Silver heard before Jasser's big arm clobbered her upside her head, dropping her to the ground.

NINE

Silver rolled in and out of consciousness, every jolt of the litter pulling her awake before she tipped off again into darkness. In the brief waking moments, she gathered as much information as she could: They were traveling down the glacier, switchbacking to keep from plummeting down the ice. She was tied next to Nebekker on a sled. Sometimes, it was snowing. Kirja and Hiyyan were harnessed together on a raft-sized contraption made up of dozens of planks of wood and pulled by a rope tied around the waist of the huge man, Jasser.

I'm going to die. I'm going to die. I'm going to die.

No.

Hiyyan?

No die.

"Mele?" Silver said weakly. Where was her friend? Surely not suffering . . . surely on her way home, back to where she once was safe, far away from Silver, who had done nothing but make her life miserable.

The woman heard. "The other girl and dragon? We're not getting paid for them. Left them where we found them."

Mele and Luap. Left on the mountain. To die.

"No! No, you can't leave them there!" Silver's breath came quickly. Her friend . . . alone.

"Not one more word." The woman loomed over Silver, her arm raised, a small wooden club held high.

Before the woman could swing, Silver clamped her mouth shut. After a few minutes of a racing heart, anticipating a blow that never came, Silver watched the woman turn away, then swiveled her stiff neck slowly to see Nebekker staring back, snow powdering her eyebrows.

Silver shivered against the cold seeping into her clothes. "Snow's getting wetter."

"Good."

"Terrible!" Silver argued.

"Don't be ridiculous, girl. Weather change means unstable snowpack," Nebekker said, frowning. "And now that we're getting closer to the snowbank . . . ah. Here." She raised her voice. "Ooohh, I don't feel weeeeelllll. Please stooooop."

Silver glanced at the trackers. The woman's shoulders stiffened, but they didn't stop walking. Whatever Nebekker was doing, it wasn't working.

Hiyyan, are you awake? Silver bond-said.

Awake. Not. Fun.

Silver pressed her lips into a tight line and probed his injuries. The poison was spreading slowly, as though it, too, struggled with their thick, cold blood. A small victory.

Silver rolled her eyes up to catch a glimpse of the tracks they'd made down the mountain. The mercenaries marched across the ice field steadily, switchbacking the whole way down, Silver assumed, to keep the sleds from racing to the bottom of the glacier. The woman and the man whose names Silver didn't know kept up a steady stream of low conversation, while Jasser said nothing.

She switched her gaze to the sky. Low granite-gray clouds had settled in heavily, blocking the minuscule warmth and light that had rolled off the sun. Sleet stung her cheeks.

Silver saw Nebekker test the ropes that bound her, then wriggle left to right under layers of furs and tunics.

"Ooohhhh, the pain . . . the fever . . ." Nebekker moaned a little louder. Still, the mercenaries ignored her.

Silver's breath quickened as the old woman's thrashing pulled her dragon heartstone out of her tunic. It slid down one side of Nebekker's neck as she continued writhing. As Nebekker twisted in the opposite direction, the pendant caught between two slats and, with one sharp movement, the chain snapped.

"Gah!" Silver yelled.

Hiyyan growled.

The sleds halted.

"*What* is going on back there?" the woman said, finally coming around to check on them.

Silver thought quickly. "I have to . . . relieve myself."

"Hold it."

"I really can't."

The woman jammed her gloved hands into her waist. "Even the queen can't pay me enough to clean up the mess you'd make."

"The dragons also need to go," Silver added. "Their mess would be even—"

"No," the man said firmly. "The dragons are not to be released. You two can go, but you must go one at a time."

". . . turmeric cauliflower," Nebekker muttered, shaking her head side to side. "Ooh, OOOOOOHHH!!"

Silver wondered if Nebekker realized the dragon heart-stone had fallen on the snow behind them. Surely she'd felt the chain break?

"MISSsssseerrryyyYYyy," Nebekker moaned.

"She needs food," Silver said. "And water. She's . . . feverish." *At least,* something's *wrong with her head.*

The man crouched next to Nebekker and prodded her with a finger. "She's teetering on the edge."

"Aaaaahhhh heeelpp meeeeee . . ." Nebekker theatrically rolled her eyes into the back of her head. On the dragon sled, Kirja mewled, echoing Nebekker's despair.

"Tell your dragon to knock that off." The man unknotted several lengths of rope around Silver. Without the pressure against her lungs, Silver took as deep a breath as she could, the air swirling around the liquidy areas brought on by the poison. She coughed and sat up. Her legs wobbled as she stood, but she forced them to be strong.

Silver shot a glance at Nebekker, but the old woman continued mumbling to herself. Kirja kept whimpering. And Hiyyan watched the three of them with shining eyes.

What's happening?

Silver blinked at Hiyyan. *I'm not really sure myself. But at least we're stopped for the moment.*

Aloud, Silver said, "I can't make her dragon do anything. Besides, I really have to *go.*"

"So go," the woman shot back.

"Giiiirrrlllll," Nebekker moaned. When Silver looked at

Nebekker, the woman's face went stern and her pupils darted over and over again to the perimeter of the glacier, where snow gathered thickly among the trees. Confused, Silver began walking in that direction. "The pain STOOOOMPS at my heaaart."

Silver knew that was for her, but when and where was she supposed to stomp? Her boots lifted and smashed down in the direction of the trees, the jarring sending threads of pain through her shoulder.

"Where do you think you're going?" the male mercenary said, seizing Silver's arm. She gasped.

"There's shelter over there."

The man laughed. "You fleas don't need privacy. Omelda," he said to the woman, "take the girl. I'll dump the extra weight."

By the time Silver's ice-addled brain worked out what the man meant by extra weight, Omelda had already begun dragging Silver away from the group. As the man's intentions dawned on Silver, she dug her heels in and shouted over her shoulder.

"Nebekker! Don't you . . . You better leave her on the sled!"

"Keep walking." Omelda forced Silver along, but her irises darkened with something resembling sympathy.

"Please," Silver pleaded, catching sight of the dragon heart-stone in her path. "She'll die out here alone. She's old . . . She's sick. And we have to go back for my friend Mele. She'll . . ."

Omelda looked away, the lines around her eyes hardening. "Our orders are for one girl and one water dragon. The rest are outside our jurisdiction."

"Then why take the others at all?"

"Certainly not out of the kindness of our hearts. Kindness doesn't pay the bills. But that dragon will. Every bill for the rest of my life."

"You can't!"

"Walk."

Forgetting Nebekker's order to stomp, Silver sank every ounce of her weight into her ankles and dropped to the ground.

"Ungh." Caught off guard, Omelda lost her footing on the glacier and fell to her knees. Silver scrambled away, the nubby ice cutting into her palms. The dragon heartstone gleamed only a few feet away. Silver reached for the stone.

"Aaaggghhh!"

A heavy boot crunched her hand. Jasser glared down at Silver.

"WwwwHHHAAAAAAAAAAaawwahhhaaaaAAA!" Nebekker's wail, surely, could have been heard all the way to the Island Nations. Silver glanced at her friend and got a stink eye back for her efforts before the old woman continued crying out. "By the . . . shifting duuuuuunes."

Silver furrowed her brow. Shifting dunes? It was obviously a clue, but for what? Before she could work it out, Jasser lifted his boot from her hand.

"What's this?" Omelda ignored Nebekker's yells and flicked Silver's wrist out of the way, picking up the dragon heartstone.

"A token from my father. Please. It's the only thing I have from my family."

Another flicker of sympathy crossed Omelda's face. She shrugged and gave the heartstone back to Silver. "If I see it again, it becomes mine."

Silver nodded, palming the stone. Jasser curled his big hand around hers as the smaller male mercenary added to the conversation:

"Not so fast. If we're selling the other dragon, we're selling this jewelry, too."

By all the sands, Nebekker, did you have to lose your heartstone?

"If you take it, you become a thief," Silver cried. "There's terrible punishment for thieves!"

As one, the three trackers threw back their heads with laughter.

Omelda looked at Silver, but her next words were lost on the wind as a much louder voice sounded in Silver's head: *There's those dragons!*

"Snuf-fle," Silver said. Her eyes widened, and she clapped a hand over her mouth. In her other hand, Nebekker's dragon heartstone grew warm. She quickly slipped it into her pocket.

Omelda glared. "What did you say?"

We can get them fast.

"Noth—*ffle.*"

"Get up, you pest. You think this is all a joke? We don't have time for rest, for food, for anything. Do you know what else is out here?"

Which one first?

Wounded one easiest.

Wounded one smells bad.

"No! I—" Silver pressed her lips together but couldn't keep back the next snuffle. *"Snuf-fle!"*

Omelda gripped Silver under her chin, her face furious. "Knock that off."

The two separated from the herd.

Yes, those. Wait. The tall one's going to kill the little one.

Easy carrion.

Silver's breath rattled up her nose. Instead of pushing away at the voices in her head, she focused on them, picking out individual strains from the din. Her brain seemed to reconstruct itself, her senses zeroing in on new planes of space and sound as if she were being lifted from her own skin to become part of the air around her. She could hear song convert to words, she could smell the creature behind the voice, she could see the basic curves and angles of their faces and bodies.

Her head thrummed with the effort, overwhelmed by the intensity of the world around her. Blood dripped from her left nostril and froze on her upper lip. So many voices rose in excitement that Silver could no longer focus on just one.

Yes.

Yes.

Hee.

Soon.

Food.

"You . . . can't . . . have me," Silver gasped.

Omelda laughed. "I take what I want, girl."

Silver's throat constricted. She couldn't tell the mercenary that she wasn't talking to her.

You are my kind. Help us.

Hiyyan's song rolled across the glacier. To Omelda and all the other humans in their party, it sounded like he was cooing. But Silver knew the Aquinder was in conversation with the same dragon voices that filled her mind. She searched the edges of the glacier, squinting against the glare of light against the ice, until she could make out the dozen or more little figures waiting where the glacier faded into rock and dirt.

Snuckers.

He wants us to help.

He doesn't know he's a nice meal.

He's the stinky one. Don't eat him.

The rest smell tasty.

Hurry. Crust shifting.

Yes. Danger.

Crust shifting? Silver's ears pricked as Hiyyan sent her audio: cracking, groaning, slithering slush.

Stomp. Shifting dunes.

The snow was shifting. Nebekker wanted Silver to help it along. She wanted them to cause an avalanche.

Was the old woman daft as a dung beetle? An avalanche would kill them all! Except . . . for those who could rise above it. Silver's gaze swept to Kirja to find the Aquinder's eyes on her, too. They locked with understanding. Silver had seen Kirja burst through an ice cave ceiling and fling a Screw-Claw nearly twice her size into a rock prison. She'd seen Kirja lift Hiyyan up from a waterfall. Moving her and Hiyyan and Nebekker out of the way of an avalanche?

Yes, Kirja stiffened her muscles and sent Silver warmth.

The problem now, though, was the band of Snuckers waiting for Silver at the edge of the glacier. She couldn't go over there alone and stomp an avalanche into existence. She'd be eaten first.

Silver cut through the voices to find the Snucker who kept warning the others about the smell. *Sick. Poison. Death.* She pushed the words at that Snucker as a warning: Eat us and you'll die, too.

Help us and . . . But Silver couldn't finish that thought. It was terrible enough leaving the wild mountain cat to the devices of the Snuckers, but to offer up fellow humans to them? It was a dark possibility that sat heavily in Silver's belly, even as it offered their best chance of escape now.

Omelda dragged Silver back to the group. Hiyyan watched her approach, his breathing light and slow.

What do we do? Silver asked him.

There weren't many moments when Silver felt she and Hiyyan were any different. Sure, their bodies were different, but their hearts, as far as Silver was concerned, were the same. Now, though, Hiyyan's pause as he mulled over Silver's question was a reminder that they were, indeed, different species with sometimes different ways of looking at the world.

To Hiyyan's way of thinking, humans were simply another kind of animal. Why the hesitation in leaving them to the Snuckers?

Her hesitation gave Omelda time to shove Silver back into the sled and begin knotting the ropes around her. Nebekker groaned, as though it was important to keep up the ruse of illness, but her acting had diminished since Silver had ruined her avalanche plan. Now she seemed mostly to be groaning with disappointment that Silver hadn't done anything clever enough to get them away from the mercenaries. Silver looked away from the old woman in shame. Kirja protectively covered Hiyyan with her wing. And somewhere on the mountain, Mele and Luap were alone to face the wilds.

The clouds sank lower until fog obscured the edges of the glacier, where the Snuckers waited. A bitter wind dropped the temperature. The sleet that had plagued them transformed into thick flakes of snow.

"Brajon, how long before we're off this ice field?" Omelda said.

Silver drew her eyebrows together. Was her cousin here?

But it was the third mercenary, the normal-sized one, who answered. Silver almost laughed. Brajon was a common enough name.

"This looks like the beginning of a bigger storm. It's going to slow us down."

"Before nightfall, though?"

"If not," the other, more horrible Brajon said, "we're dead."

Jasser grunted his displeasure at the sky.

"But we won't survive going any faster," Silver said.

Horrible Brajon curled his lip. "You weren't invited into our conversation."

The Snucker voices became more frenzied. The little water dragons knew that they were running out of time to catch their meal. Silver closed her eyes and concentrated again.

I can provide you with a meal. A good one. Bigger and better than any of us, she thought.

How?

The dragon with the wings . . . the healthy one? If you flush a deer out, she can snap it right up. No chasing required on your part. Easy. Find two? She'll get both.

As the Snuckers argued among themselves, Silver refocused her attention on the people around her.

"The queen's after live water dragons, not dead," she said to Omelda. "Please. He needs help. I know we're near the Watchers' Keep—"

"Quiet, girl!" Omelda snapped. She scratched her head, looking thoughtfully at Horrible Brajon. "But she has a point. We're closer to the Keep, even if it is up rather than down. It's neutral territory. A place to wait out the storm and heal the sick dragon. Two dragons could fly us all off this mountain."

"And give them a hundred chances to escape? Not

happening." Brajon gnashed his teeth. "Get them all secure, and let's move!"

"Put the girl with the wounded dragon and leave the others here," Omelda said. "If we're not going north, we're decreasing our load to outrun the storm."

"No!" Brajon shouted. "Not north, and not leaving the bounty!"

Omelda raised an eyebrow.

Brajon stuttered. "Th-they're worth too much!"

"Are they worth our lives? There's something funny about you. You were the one who insisted we bring the others." She licked her lips and surveyed Brajon. "Whom have you already promised them to and for what price?"

"Someone who will pay higher than the queen?" Silver asked.

Horrible Brajon tugged his jacket sleeve. "Why does she keep assuming that's who wants her? Does Queen Imea have it out for you? If so, that's *certainly* someone who'll pay."

Silver's toes curled. The mercenaries weren't there on order of Queen Imea? Who, then? As she pondered, something tickled her nose. She crossed her eyes, peering at what she thought was a snowflake. But the little puff of white didn't melt on her skin. It unfurled, slid down the slope of her nose, and flung itself off to the ice, where Silver lost sight of it.

The softest *Wheeee!* reached Silver's mind before fading into the distance.

Was that a tiny water or . . . *ice*? . . . dragon among the real snowflakes?

*Snow*fluff, a miniscule voice corrected her thoughts before that one, too, faded into the landscape.

"Queen Imea . . ." Omelda mused.

"We can't involve the queen," Brajon said quickly. "We . . . have reason enough to avoid her."

"I don't," Omelda said. She took a step toward Brajon. "And I'd love more coin. You don't know anything about more coin, do you?"

"I, uh . . . uh . . ." For all his bravado, Brajon weakened under Omelda's questioning. And then, when he bumped into Jasser, whose folded arms and well-planted feet made him akin to a wall, he broke. Yanked a pouch from his tunic and tossed it into the snow, where it landed with a jingle. "There was more! Payment for the others—"

"Liar! Cheat! Swindler!"

While the trackers fought among themselves, Silver made a quick choice: She would call the Snuckers over. The pack of little water dragons still hadn't agreed to Kirja's finding them a meal, but even so, the ensuing chaos of their arrival was the only way they'd have a chance to escape and get to the snow. And stomping Aquinder would do an even better job of getting an avalanche going than Silver alone.

Silver closed her eyes and reached out to Hiyyan. *It won't be easy, but be ready to run. The Snuckers might chew the ropes for us.*

Might?

And if they don't, they'll eat us. Either way, we're getting away from these mercenaries.

Hiyyan stared at her as though she'd gone mad.

I never thought I'd get off this mountain in the belly of a Snucker, Hiyyan finally bond-said.

Well, they probably won't eat you, all oozing and slimy.

In that case, bring on the chaos.

"How long did you think you could keep this secret?!"

Omelda yelled. Jasser lifted Brajon right off the ground and shook him.

Determination flowed into Silver's body. She stretched to make herself as long and imposing as she could. They *would* survive, she and her friends. The Snuckers sensed the change come over her. Their voices amplified in her mind. The sky opened suddenly, dumping so much snow Silver couldn't see Hiyyan in the distance. Horrible Brajon yelled something unintelligible to Omelda, and she shouted back. A series of snuffles and yips drowned out all other sound.

They're here, Hiyyan bond-said.

TEN

Through the increasing blizzard, red eyes flashed. Silver's pulse raced as she tried to keep track of the small, darting Snuckers. Jasser howled—why? What was happening to him? Kirja roared. Was that in pain or in triumph? Too much was happening for Silver to track individual voices. Along with the increasing crackling of the mountain, it all blended into a deafening flurry of sound.

Silver furiously blew on the snow that landed near her mouth, but it was piling up on her forehead and cheeks. Even blinking it away didn't clear a line of vision to what was going on just feet away from her. Her belly flip-flopped. Would the Snuckers help? Or make a meal of her?

Cut our ropes.

They heard. Two or three sets of red eyes bounded through the snow to Silver and Nebekker's sled. Silver held her breath as one Snucker opened its maw wide, revealing those razor-sharp teeth. She squeezed her eyes shut as it brought its mouth down.

Chomp.

The ropes loosened.

"Get up, Nebekker!"

Her quickest movements were painfully slow, but Silver's old mentor pushed to her feet and brushed snow from her clothes. Just in time to see Hiyyan and Kirja's sled zoom past them down the glacier.

"Grab it!" Silver screamed.

Nebekker flung herself toward the sled, catching and gripping the frayed ends of the ropes with all the fire she had in her.

"Wait for me!" Silver yelled. She dove to the ground, snatching one of Nebekker's trailing feet. "Guh."

Silver's one useful shoulder was nearly yanked from its socket—again—as her body dragged over the glacier, nubbly ice scraping against the layers of her clothing, tearing and tossing aside bits of fur and wool. The thickness kept the ice from ripping her skin, but she knew that would last only as long as her furs held up against the onslaught.

Silver and Nebekker grunted with the effort of holding on.

"You're heavy."

"And getting dizzy." Silver swept left to right, rolling from shoulder to shoulder as she redoubled her efforts to hold on. "But don't let go!"

The faster they sped down the glacier, the more space they put between themselves and the mercenaries. And the Snuckers. She knew they were going the wrong way for the Keep, but they would deal with that when they could. For now, Silver's eyes widened as she banked left and caught sight of a snowdrift in their path. "Watch out! Dig your talons in!"

Kirja and Hiyyan did the best they could to slow the sled

down, clawing until the tips of their talons snapped off, but there was no stopping them.

They slammed into the lump, went airborne, flipped once, and landed in a heap on the edge of the glacier, the newly fallen snow breaking their fall. Still, the four didn't move for some time, letting the flakes gather in a thin blanket over them, catching their breath and assessing their limbs for breaks. Other than the Aquinder's ragged talons, and the old wounds that plagued them, they were in better shape than Silver could have hoped for.

Gingerly, she got to her feet and walked several paces away, looking around.

"I don't think we went too far down the mountain," Nebekker said at her shoulder.

"It's hard to tell. It feels like we're on a different *side* of the mountain," Silver said as she nibbled the inside of her lip.

"Let's go all the way down, then," Nebekker said. "The queen knows we're here—"

"Or whoever it is hunting us," Silver corrected.

"Correct. We can't go to the Keep now. Stop fighting me on this, girl."

Silver shook her head. This argument of Nebekker's was getting old. "We got away from the trackers, and without even needing to cause an avalanche—which could have killed us! Now, I need to ask the Watchers for help. You know that."

"Don't tell me what I know. I know Kirja would have gotten us out of the avalanche."

"She didn't have to. Now, she can focus on helping her son, who she won't leave," Silver said.

"And I won't leave her," Nebekker mumbled.

Silver nodded triumphantly. "Back up the mountain we go."

Nebekker didn't just look defeated, she looked *angry*. To soften the mood, Silver turned the conversation to the one Nebekker cared about over all others.

"How are Kirja's claws?"

"We'll see now."

The two humans returned to their dragons. Silver wanted to go right to Hiyyan and run her hands through his thick, soft fur, but first she inspected Kirja's talons with Nebekker. All ten claws on her front paws were broken, though some had only the very tips chipped off. Others were worse, and one was even split up the center, all the way to the quick. It oozed slightly, the cold freezing the blood before it could flow too much.

Silver frowned. "I'm sorry, Kirja."

Kirja folded her paws under her body. *We got away. That matters the most. Let's focus again on healing Hiyyan.*

Silver blinked at Kirja. Her words, like Hiyyan's, had suddenly gotten much more complex. Or maybe it was Silver's understanding of the water dragon language that had grown.

Silver moved to Hiyyan, checking the wound on his wing. She, too, felt the poison seeping into her central organs. If the Watchers didn't have any healing ideas—or some insight on how Silver could get her hands on her own heartstone—the Keep was the last place the two of them would ever step foot.

We'll get better, Hiyyan said.

"I appreciate your optimism," Silver said.

Snuf-fle.

Silver sighed. Looked to the trees in the distance. Were

those the same Snuckers that had helped them up-glacier or a new troop of hungry mountain critters?

You promised.

They were the same.

I know I promised. But Kirja's claws are broken. She can't hunt now.

The Snuckers snuffled, their voices rising angrily.

You said . . . you said!

Aren't you full after eating . . . them, anyway? Silver's stomach roiled with the thought of the Snuckers making a meal of the mercenaries. Just because they were her enemies didn't mean she wanted . . . Silver squeezed her eyes and shook her head.

Eat them? The Snuckers' tone was incredulous. *Disgusting. Our kind don't eat your kind. Not if we can help it. Do you even know how you taste?*

Do you? Silver shot back.

For hundreds of years, dragons have passed down the decree banning our kind from eating yours. You are simply too gross. Do you even know what your kind eat?

Silver's stomach rumbled at the idea of Aunt Yidla's rich and redolent feasts. But then she recalled something Sagittaria Wonder had suggested: Her Dwakka had eaten a human before. And then there was the Screw-Claw beneath the glacier down-mountain.

The Snuckers snuffled with indignation.

That is not representative of our kind! The Screw-Claw faces winter desperation! And that Dwakka water dragon is rebellious, it was coerced, it was—

Okay, okay, Silver soothed. The Snuckers, for all their ferocity, were genuinely upset at the implication. But what about the first time she'd encountered the Snuckers? Silver's glance went to Hiyyan, and her heart felt like gold pinched between pliers. Humans may not have been on the menu, but other water dragons?

A hiss sounded across the glacier, and when Silver looked back in the direction of the Snuckers, she saw a flash of light against teeth.

They're not our preference, but when winter falls, we eat what we can.

Silver shuddered. The snow eased, and the wind picked up, pushing the clouds across the face of the mountain. If the mercenaries were still out there, Silver and her friends weren't safe.

What did you do with the other humans?

We sent them down the chute.

The . . . what?

The burrows. Now where's our feast?

Wait. Burrows as in an underground travel system? There were desert foxes in all climates, weren't there?

Of course. There's a particularly steep one that slides all the way to the valley at the base of the mountain. It's the one we use to exile bad Snuckers.

Or bad humans.

Yes. Ones who break their promises.

Silver swallowed nervously and reached a hand out to Kirja's talons again.

"We've rested long enough," Nebekker said. "The snow's stopped. Time to move."

Silver remembered that Nebekker couldn't hear the conversation she was having with the Snuckers. "One more minute. I'm putting a plan together."

"Oh, *now* you have a plan?" Nebekker mumbled.

To the Snuckers, she asked, *Does the chute also go to the top of the mountain?*

Yes.

Can the Aquinder fit through?

No.

Silver frowned. The chute sounded like the ideal way to get to the Watchers' Keep: out of sight, out of the elements, likely faster, too. But no way was she going to abandon Hiyyan and Kirja to go underground.

I will carry him up, Kirja said, pulling her shoulders back and lifting her chin regally.

"Out of the path of an avalanche is one thing. But all the way up the mountain? It's impossible."

Kirja growled.

"Besides, what about Nebekker? I could climb the chute, but not her. Plus, going up the chute means leaving Mele and Luap behind for certain."

"What chute?" Nebekker said. "What are you talking about?"

"The Snuckers have a burrow system under the mountain. One line runs to the top. We'd fit, but Hiyyan and Kirja won't."

Nebekker rubbed her gloved hands over her cheeks. "What is it with you and small, underground-dwelling creatures?"

Small and *big underground-dwelling creatures,* Hiyyan joked.

"We all have our specialties." Silver rubbed the back of her neck. "The trouble is, I promised a nice meal for the Snuckers. A deer."

"Go find one, then." Nebekker slumped to the ground, exhausted.

"I told them Kirja would find food, but now . . ."

Silver looked at Kirja's claws. The Aquinder, though, pulled herself up even taller, unabashed. She curled and uncurled her talons, the muscles in her face contracting, her eyelids drooping majestically. Without a word, Kirja took to the skies.

"You shouldn't have underestimated her," Nebekker said. "And you shouldn't make decisions for her, either."

"I was doing my best to get us away from the trackers," Silver said.

"She'd have done that better than any of us could." Nebekker examined Silver's battered furs, then sighed. "Still, here we are. You did well, Silver. Now, we'll go underground. We must. You have a habit of underestimating this elderly lady, too. I'll keep up."

Nebekker gingerly got to her feet again and turned her back to Silver, as miffed as Kirja had been.

A roar of excited snuffles filled the air. In the distance, a blue blur crested the tree line and returned to them. Kirja landed on the glacier with a triumphant stare at Silver.

Silver felt as small as a Snucker.

"Imagine being made to feel unequal, unworthy," Nebekker said quietly as Kirja turned away to lick her sore paws. Nebekker's weathered face tipped up to meet the weak sunlight, and her hands folded over the top of the walking stick that she'd somehow managed to keep hold of this whole time. "Imagine being made to feel you're living in someone else's world, that you're a secondary character in all their adventures."

"What do you mean?" Silver said.

"Your whole life you've wanted a water dragon. Start with that, Silver Batal. You can want a tasty meal or a pretty new dress. But can you want a water dragon?"

"I don't understand."

"Can you want another person? And if you do, what does that mean?"

Silver was saved from digging deeper into Nebekker's questions by the arrival of two Snucker emissaries. Their eyes were more pink than red, as though softened by having the edge taken off their hunger.

Delicious deer.

"Deer?" Silver said.

Oh yes, the Aquinder brought three! they snuffled. *Enough to repay sending the other humans down the chute, and to pay for getting your party up the chute.*

Silver's gratitude warmed her better than her layers of tattered furs.

And now we take you up the chute. Come, come.

Silver quickly gathered their few remaining possessions and went to Kirja.

"Thank you for repaying our debt," Silver said. "For keeping the promise *I* made. And for making it possible for us to go up the chute, too. You can . . . help Hiyyan get to the Keep?"

Silver knew the question was another insult—of course Kirja would get Hiyyan to the Keep—but Silver had to know. Had to hear it firsthand.

A mother carries their child as needed.

Kirja held back as Hiyyan twisted himself around Silver's legs. He was unhappy that they would be separated, but they both knew it was necessary and hoped it wouldn't be for long.

"I'll be right below you the whole way," Silver assured him. She marveled at how young Hiyyan was, compared with Kirja. He was barely out of his baby stage. It felt as if they'd done so much together in his short life: crossed deserts, swam

96

in oceans, climbed mountains. But he still counted on Silver to make the best decisions for both of them.

Or did he?

Kirja didn't need Silver to make decisions for her. In fact, Kirja seemed to be growing frustrated. And perhaps rightfully so. When was the last time Silver treated Kirja like more than . . . Nebekker's companion? Had she been treating Kirja like a pet? A thing to possess?

For so long, Silver believed dragons existed in *her* world; did water dragons view her the same way, as something they possessed, as something that existed in *their* world?

Silver hugged Hiyyan tightly, then reluctantly untangled herself, her chest squeezed with worry.

"I'll see you at the top. Promise."

You're slow. Only two legs. I'll get there first and eat all the hot food. Hiyyan's double row of teeth gleamed as he grinned at Silver. Kirja's mirthful snort sent up a cloud of mist.

Silver combed her fingers through Hiyyan's mane. She wanted more of his teasing, every day of the rest of her life.

Hiyyan's grin faded from his face, though the smile in his eyes remained, and the hum of a soft song filled both of their minds.

Soon, they thought at the same time. *Always, soon.*

Reluctantly, Silver turned away from Hiyyan and Kirja and marched to the Snuckers waiting to escort her to the burrows. The pain she felt at walking away from Hiyyan was laced with the sweetness of hope: a thing that had carried them this far.

"Thank you again," she said to the Snuckers. Because they, too, didn't only exist to help Silver on her path; they had their own lives, their own reasons for doing the things they did.

Come, come, follow us here.

Even in their new friendliness, the Snuckers' red eyes and razor teeth made Silver shudder. She followed them into the tree line and to the burrow entrance, tucked behind a boulder and encircled by several feet of snow. Silver peered into the darkness, smelling the earthy depths of organic matter and the musky scents of furry water dragon oils. She guessed the oils were essential to keep the Snuckers' coats dry and warm, but still she wrinkled her nose, thinking about how she was going to smell riper than fermenting fruit in the crocks of Aunt Yidla's kitchen by the time she reached the top of the chute.

Silver looked around. "Where did Nebekker go?" she asked the Snuckers.

Up ahead. Far, very far. She is carried fast and demands faster. We'll try to catch up. A race.

Silver laughed. Somehow, Nebekker always seemed to rise to the occasion. Why not show off a bit of speed?

Go down there.

"It's very dark."

It's nice to see in the dark. The Snucker who conversed with Silver grinned and snuff-chuckled. He knew of Silver's vision limitations and thought it funny. She wasn't impressed.

Silver twisted her mouth. "Do you know how ferocious you look?"

Thank you very much. The Snucker sat back on his haunches proudly, his tall ears flicking in the wind.

"That wasn't really a compliment." Silver sighed. How she missed spending her days on the desert sands, the sky big and endless above her. She'd spent more time underground in the past few weeks than she'd ever expected to in her whole life.

A loud *BOOM* followed by a splitting *CRACK* tore across the air.

The slide!

One boot was dipped into the burrow when two Snuckers rushed up behind Silver and shoved her in, just as Silver caught sight of the landscape rushing toward her.

"Hey—*ooooogaaahhh!*"

Silver slid down a narrow, frozen-earth slide, one arm pointed down and the other thrown over her head. She dug in the heels of her boots, to no avail. Her rear bounced painfully, and her fur collar snagged on roots, choking her before being yanked away again, sending broken roots and dirt down her back.

Then she hit the bottom.

"Oof."

She couldn't see them, but she heard dozens of Snuckers laughing at her landing. Silver tried to stand and bumped the back of her head on the top of the chamber. It was only high enough for her to rise while doubled over at her waist. That dark, suffocating feeling of being trapped creeped in, and Silver closed her eyes—even though she couldn't see anything, anyway—and took several deep breaths. *It's better than being buried alive by the avalanche,* she told herself.

"Please. Just get me out of here."

The tops of furry heads deposited themselves under her palms. More nudged the backs of her legs. Six Snuckers carried her on her back. If she kept her eyes closed, Silver could pretend she was in an open space, something as grand as the palace rooms of Calidia, with their views of the stars above.

Sleep for a while. Relaxed body is easier to carry. We'll watch over you. Nothing will eat you. The Snuckers laughed. What could get to Silver in that belowground tunnel?

Silver felt a little uneasy, but soon exhaustion took over.

◊ ◊ ◊

WHEN SHE WOKE, Silver's mind was refreshed, but her body ached even more. As the Snuckers continued to carry her, she sent a question to her Aquinder.

Hiyyan, where are you?

We see the Keep. Hiyyan's quick reply excited her. So close!

Hiyyan gave Silver a play-by-play of what he was seeing as he and Kirja approached the Keep. *Fewer trees. More snow. I smell . . . figs and bread.*

Images of figs and bread and Aunt Yidla's kitchen and her own mother laughing around the table at Brajon's house and . . . and . . . Silver rubbed her forearm under her nose as the Snuckers climbed onward.

Almost at the top! Almost there! The Snuckers were nearly as excited as Silver.

Nebekker! Hiyyan said.

They'd made it.

The air around her ears surged with frost. Silver dared open her eyes to discover a faint light over her head. She reached up with her good arm and emerged from the chute with a sucking breath like a swimmer elated to discover they hadn't drowned.

Good-bye, humans.

"Thank you. Good-bye."

Silver spared a glance to see that Nebekker looked no worse for the climb up the chute and then went to Hiyyan, hugging his neck tightly. His breath was mist in the cold, and

Silver's lungs burned with the thinness of the air. Her head swirled, spotted with fits of darkness.

"Hello, my friend, my Hiyyan," Silver gasped. She never wanted to let him go, but she pulled back slightly to look north, where the mountain peak blended with an imposing building of gray stone.

They'd reached the Watchers' Keep.

ELEVEN

The Keep frowned down at them with its stern black stone lines dusted over with glistening white snow. The structure perched on the side of the mountain summit, rising nobly into the uppermost reaches of the atmosphere, and before seeing it, Silver would have thought it was carved from the rock that was already part of the mountain, just as Jaspaton was carved from sandstone cliffs. But now she saw that the stone of the Keep didn't match that of the mountain. What madness would have compelled people to carry those huge stones up the mountain so many hundreds of years ago?

Silver's neck ached from tipping her head so far back, but even so, she couldn't see the top of the Keep. It rose into the clouds as though touching the very homes of the ancient goddesses. Mele would have loved to see this. Silver pressed a palm to her eyes. As soon as Hiyyan was healed, they were going back for Mele and Luap.

About those figs and that bread . . . Hiyyan nudged her gently. He was right: No one was getting saved if they weren't fit and fed.

"You would think their diets would be spare, all the way up here on the mountain, but the Watchers always manage to put out a good spread," Nebekker said.

"With medicine stores to match, hopefully," Silver murmured.

Despite the imposing majesty of the building, the Keep doors were simple wood, hinged with long black iron findings. Silver swallowed, raised her fist, and knocked.

It was possible no one inside heard her. The doors were so thick she barely heard the knock herself. Even so, the bass sound of a heavy lock dropping meant someone had come. Slowly, the huge door was pulled open, the hinges moaning their protest, and Silver's name was hollered into the mountain range.

Mele reached an arm through the doorway and yanked Silver inside.

"We thought you were dead!" she exclaimed. "Killed by the hunters or frozen to death."

"Eaten by wild animals," Nebekker added, as though it were a game.

Kirja let loose a disapproving snort.

"Mele!" Silver threw herself at her friend. "You're okay! You're here!"

"We're all alive." Mele held Silver at arm's length and grinned. Her glance swept over Silver's tattered clothes and the thick layers of mud on Nebekker's knees. "Come inside and get warm."

Silver curled her fingers to hide the dirt caked under her nails and used her forearm to push some errant hair off her forehead. Mele looked as fresh and clean as the first time Silver had seen her, in Calidia. The Watchers' Keep would be good for a bath at least.

They entered an echoing great room, and Mele pushed the heavy door closed with a scraping *thud* behind them. Silver craned her neck, taking a deep breath to steady her balance as her head shot through with pain, but at least the voices that had assaulted her brain on the glacier, upon Silver's first touch of Nebekker's heartstone, had been silenced by the thick walls of the Keep. The ceilings were three stories high and braced with thick wooden beams. Heavy tapestries lined every floor and wall, including being draped back over the door that had just been closed behind them. A massive fireplace, taller than Hiyyan, threw off roars of heat. An entire tree must have been burning in that pit.

There was little else to recommend the space. A few spartan chairs that would do nothing to ease aching bones. Low tables covered with an arm's-thick layer of melted and cooled wax and with candles stacked on top. Metal chandeliers hanging from impossibly long chains dripping yet more wax all over the floors and rugs. It was, indeed, warmer than outside, but not by much.

Silver pressed the back of her hand to Hiyyan's flank. As one, they both sucked in air through their teeth. Silver because Hiyyan's skin was burning up, and Hiyyan because her hands were like ice.

"Sit and res—" Mele began.

"No time for rest. Hiyyan needs medicine. Food. Quickly."

Mele twisted her fingers together. "I'll try to find Lers, the tender here at the Keep. He's the one who found us. He was out in the forest clearing the path to the Keep—to the other entrance—and stumbled across me and Luap."

"It's a good thing you were so close," Nebekker said darkly. "Had Lers not found you, we would never have seen you again."

Silver's hand moved from Hiyyan, shot out to grab Mele's fingers. She knew the Calidian girl had conflicting emotions— she watched them cross Mele's face, one after the other: relief, blame, fear, anger. But they had all made it to the Keep. Things had to get better from here on out.

"Last I saw, Lers was taking supper to Luap."

Supper! Hiyyan said.

"What's this bedlam, then?"

As if summoned, a bearded man Silver surmised to be Lers entered the room. He was a short and stout man with arms the size of tree trunks. His bald head was revealed when he pulled off the thick wool hat he wore and stuffed it into one of the huge pockets on his coat.

"Your water dragon looks sick, young one."

"*Obviously,*" Silver burst out. "He's dying!"

"Silver." Nebekker stepped in. "Hello again, Lers. I'll assume that the healing stocks are in the same locations as before?"

"If it's stored warm, it's next to the kitchens. Cold storage below," Lers confirmed. "I'd guess the dragons are peckish, too. Let's get you critters fed. Off to the den!"

"Where's the den? Why are you taking him there? Wait for me," Silver called out, but Nebekker stopped her with a hand on the elbow.

"Stay. Get some food."

"It's all right, Silver," Mele added. "Luap's in the Dragon Den, too. It's safe there. Warm. There's food. The rest of the Keep isn't built for the size of our dragons."

"Is that the reason they gave you?" Nebekker's mouth twisted wryly.

"I have to take care of him. It's my responsibility." Silver swallowed a painful lump.

Nebekker nodded knowingly. "Taking care of yourself is the first step to taking care of him."

The scent of nourishment wafted in from somewhere down one of the dark hallways at the back of the great room. Silver's stomach growled.

Nebekker smiled. "Smells like there's supper for the humans, too. I'll go with Hiyyan. Lers knows all about the creatures on this mountain. If there's a—if all goes well, he'll be a new water dragon by the time your meal is over."

Silver's exhaustion, body and mind, settled over her in a fog. Hiyyan's nostrils flared as though he was going to take in a deep breath full of smells that would reveal some clues about the Watchers' Keep, but instead he only sighed.

We'll meet again with full bellies.

Silver watched Lers and Kirja help Hiyyan across the room and out a side entrance. Her chest hollowed with worry and fear. She reached into her pocket to warm her hand and bumped into something hard. Nebekker's heartstone. She'd forgotten to return it amid all the Snucker chaos on the glacier.

Silver opened her mouth to call after Nebekker, but as a flash of firelight ricocheted off the heartstone, a boot step echoed on the far side of the room. Silver turned at the sound, surprised to discover a hidden staircase carved into the stone of one wall. One figure stood high above them, looking down, while another one slowly descended to the great room.

The man who remained at the top gazed down at them, his thick eyebrows raised high. His pale skin sagged, but even from far away, Silver could tell his eyes were as bright and curious as a child's.

"And so," he said, his bass tones carrying into all corners

of the great room. "You have found a dragon heartstone. How very intriguing."

Instinctively, Silver's fingers curled around the stone, hiding it from sight.

"It's not mine," she admitted. "But I've come here to find my own!"

The woman descending the stairs chuckled. Her amethyst-colored bell sleeves fell over the tops of her slim, gloved hands. Around her head, a narrow silver band held her hair flat. It was a circlet much like the one Silver's father wore. "No need to worry, Silver Batal. We do not want your friend's dragon heartstone. Nor your Aquinder. Nor anything else you could offer us. Our needs are seen to, and our wants are very, very small and can hardly be met by the things of this earth."

"How do you know my name?" Silver asked. "You won't tell Queen—anyone—what I have? Or that I'm here?"

"We don't converse with the queen of the deserts," the woman said. "Unless she comes to our doorstep seeking wisdom. In that case, we won't turn her away. We don't turn anyone away."

The last part of that statement was nothing more than fact, Silver knew, but she also heard the warning behind the words.

"But few visit. Most seek alternative paths to wisdom or ruin," the woman continued. "Our ways are dusty, musty, and old. The young have little use for our silly mythologies and methods."

The woman and man shared a private smile that Silver didn't quite understand.

"I seek wisdom," Silver blurted out. "My water dragon has been poisoned. I need a cure."

The woman had reached the floor of the great room by now and swept toward Silver, her heavy robes dragging across the stone. She was a formidable woman, tall and large of stature, but her face was welcoming.

Silver felt her shoulders relax—she hadn't realized how tense she'd become since the Watchers had entered the room.

"My name is Lothilde. And that is Gavi at the top of the stairs. We're happy to welcome you, and to do our best to help your water dragon companion."

Gratitude rushed into Silver's chest like a desert heat wave. "Thank you. It's been a while since we've felt welcome anywhere. And thank you for helping heal Hiyyan." Silver squeezed the heartstone. Boldness replaced gratitude. "Just in case you can't heal him . . . can you tell me more about dragon heartstones? Where to get one myself?"

Lothilde shared a quick glance with Gavi. "There certainly will be some kind of information about heartstones in the Keep."

"How common do you think they are, girl?" Gavi growled.

"Not . . . very?" Silver knew of only one, but surely there had been more in the history of the world.

"Certainly not many in this generation. You'd better put that one away"—Lothilde nodded to the dragon heartstone—"and join us for a meal. You will be tired and cold, still. Whoever built the Keep didn't seem to understand how chilly these big, open stone rooms get. And you all look more used to the warmth of the desert. The dining hall is upstairs, where the heat rises. After some rest, we'll help you with your search."

Silver hesitated. When Silver held the dragon heartstone out in the open in her hand, the Watchers commented on it. Shared a glance that Silver couldn't read. But that was it.

She remembered how Sagittaria Wonder's eyes had flashed the first time she saw Nebekker's heartstone, and she could imagine how Arkilah's expression would darken and deepen. Even now, a voice came to her through the stone walls.

You have our heartstone.

Kirja.

I will return it as soon as possible.

But the Watchers? They simply watched.

Silver didn't entirely trust them, not with Gavi's *very intriguing*, but it was possible they really had no interest in capturing illegal water dragons or stealing dragon heartstones.

"I am cold. And hungry," Silver finally admitted. Lothilde pulled a blanket from a chair and draped the colorful fabric over Silver's shoulders.

"You look like you're leading a festival parade with that getup," Mele joked.

"Someday I will. Hiyyan and I both will. Closing out the festivities, holding our race cup high, world champions."

"You sound like yourself again," Mele said. Then her voice took on an edge. "It's good to hear you haven't given up on what you really want."

Maybe Silver deserved that reminder that she often rushed headlong into what she wanted without thinking enough about others.

"Yes, I want to race," Silver said softly. "But more than that, I want Hiyyan healed. I want us all safe and free and happy."

Silver locked eyes with Mele. "Let's make that happen."

TWELVE

*F*ish.

The single word came to Silver faintly, but it was lined with delight. Hiyyan was eating. That made Silver happy, but worry still lapped at the edges of her heart. Her left arm was growing weaker, unable to grip the edge of the blanket as it slid down her shoulder. When she pulled out a chair in the dining hall, she noticed the tips of all her fingers were still a dangerous dull-blue color.

"Here." Gavi noticed Silver examining her hands and passed her a metal cup. "Wrap your hands around this. You might be able to keep your fingers."

The liquid inside the mug was steaming hot and warmed her palm so quickly that the pain increased. *Might?* Silver winced and held her face over the steam, inhaling the rich scent of milky, hot molten chocolate laced with cardamom and almond cream.

Silver drank deeply and smacked her lips. "It does help me feel better. If you have hot chocolate way up here, what else do you have? An antidote to Screw-Claw poison?" Silver would give up sweets for the rest of her life if it meant an easy and quick way to heal Hiyyan. "That's what we had a run-in with on our way here."

"I was wondering about the way you favor your arm," Lothilde said. "Screw-Claw, you say? A treacherous water dragon breed."

Silver nodded. She debated telling the Watcher everything, but what did the Watchers know of water dragon bonds? How much did Silver want to reveal yet? Not much. Not until she trusted the Watchers.

"We don't have a specific medicine for that. It's never been needed. Screw-Claws are reclusive, and humans aren't common in the mountains, either. When they meet, well . . ." Gavi made a sinister expression and drew a line across his throat.

"But you survived and you're here," Lothilde said cheerfully, giving Gavi an impatient look.

"For now," the cranky old Watcher muttered.

The group sat around a long wooden table, and the first of three courses was brought in by another of the Watchers, this one a petite woman who frowned at the number of people seated around the table.

"Thank you, Dasia," Lothilde said. "You outdo yourself— and all of us—each time."

Lothilde turned to Silver with a conspiratorial expression and lowered her voice. "We take turns cooking daily meals. Some of us are better at it than others. Dasia is the best. You came on an opportune day."

As soon as she was served, Silver's appetite hit her like a desert storm. It was all she could do to keep herself from licking clean her bowl of broth, before asking for another plate of the spice-crusted game bird with lemon rice and pine nuts, and the hearty, simmered dried fruits that came next, and finally, falling face-first into the farina with mastic and orange-blossom water. Next to her, Mele ate with the same gusto, too busy eating to speak beyond murmured words of appreciation.

In the lull, Silver quickly sent her thoughts to Hiyyan.

Are you warm? Is your food as delicious as mine? Hiyyan? Can you hear me?

When the reply finally came, it was quiet. *Yes and yes.*

The Watchers say they don't have the antidote. Is Nebekker tending to you? Keeping you comfortable?

When Hiyyan didn't answer right away, Silver tuned out the people in the dining hall and focused on Hiyyan: his long tail, his strong haunches, his wings—one badly hurt, one healthy—his aching shoulders and front legs, his too-taut neck muscles, the matted fur that she would brush until it was magnificently soft and lush.

A strong and bitter herbal smell shocked her nose. *What is that? It nearly knocked me off my chair!*

All the medicine Nebekker could find.

A cure?

No. But it helps with the pain.

Silver's heart squeezed. *I'll come down to tend you. I'll—*

No. Find out about a heartstone. That's what we need.

Silver nodded to herself and looked longingly as her empty bowl of pudding was carried away. But soon enough her mug of hot chocolate had been refilled, and she sat forward in the stiff wooden dining hall chair and appraised the Watchers.

During the meal, five more had wandered in until Silver had seen eight of them, each swathed in colorful robes with fur trim on the collars and cuffs. Their faces were old, but not terribly lined, and had a wide range of pale to golden to very dark complexions that told Silver they came from all over different parts of Alsa, their world.

Surely, they knew many things. But where to begin?

"Can I ask some questions?" Silver said. "About being a Watcher?"

"Of course," Lothilde said. "We hold no secrets."

"That's not what people in Calidia think," Mele said. "They think you do all sorts of weird and mysterious things up here."

"Same for Jaspaton," Silver said.

"Let me guess." Lothilde counted on her fingers. "We sacrifice creatures to the ancient goddesses. We roam the tunnels and caves below the mountains looking for riches. We can alter the course of entire nations with a wave of our hands."

Silver and Mele looked at each other and nodded. The Watchers also looked at one another, but they smirked.

"We only watch," Lothilde said, "and catalog what we see."

"But you do choose the desert rulers," Silver pointed out.

"A grave responsibility, that," said Dasia, finally sitting to enjoy her own cup of hot chocolate.

"A grave curse," Gavi said darkly.

The Watchers shared a look that held layers of meaning.

"What do you mean?" Silver said.

Lothilde buried her face in her mug. Her voice echoed out of the little chamber. "That's what the nomadic tribes believe."

"Arkilah and her ilk, you mean?" Mele said.

Silver didn't know how her friend could say Arkilah's name so easily. Just hearing the syllables made Silver cringe.

But then Mele rolled her eyes. "There are no such things as curses."

"So you say," Gavi said. "But the nomads believe in an ancient group of people who once did something so terrible that the goddesses cursed them to live forever, with one grand task to perform and otherwise allowed only to watch the fallout of their decisions."

"What did they do?" Silver asked.

Gavi's eyelids lowered to slits. "They released a darkness."

Silver shivered. She didn't believe in the goddesses—no one in Jaspaton did anymore. And she didn't believe in curses, nor had she ever heard of a "darkness" being released. But the way the Watchers hid in their Keep, only emerging to seek a new desert ruler, as needed, fit the story.

"Then again," Gavi continued, shrugging, "perhaps the Watchers are simply wise people who shun the monotony of human life and nothing more."

The seven other Watchers each reacted differently to Gavi's words. Dasia sighed and looked sadly into her cup of hot chocolate. Lothilde pressed her lips into a fine line, her eyes going steely. A man, exceedingly tall with dark brown skin and furs across his shoulders to match, tipped his chin up proudly. Another man, the shortest of the group, pulled his eyebrows together and sucked on his teeth.

And Gavi stared at Silver, his face as unreadable as rock.

"Come, it is time to continue our catalog," the tall man said in a deep, rolling voice. "Until our shift ends."

"Until then, Baana," Lothilde said.

Accompanied by hollow laughs that confused Silver, five of the Watchers retreated once more, leaving only Lothilde, Gavi, and Dasia behind.

"You watch in shifts?" Silver asked.

"Endless shifts," Gavi said.

"Or so it feels," Dasia quickly added in her high-pitched voice. "So many events, so much cataloging."

"What do you mean by cataloging?" Mele leaned forward, her eyes lit up with interest.

Silver rested her chin on her palm, covering her small smile. What sort of upheaval could Mele cause with hundreds upon hundreds of years of knowledge?

"We catalog as many events of the world as we possibly can," Lothilde said.

"Do you include water dragon history in your histories?" Silver said.

"Of course. They are the other dominant race in our world," Lothilde said. "Their history is tied to our own."

"I'm ready to search that history." Anticipation made Silver's toes curl and uncurl in her boots. The Watchers had said there wasn't much information about heartstones in *their* generation, but since the beginning of all time? The answers she needed to help Hiyyan *had* to be in those catalogs.

As if summoned, Hiyyan's thoughts erupted in her mind.

Fifteen fish! Each one more delicious than the last! Whatever sad thing you're eating can't compare.

Silver couldn't keep back her laugh—how could she not be overjoyed at a sudden burst of energy from her Hiyyan? Then she quickly coughed to cover the laugh once she noticed everyone looking at her as though the ice had frozen an integral part of her brain.

Mele raised her eyebrows. Silver cleared her throat.

"It's nothing. Just remembered an old joke is all."

I'm happy you enjoyed your fish, Silver bond-said. *My chocolate is better. And now I'm trying to find out everything about dragon heart-stones. Healing, soon!*

Soon. Hiyyan's thoughts grew drowsy.

Lothilde pressed her fingertips together. "You underestimate the enormity of the search."

"I'm ready. In school, we learned that Watcher knowledge belongs to all," Silver said. Emboldened by Lothilde's nod, Silver rushed on. "Where do I find the knowledge?"

"It begins in the Chamber," Lothilde said. "And is recorded in the library."

"Can you show us?" Mele asked.

"Lothilde . . ." Gavi's voice was low.

"Oh, stop, Gavi." Dasia waved her fellow Watcher away and leaned in close to Silver, her stage whisper loud enough for everyone to hear. "Sometimes, we call him Grumpy Gavi. But it's in the oath we took when we were called to Watch: Knowledge belongs to all."

"If that's true," Mele said, "why don't more people come here in search of it?"

"I imagine many fear they'll be made into our next sacrifice," Gavi said, echoing some of the rumors that the girls had heard about the Watchers.

"Others can't or have no interest in making the trek all the way here," Dasia added. Silver grunted her agreement with that. She'd never have scaled the mountain had she not truly needed to.

"And others," Lothilde finished, "do come. Learn a few things. Take that knowledge into the world with them and share it in various ways. But that is rare. More often, they come, find themselves buried under knowledge, and become more confused than when they came."

"How long do those people stay?" Silver asked.

"Without fail," Gavi said, "they perish here."

Silver caught Mele's glance, knowing her friend's wide eyes mirrored her own. Silver's breath came quickly when Lothilde stood and indicated with a nod for Mele and Silver to follow.

"To the library," Gavi mumbled.

One corner of Lothilde's mouth twitched. "And then to the Chamber."

Gavi's jaw clenched once more, but he held his tongue as the five of them all filed out of the dining hall and back to the grand staircase. At the top, Silver paused, studying the huge room below, ready to learn the most valuable piece of knowledge of all: how to find her own dragon heartstone.

◊ ◊ ◊

LOTHILDE'S SLIPPERED FEET *shushed* quickly as she guided the group down a flight of stairs that twisted narrowly to what Silver assumed was a space below ground level.

They reached the end of the stairs, and the Keep once again opened up into a massive room. Unlike the sparsely decorated great room above, however, the library was packed side to side and top to bottom with furniture, shelves, supplies, stacks of parchment, and—

"Books," Silver and Mele breathed in unison.

Thousands upon thousands of huge tomes of history. The majority of the books were bound in burgundy leather, with nothing more than a range of dates stamped into the spine, but Silver noticed that one corner of the library was dedicated to brown leather-bound books, the tan creases an indication that they'd been read many, many times, and in between the burgundy books, here and there, sapphire-blue-bound pages.

Silver turned in a slow circle, overwhelmed by the display of human history in one single room. Her skin tingled, and her nose twitched. The room, despite the many items inside, was meticulously clean to a degree that even Aunt Yidla would approve. It was cold and dry, as well, she assumed to keep all the parchment in good, archived condition. Binding materials were arranged neatly across several of the tables, and at one, the Watcher Baana worked in silence, neatly transcribing a set of notes from one stack of parchments into a book. Silver waved a greeting in his direction, but he was too engrossed in his work to look up. There were no other Watchers working in the room.

Silver walked over to the brown books. "Why are those bound in a different color?"

"They are prehistory," Lothilde said.

"Lore and myths," Gavi said. "Stories of things that may or may not have happened before the discovery of the Ever."

Silver frowned. "Stories of the ancient goddesses, then?"

"Yes," Lothilde said.

"And what about the blue books?"

"Ah." Lothilde swept across the room, as though relieved to get away from the brown books. Silver kept right on the Watcher's heels. Lothilde reached for one of the blue tomes and opened it, the spine creaking with the effort. "The Ever shows us six views of the world at once."

"Literally?" Mele scrunched her face disbelievingly. "You're supposed to write the history of the whole world by only looking at six things?"

"The Ever shows us things that, over time, allow us to piece together a holistic view of modern life. How people in various regions cook and speak and work and celebrate and educate.

And it shows us unusual things, as well. Changes of power, seminal events like major water dragon racing events, shifting of landscapes under storms, for example. We believe the Ever shows us the most important things for us to see, because we must believe that. We have no choice. There are, surely, things we never see. But isn't that always true of recorded events?"

Silver pressed a thoughtful finger to her chin. Beside her, Mele let out a soft *hmm*.

Lothilde continued. "Almost always, these views center on the experiences of humankind. But sometimes, and for reasons we don't understand, one view of the Ever focuses on water dragons. Here, in these blue books, we keep track of the history of water dragons as it happens in concert with our own."

"May I?" Silver asked breathlessly. Silver balanced the book on her hip. The answer to finding a heartstone for Hiyyan could rest within those pages.

She rushed over to a table and struggled to open the book with her good arm. The pages were nearly as big as Silver's chest and weighed more than one of Brajon's dinner platters on a feast night. "Ugh!"

Mele joined her, peeking over Silver's shoulder.

"Watchers are artists?" Mele said.

On the parchment, a lovely charcoal sketch featured Abruqs, the little water dragon guards of Calidia, frolicking on a pebbly beach, with tall evergreens for a backdrop. Their trumpet snouts lifted to the sky playfully, but hiding in the trees was a sinister shadow: a human. The note on the page said: *Initial Abruq-human contact.*

Silver put a finger to the page to trace the illustration, but pulled her hand back when Gavi sternly cleared his throat.

"No touching!" Gavi snapped. "The oils from your skin eat away the parchment."

"We wear gloves when we fill the books, dear," Dasia said. "It was a hard-learned lesson. Some of the very earliest pages have been eaten away. But we do have excellent archivists here in the Keep, so we've saved all we can."

"Has much been lost?" Silver asked.

Dasia waved her white-fur-clad arm. "Oh, nothing of importance, as far as we can tell."

"Most of what is contained in these books is nothing of importance," Gavi grumbled. "Imagine spending your days detailing the process of making bread or crossing a desert. You lowlanders might think we're wise, but really all you need to be a Watcher is an endless supply of patience for the utterly mundane lives most people live."

"Imagine forgetting how to make bread or cross a desert," Lothilde said. "These books would be put to good use then."

"The kind of earthly event that would wipe out the knowledge of bread baking or desert crossing from humanity would destroy this library, too." Gavi's entire beard seemed to droop when he frowned.

He cleared his throat again and shot a look at Silver and Mele. "As mealtime has concluded and I'm no longer entertained by the novelty of our guests, I will relieve one of the other Watchers' shifts at the Ever. How delighted I am to fill yet more pages with mediocrity and uselessness."

"Has he always been like that?" Silver said.

"He really has, my dear," said Dasia, shaking her head solemnly.

A soft chuckle came from Banaa across the room.

Silver read a few sentences on the open page. It was the

history of the Abruq water dragons becoming part of the royal protection unit. Silver smiled, recalling her first encounter with the silver-and-black-striped water dragons. They were so cute and just the right size to hold in her arms and snuggle, which belied their stoic dedication to duty. Silver saw how their horn-shaped snouts were perfectly shaped for sounding an ear-piercing warning at any sign of danger around the royal palace in Calidia.

She pressed a finger to her lips. Now she understood what Lothilde meant by the chronicling of water dragon history in concert with human history. Which meant that somewhere in those blue books had to be the answer she sought regarding dragon heartstones.

Silver gently closed the cover of the book she was reading. There must be thousands of burgundy-bound histories and several hundred blue. It would take ages to get through them all.

She stepped closer to a set of shelves and glanced at the spines. "They're all organized by date . . . but is there any other way of knowing what they contain? Specific volumes, I mean. If I wanted to know one particular thing, how would I find it?"

"Banaa is the best for that!" Dasia said.

"You're in charge of keeping track of what each book contains?" Silver called to him.

"I do. It's all up here." Baana paused his writing and tapped his temple with a raised finger. Silver's heart sank. There was no way she could tend to her task privately. As she looked at Baana's cloudy gray eyes, she wondered if she could trust him. Any of them. The Watchers seemed unconcerned by the presence of Aquinder, and, when it came to knowledge, they were open and ready to share. Nothing to hide, as Lothilde had said.

"What about the Ever?"

Lothilde clapped her hands together once, her slender cheeks rounding with a smile. "It is the most incredible thing. The entire Keep was built up around the Ever, you see."

"It was here before the Keep was here?"

Lothilde's eyes sparkled. "It was."

She beckoned for the girls to follow her into a narrow stone passageway that led to yet another staircase. This time, though, Silver and Mele took only seven steps down before reaching their destination. Here, the stone walls were as smooth as obsidian, as if time had worn them to a glittering luster. The room contained three stone tables with just enough room for one person to sit at each. Atop each table, there was a stack of parchment, a jar of ink, and several styluses with sharpeners. All the tables were occupied by Watchers, including Gavi, whose brow wrinkled with displeasure at their appearance.

Silver didn't care. Her attention was stolen completely by the object in the center of the room.

"That's the Ever?" Silver asked.

"That's the Ever," Lothilde confirmed.

The Ever was like a glass box, or cube. Perched on a stone dais that rose to the height of Silver's shoulder, its six sides rotated slowly on a spindle about the same thickness as Silver's mother's favorite fiberworking needle. Silver thought the Ever looked like an oversized version of the dice used in children's games in Jaspaton, except that a scene played out on each side of the Ever.

"What interest can *mere* children have in the Ever?" Gavi

was so worked up that his words were accompanied by a spray of spittle. "You shouldn't have brought them here."

"It's within their rights to see it, no matter how young they are," Lothilde said firmly, sending Gavi back to his work, grumbling.

"How did the Ever get here?" Silver asked, peering closer. On one side of the cube, in a harsh landscape that mirrored the mountain, a small Snucker made its way along an underground stream.

"The Ever has always been here. There's no answer to that. The first book begins with the actions of those observed in the Ever, but there's no account of the first Watcher who found it. Interesting, don't you think?"

"So the Ever was just lying here. In the snow." Mele raised one eyebrow. "For anyone to find."

"That is our understanding."

"And the Keep?" Silver said.

"It grew up around the Ever."

Mele's expression was still one of deep disbelief. "It *grew*?"

"I see there is no mincing of words with this one," Gavi said sullenly.

Lothilde laughed. "The Keep was built slowly, over many . . . generations. To protect the Ever, and to provide comforts to Watchers as their needs and desires for, well, warmth and space evolved. This room is the oldest. Then came the library and"—Lothilde winked at them—"not long after, the kitchens."

"Kitchens are essential!" Mele said. "So, can I watch the Ever? Like you do?"

Now even Lothilde looked uncomfortable. Her wide

brown eyes scanned the room. "There are only enough tables for Watchers," she finally said.

Mele nodded, but her clever face shadowed. Silver had the feeling her Calidian friend would find some way to become a Watcher of the Ever, even if unofficially.

Silver glanced at the Ever again and bit her tongue to keep from crying out. This time, she caught a glimpse of a boot on ice just before the scene shifted to somewhere else in the Desert Nations. There had been a sled in the background of that scene, she was certain of it. A huge one, mostly broken.

Silver elbowed Mele. "The trackers are back on the trail," she whispered.

They had to hurry.

The Watchers didn't seem in any kind of hurry, though.

"Well, that's enough of the Ever. You've had an exciting day. I think two girls should be heading to bed now." Lothilde's grandmotherly tone, suddenly firm, was the kind you didn't question.

Silver bristled and pulled Mele close as they followed the Watcher back upstairs.

"I need you to help me go through all those books in the library," Silver whispered. "As fast as possible. Surely somewhere in the history of human and water dragon kind, there is an answer to where I can find my own dragon heartstone. And once we do that and I heal Hiyyan, we can get to King A-Malusni and put all our troubles behind us."

Mele nodded.

"I am *so* tired," Mele announced. Lower, so that only Silver could hear, she said: "For *now*."

"We have rooms prepared," Lothilde said. "They have every creature comfort we can manage up here in the Keep, but please, if there's anything else you require before the morning, do not hesitate to ask."

Silver met Mele's eyes again, but the girls didn't have time to say anything further before Dasia reappeared with two mugs of freshly warmed chocolate.

"Can I check on Hiy—the Aquinder—before we go?" Silver said.

"I just spoke with Lers," Dasia said. "They've settled in nicely. No need to worry! Lers is the best water dragon caretaker we've ever had here at the Keep." Dasia led them up the stairs, her fat gray curls bobbing up over the top of her robe's hood. "I think he likes them better than he likes us, if I'm being quite honest. Even the surly ones melt to pudding under his thorough care."

They were led down a hallway lined with doors and yet more tapestries. For the first time, Silver noticed the images crafted with thread: They were portraits of desert rulers. Some Silver remembered from pictures in her school texts. Others she didn't recognize. They were an unusual topic for art. The Desert Nations tended to create abstract art focused on shape and pattern, or sometimes they would portray scenes of animals in their habitats, like herd animals in pastoral valleys or water dragons on the seas. Images of faces were reserved for family members. Silver's father had crafted many a simple pendant or bracelet to hold the miniature portrait of a loved one. He, she knew, even wore a ring whose clasp, once sprung, opened to reveal her mother's beautiful face.

"I have put you side by side," Dasia said to Silver and Mele. "I hope you like it. Isn't brownish-red the loveliest color? Of course, the incident with the beets is the reason the bedding is dyed that shade, but a happy accident, I always say!" Dasia's laugh was meant to be light; the end of it nervously rose an octave, surprising even Dasia. The Watcher cleared her throat.

"Good night, Silver."

With a brief twist of her mouth, Dasia left Silver's room. The Watcher woman had hardly shut the door behind her before Silver darted back into the hallway and right into the back of her friend. Mele let out a cry before Silver quickly hushed her.

"Are you sure we should be doing this?" Mele whispered. "How will we hide from Banaa?"

"Carefully! If a heartstone is out there waiting for me, I'm racing to it. I'll be in the library until I fall over dead."

"I'm shocked you aren't already."

Silver swept her gaze over her friend. "I could say the same for you. How did you make it here?"

"I sat." Mele sighed. "After the trackers left me, I sat against a tree with Luap across from me because then nothing could sneak up on us, and we nearly froze waiting for daylight to arrive. When it did, and the river began melting again, we swam. Luap's fast, but I've never known her to swim that fast before. We would have beaten you in any race, Silver Batal."

"I can't tell you how I felt when I thought . . ." Silver shook her head. "I'm sorry you were left."

"And I was sorry you were taken." Mele laughed. Then she raised her eyebrows dramatically. "But here we are now, so let's just focus on the wild and wonderful secrets contained in those books."

"Good ones, I hope. But first, I need to see Hiyyan."

"And I know how to get you there. I've been visiting Luap."

Mele led Silver to a door to the side of a fireplace and

down a swirl of lightly white-frosted stone steps. Silver could tell they'd been recently scraped clear, but snow had started falling again. She peered around hopefully for another tiny Snowfluff dragon, but she didn't see any. Mele slipped through the narrow opening between two sliding doors, disappearing into a plume of mist.

When Silver entered, she grinned.

In a room decadently decorated with thick piles of fur rugs, metal basins of spring water, dueling tile-bordered fireplaces on opposite sides, and, through the center, a bubbling brook brimming with fresh fish, lounged two content water dragons and one more, as comfortable as was possible under the circumstances.

"Hiyyan!" Silver ran to her Aquinder, throwing her healthy arm around his neck and relishing how his good wing automatically curled around her back.

Kirja opened her eyes to blink once at Silver, then rolled onto her back with a snort and a squirm as though to reach an itch. Mele rubbed Kirja's exposed belly. Kirja let out a satisfied sigh. On another pile of rugs, Luap stretched her tail and yawned, then dipped her head into the brook, slurping up an easy catch. Mele took one hand from Kirja to pull apples from her pockets and roll them to the water dragons.

"Where did you get those?" Silver asked. "It's frozen out there!"

"I've figured out my way around the Keep," Mele said mysteriously before going over to Luap.

"I see you all have been treated terribly down here." Silver laughed as Hiyyan scooped up his apple with a darting tongue and crunched through the fruit. "Where's Nebekker?"

More medicine, Kirja said. *Everything the Keep has.* As before, Silver startled at how clearly the water dragon's words came to her, even though they weren't bonded.

I am poked and prodded and given sour things and also sweet things to drink. But I'm getting lots of tail massages, too. Hiyyan's round cheeks rose with his smile, and he curled into a C-shape, gathering Silver close.

Lers and Nebekker entered, both with arms full. Lers fed the roaring fires with logs, while Nebekker set a series of jars on a table to join other vials and bags.

"Dasia said you were in your quarters, but I had a feeling you might be here," Nebekker said. "Lers has something for you."

Lers passed Silver a small metal tube with "Silver" etched in it. "This arrived long before you ever did. Was confused when it weren't filled wi' silver coin, but I understand now." Then he tipped his chin at Hiyyan. "His wound is oozing. I hear a Screw-Claw got at yer boy?"

"Are you closer to finding an antidote?" Silver asked while removing and unrolling a small bit of parchment from the tube.

> *In case you make it here before my invite to the Islands does, stay put. I've sent help.*
> *—Your Favorite Glithern Rider*

Silver couldn't hold back a grin. Ferdi! And he's sent help. Hopefully an escort to his home nation. Protection as they traveled off the mountain. When would they arrive? Hiyyan *must* be healed before then.

"Not yet." Lers stroked his beard thoughtfully. "I've told

Nebekker here all I know about them Screw-Claws, but I'll do more looking around tomorrow. Ain't never looked for a Screw-Claw antidote, but there's got to be some critter what's evolved alongside them big beasts and developed a good defense. You let me know if you fancy coming out with me."

"I'd prefer spending my whole life never seeing another cave beast," Silver said with a shudder.

"Mrumph," Hiyyan agreed.

"Besides, I have another cure theory I'm looking into," Silver said.

"That's good. Yer boy needs all the help he can get," Lers said as he left the Dragon Den.

"What does he mean?" Silver asked Nebekker.

"He means these medicines aren't working," Nebekker said gently, her eyes glistening.

Silver blinked back her own tears, knowing Hiyyan would sense her worry. Instead, she sent Hiyyan images of the library, of the Ever, and of each of the Watchers' faces, in turn.

Mele and I will search those books all night. There has to be a clue in there! I wish you could come. I miss you when you're in a different room from me.

Humans are soft, Hiyyan bond-said.

Silver knew he was teasing her for missing him, but she wiggled her good arm as if he'd meant her squishy muscles. *But not edible!* she reminded him. *We're so grooooss.*

What are you two laughing about? Speak to everyone in the room. How rude. Kirja glared at them but she couldn't hold her stern expression for long before it dissolved into a teasing smile.

Silver smiled, too, but only briefly before her eyes hardened with determination. "Nebekker, you know something about the library. Where should we begin our search?"

"Perhaps with someone we know had a heartstone: Gulad Nakim."

Silver nodded. Interesting, she thought, that Nebekker didn't mention herself. Was there a record of the moment Nebekker received her heartstone in the library?

"Okay. Gulad, it is. I'm going to figure this out, Hiyyan." Silver stood, dug Nebekker's heartstone from her pocket, and returned it to the old woman, then she turned on her heel and walked out to the cold steps, Mele right behind her.

"Enjoy snooping through those ancient books," Nebekker called after them. "I delight in seeing cranky old Gavi foaming at the mouth."

But before Silver and Mele got very far, they heard the sound of fast boots crunching through ice. Lers came around the corner, shouting, "They're here, all of them!"

They're here.

Silver's heart began pounding. Whom did Lers mean? Sagittaria Wonder. Queen Imea. Arkilah.

"Get out of here, Silver!" Mele pushed her friend forward and flung her body against the door, arms wide, as though she could block a whole herd of Snuckers.

Then Mele caught sight of something over Silver's shoulder, her eyes going wide. Before Silver could turn, darkness covered her face. She felt a heaviness on her back and shoulder muscles, and the ground fell away.

THIRTEEN

Silver!" She heard Mele cry.

"Mele!" Silver's legs kicked and flailed, tangling in the blanket that had been thrown over her. Fear rushed like a spring river. What held her? Where were they taking her? "Let me go!"

Images of foul prisons, of being thrown into the sea, of being eaten by a Dwakka all came to Silver in her panic. She didn't know how long she was in the air—or how high, or how far she was taken, nothing—but eventually she was dropped to the ground and the blanket was whisked away.

She jumped to her feet, ready to fight, and surveyed the dank and dark place. The skin on her arms puckered in the cold, and her feet sank into soft ground. There were trees, millions of evergreens blocking the sky, but no snow. Silver couldn't be sure she was still anywhere near the Keep. She *was* sure that she was alone, the teasing sway of the trees the only hint of other life.

"Hello?" Silver called out. She tried to sense Hiyyan's thoughts to see if he was nearby, but she didn't pick up anything.

Before her, Silver saw two paths, both shrouded in mist. Instinctively, Silver looked for Hiyyan and, when her Aquinder wasn't found, for Mele or Nebekker. Anyone who could explain where she was and how she'd gotten there.

A branch crackled in the tension of the stillness, and Silver pirouetted, her chest painfully sucking air, her eyes scanning every shadowed nook and cranny of the forest. There was no other movement.

She knew Brajon would give her an earful for not gathering more research, but Silver picked a path for no other reason than it seemed slightly brighter. As she walked, her steps were sometimes clear and sharp. In other moments, a fog seemed to take over her brain, and she seemed to walk for long stretches without realizing she'd gone anywhere at all.

Silver wished Hiyyan were there with her. She imagined reaching out her palm and patting his side. She put out her good hand and jumped when her fingers brushed scales.

"Hiyyan!" Without warning, he was there. "Where did you come from? Have you been here this whole time? I'm so glad the trackers didn't catch you!"

His expression was as puzzled as hers must be, but no words bubbled up in Silver's mind. Her eyebrows drew together. No communication . . . but at least Hiyyan was walking.

The fog grew thicker suddenly, and Silver saw a figure emerge from the mist and walk toward them. Silver shrank back for a second, then her wariness turned into confusion.

"Father?" Silver called out. Her heart leaped.

He's forgiven me. He's come to help us.

Silver ran to Rami Batal but stopped short of flinging her

arms around him. He was exactly as she remembered: tall and stoic, his sharp jawline softened by his long black hair, which was held back by a thin gold circlet. His thick eyebrows were drawn together, eyes unreadable as he glanced over Silver.

"Silver, where have you been?" Rami Batal said. He spread his hands wide, and his body slumped, seeming to carry the weight of the world on his shoulders. "Queen Imea didn't accept my scepter. Now it's up to you to return glory to the Batal family. You're the last hope we have, my brilliant girl."

Silver's breathing came fast. The fog in her mind cleared momentarily, and she realized she couldn't be in the forest near the Keep. Not if Rami Batal were here.

Am I dreaming? Delirious? Or, am I . . .

Silver refused to finish her thought. Instead, she met her father's eyes.

Before Hiyyan was part of her life, Silver's father had raised her to believe her place was upholding the Batal family dynasty. But Silver had rejected her father's dreams and broken his heart when she decided to become a water dragon racer. How could *she* now pick up the pieces and return the Batals to their former glory?

"I don't have anything to show the queen," Silver said, holding her empty palms out to her father.

Rami Batal studied her hands and frowned. "Your fingers are nearly frozen. A jeweler's hands are their tools. You spent all your time dreaming of water dragons, but now you can't even take care of the one bonded to you. You fail before you begin, every time."

Dizziness overwhelmed Silver, and she fell to her knees. "I can't do anything to make you proud," she whispered.

"Rami."

Another voice came to Silver. A softer one, missing the thick lashings of disappointment in her father's voice.

"Mother." Silver looked up. Sersha Batal stood before Silver, draped in a gold gown just a shade lighter than her skin. Her dark hair fell in thick waves over her shoulders, and her wide eyes were rimmed in kohl. She was as queenly a sight to Silver as Queen Imea had ever been.

Sersha reached down for Silver's hand and drew her daughter to her feet.

"I would have helped you, had you only trusted me," Silver's mother said. "You are a spring desert storm, Silver. Fresh and cool but still more gentle than a summer squall. You are not ready to face the world."

"I didn't have a choice," Silver said. "The world came for me."

"And now it comes for all of us. Queen Imea will stop at nothing to get the Aquinder; then what will be left of Jaspaton, of your family?"

"I'll never lead the trackers to Jaspaton!"

"And so you'll never come home to me?" Sersha asked with a sad smile. "Our children grow up and leave us too quickly."

Rami and Sersha Batal held their hands out to Silver.

"We know that Nebekker took you away and that you made a mistake. That's all behind us now," Silver's father said. "You can come home. Leave all this fear, this cold, this running away."

Silver let out a relieved breath. She hadn't realized before how much she wanted to go home. With a wide smile, she fell into her parents' arms.

"Come on, Hiyyan. Let's return to Jaspaton."

"No." Her father pushed Silver back to arm's length. "He can't come with us."

"He's too dangerous," Silver's mother added. "An illegal breed! Look at all the problems he's brought you."

"You mean, the problems I've brought *him*," Silver said as she took a step back, reaching behind to brush her fingers over Hiyyan's scales. He steadied her wildly beating heart. "I can't leave him."

"Take care of your*self*, Silver," her father said.

Silver moved to Hiyyan's side and wrapped an arm around his neck. "Taking care of him is taking care of myself, too."

"So you're choosing the water dragon over us again?" Silver's father asked.

Silver looked up, expecting that anger and disappointment she remembered from the last conversation with her father. But there was only sadness, and that cut deeper than anything else.

"I'm not choosing," Silver said. "But Hiyyan needs me now."

"You can't have everything. Pick. Him or us."

"Don't make me pick," Silver said. "Please."

Silver's mother wiped the tears off her cheeks. "You already have, my girl. Good-bye."

"Wait!" Silver reached frantically for her parents, but they disappeared like mist through her fingers.

Were they ever really there? Silver turned in a slow circle, focusing on the solid ground beneath her boots and the cold air searing her lungs. The forest was real, and she was real. Were dreams real? Silver's head pounded with confusion. *That* was certainly real. She pressed her fists to her forehead.

"Think, Silver. You know your parents can't really have

been here, or have disappeared. It's an illusion or a game of some sort. Why? From whom?"

She faced the pathway once more. There was a thin, whistling air of loneliness on the forest path. But how could she be lonely? She had Hiyyan with her.

Hiyyan mewled. A sharp pain ricocheted through his wing joint, and through Silver's arm, too. She winced.

"It will be all right," she said to Hiyyan. But seeing her parents like that . . . seeing their sadness over her choices . . . nearly extinguished the little flame of hope that burned in Silver.

Silver pressed her back against a tree trunk, hoping the cold would shock feeling back to her arm. She'd hurt so many people along the way already. Would it ever end? Why was she working so hard to find a dragon heartstone when what waited on the other side was even more heartbreak?

"No," Silver said, shaking her head. The fog was settling in her mind again, making her thoughts sluggish. "I can't think that way."

She reached for Hiyyan and curled her fist in his mane.

◊ ◊ ◊

"IT'S A TRIAL," Silver breathed. "I know it is. Like in the old desert fables. But I don't know if I'm passing or failing. Or who's testing me. Hiyyan . . . I don't even know if you're real or part of the mirage." Silver pressed a palm, a cheek, against her water dragon. He certainly felt real. Smooth and warm. "Either way, we must find a way out of this forest. Let's go."

Silver hadn't realized she was almost running until a regal voice stopped her. Silver skidded forward on the humus, then fell to her knees. Right at the feet of Queen Imea.

The queen smiled. She was very beautiful, with bronze skin and hair the color of moonbeams. Her dark eyes were ringed with the deep purple of a rare sapphire, and her platinum gown sparkled more than even the icicles glistening at the top of an ice cavern. Jewels gleamed, and in one hand, she held aloft a stunning royal scepter made of pure gold and silver and dotted with the finest gems in all the desert. The kind of jewels a great master jeweler would spend his whole life searching for.

After Silver processed all the beauty of Queen Imea, she realized a group of people was behind the queen, all on their knees as Silver was. Unlike Silver, though, each had ropes around their wrists, prisoners of the queen.

Queen Imea was quick to remind Silver of her crime. "My dungeon has an empty cell for you, Silver Batal. Or perhaps I will fill it with all of them? I might be willing to work out a trade."

Hiyyan mewled and lurched forward when he spied the group. Queen Imea threw her arm to the side, and Hiyyan skidded to a stop. The scepter was an extension of the queen's impenetrable power, creating a force of some kind between Hiyyan and those behind the queen.

It was Silver's mother and father. Her cousin Brajon and Mele. Nebekker and Kirja, wrapped in a net. Ferdi, the Island Nations prince. Her once hero, Sagittaria Wonder. Even the guard, head to toe in his white uniform, who had been kind to her when she was in Calidia so long ago. Who had helped her get registered for her races, who had cheered her on to victory, and who had helped her escape when the queen wanted to arrest her.

Silver repeated the queen's words in her head—*work out a*

trade—and her heart leaped. Freedom, for her and Hiyyan, was within her grasp?

Her stomach lurched as if an anchor were being pulled up from under her belly button. Why not take it? Hadn't she already turned her back on her family? Hadn't she forsaken Sagittaria Wonder—and vice versa? And the guard . . . she hardly knew him. Between her freedom and his, she could choose her own. Of course she would choose her own! Who wouldn't?

As though he could read her thoughts as he used to, Hiyyan peered at Silver disapprovingly.

No, Silver admitted to herself. She wouldn't. But she also wasn't willing to give herself or, even worse, Hiyyan over to the queen.

"It's a trial," Silver repeated to herself. "A test. There's a right answer, isn't there? An answer that doesn't turn my loved ones over to the queen, but that still allows our freedom."

Hiyyan snorted his agreement.

"All I've ever wanted was to race water dragons. It's still all I want." But as Silver's eyes went from family member, to friend, to hero, to helpful stranger, she became unsettled. If water dragon racing was all she wanted, truly, she would sacrifice everything else in pursuit of her goal. Her eyes fell on her father. Wasn't that what he'd always done? Forced Silver to give up her dreams for his own?

And yet, she could not fathom her father in a dungeon. And certainly not her supportive mother. She could not imagine her happy cousin locked away forever. She didn't even want Sagittaria Wonder taken away from the sport.

"Here are all the things in the way of water racing," Silver said, slowly getting to her feet and limping in a circle around Hiyyan. His head followed her movements as she tried to untangle the test. "My family doesn't want me to do it. Nebekker doesn't want me to do it. Arkilah wants us for other reasons. Queen Imea wants us for—I don't know why. Adherence to the law?"

Silver looked up. Queen Imea twirled her scepter slowly through her fingers so that Silver and Hiyyan winced each time the filtered daylight reflected off the perfect gemstones.

"Or even for power. Glory, I suppose. Possessing the rarest things in the land. You proved you loved precious things the day you came to my father's shop in Jaspaton."

"It's not wrong to love beautiful things." The queen's face was full of mirth.

"No," Silver admitted. "My family makes beautiful things, and I value that. But you're supposed to be an example to all our people. You have to respect and adhere to the law. Instead, you took something that wasn't yours."

"I found something that didn't belong to anyone."

"Kirja and Nebekker belong together!"

Queen Imea sighed. "I will protect you, of course. And in return, you will lead the desert to its ultimate glory."

"Winning the Spring Festival cup?"

Queen Imea threw her head back and laughed at Silver's confusion. "You are as sweet as a desert rose jelly, my girl. I will make you a deal." The queen plucked a small blue-and-violet stone from her scepter and held it out in her palm. "Look what I have."

A flame burst through Silver, warming her insides. A dragon heartstone! "You've had this all along?"

"It does not do to lay all our secrets out on the table at once," Queen Imea said. She paced in a small circle, the crystals on the hem of her glittering gown dragging along the path so that a strange winter melody filled the air. "A dragon heartstone must be earned. Succeed, and the heartstone is yours. Fail, and I leave you and your Aquinder here, not even bothering to dig you a proper grave."

Silver ached for that heartstone. Not only for Hiyyan's wing and her own arm, but for the even closer bond it would create between them. They could rule the entire world with a heartstone.

Queen Imea paused. "You do mean the world of water dragon racing, don't you?" she said, as though she could read Silver's thoughts.

Silver licked her lips. Did she only mean the world of water dragon racing? She recalled the wars of old between the Desert Nations and the Island Nations. The Aquinder were so powerful that when the deserts were about to fall to the islands, the Aquinder turned the tide of the war almost single-handedly. What could she and Hiyyan do with an even more powerful bond? Maybe more important, what could they not do?

But Queen Imea smiled. "Yes, girl."

Silver clenched her fists. She would make the queen kneel to *her*.

"Mrow?" Hiyyan cut through Silver's wild thoughts, but Silver brushed his questioning tone aside. The queen laughed again.

"What do I need to do?"

Queen Imea spun around and stabbed a finger in the direction of Silver's friends and family.

"Tell them the truth," the queen said. "You don't love them. Don't need them. Your past is nothing. All that matters is the race. Tell it to each of their faces."

Silver narrowed her eyes at her loved ones. The promise of freedom, of power, of—

No. A roaring sound filled Silver's ears, and she shook her head to rid herself of it. Where had this hunger for power come from?

"I won't."

Queen Imea walked closer, her eyes flashing in the low light. She stretched her arm out even farther.

"Tell them, and you can take this stone. All the riches and glory of the world will be yours. Isn't that what you've always wanted? To be a champion?"

Yes, thought Silver. And what was wrong with becoming the greatest water dragon racer of all time? Ambition was not a dirty thing.

Sagittaria, one moment behind the queen and the next beside Silver, placed a hand on Silver's shoulder. "Do as the queen says. Don't you admire my greatness? I achieved it alone."

"Yes . . ." Sagittaria was strong. Alone. No family to get in the way, no friends to judge her. "Hiyyan, what do you think?"

Hiyyan's feelings didn't need words; they were splayed across his face: confusion and fear, distrust and hope, all rolled together.

"We *need* that heartstone."

The trees seemed to speak to her, talking in crackling whispers and grunts, warning her of terrors to come, of dashed hopes, of promises of beauty twisted into things dark and sinister. Silver tried to curl her functional finger joints back and forth. When did blood start flowing into her hand, slow and thick? There was prickling pain.

"Think of Hiyyan," Silver whispered to herself, urging her

aching arm and legs to move. She felt like she was made of ice, and her limbs crackled with protest. "Think of racing. Think of glory and ruling the entire world."

Silver paused and frowned. "No, not that last one. Where did that come from?"

"Silver," her mother called to her.

But Silver turned away.

"Yes. Choose yourself." Queen Imea's voice was softer than ever. "Your path is clear. You and your dragon for this heartstone."

The queen held out the dragon heartstone, and with a heart that was suddenly so light it seemed to fly from her chest, Silver reached for it. Then she yanked her hand back as the fullness of Queen Imea's words reached her.

"No, that's not the deal! Deny my past for the heartstone, you said!"

"Follow my orders, I said!" Angrily, the queen flicked her wrist to the side and threw the stone into the trees.

Then she slammed the end of the scepter into the ground, causing the path to crack in a thousand places, dark lines running up and down the field like tiny rivers of dried blood. The forest began falling in on itself. Hiyyan cried out. Her parents screamed.

"No!" Silver dove into the opening, falling as fast and hard as the huge branches around her. The hole closed, and the sun was blotted out.

FOURTEEN

The voices came from every possible direction.

You should just give it to her.

Why? Because she looks so pathetic lying there? None of them are innocent.

She's very young.

That's not in her favor!

Stop arguing, you two. This decision is far more complex than anything you've said so far.

Yes.

It was that voice, the fourth one, that reached Silver's ears, that made her go still. The voice was close enough to her that she could feel the breath of it float over her cheeks, and low enough that she wondered if the other three heard the single word uttered or if it was meant for Silver only.

Her lower back ached where a rock was lodged beneath, and there was a steady, thrumming pain in her ankle. Running water sounded in the background like a lullaby. She could sleep so easily. But Silver forced her eyes open to see who was gathered around her.

They were water dragons. Four of them in a circle.

A Glithern, small for its breed but sporting the familiar iridescent, rainbow skin. He blushed and turned his face away when Silver looked at him. Next to him: a Padahu, the water dragon with a single line of black down the center of her face, one side of the line yellow and the other red, her hair the same dual shades and falling over her furry black robes. She looked left to right and back again, avoiding Silver's gaze. Her mouth seemed to turn up on one side and down on the other.

And two . . .

Silver could hardly believe her eyes. Hiyyan's joy was thick enough to spread on flatbread. His voice came to her when Silver was carrying Nebekker's heartstone, loud and clear:

Two Aquinder. There are more of my kind! In close proximity to a heartstone once more, Hiyyan's words to Silver were clear and complex.

Eyes shining, the female Aquinder graced Silver with a regal nod. Hiyyan's body blossomed with warmth, and a low hum buzzed in his throat. His happiness filled Silver to the brim.

The male Aquinder stood as erect as a stone; the skin around his ample beard and mane was wrinkled, with a gray pallor. Ancient. And he was staring at her with great disdain.

The female had a clean, smooth face and wore a white cloak fastened with sapphires, her furry chest thrust out proudly. Her dark eyes studied Silver so fiercely—and yet, somehow, kindly—that Silver was certain the dragon could see into the depths of her emotions and guess at things Silver herself didn't know.

Both were full of grace and beauty. These were no racers. These were leaders.

"Two more Aquinder," Silver whispered.

The yellow-red-faced dragon curled her talons into the soft soil of the burrow. *Do not argue on her behalf, Ssun. She can't be trusted. A typical human. One moment they're dependable and the next they've thrown our needs to the wind and taken off for their own adventures. I understand the impulse, and it doesn't make for a good ally.*

The only person she needs to be an ally to is the Aquinder, argued the Glithern called Ssun. *That should make you two happy.*

The old, male Aquinder snarled. Silver caught sight of a double row of teeth. It was like looking at a future version of Hiyyan. A healthy version, long into the future.

"Who are you?" It took all of Silver's energy to rasp out those words. "Can you help Hiyyan?"

You see, Dortaal? Ssun said, rearing back his head excitedly. *Her first words, her first thoughts. She is loyal.*

Her first words were about us, the old Aquinder, Dortaal, said drolly.

Carefully, Silver propped herself up on her elbow, her wounded arm dangling uselessly at her other side. She blinked a few times, washing away the cold blurriness. Behind the four dragons, roots and piles of rock crowded the space she was in. A wide stream ran along the left side of the burrow. There wasn't a single light source that Silver could see, and yet somehow the space was bright, full of daylight's spectrum of colors. The forest was gone.

The last thing she remembered was leaping into the hole. Before that, Queen Imea had been here . . . her parents and friends . . . Sagittaria Wonder. Where had they gone? What was happening?

Silver swallowed against the cold dryness in her throat and tried to speak again. "Hiyyan. He must be healed."

The female Aquinder leaned so close that Silver could see layers of depth in her eyes: the reflection of the fantastical light, yes, but also of seas and, deep down, a gentle orange glow. Silver looked away. The Aquinder's gaze made her squirm.

The Aquinder you're bonded to is on the cusp of death. But, for a moment, he is safe.

Silver shook her head. She knew the truth because her own life was dwindling into darkness, too. "He isn't. None of the medicines have worked. Help me find a dragon heartstone. It's the only hope we have left."

Silver remembered Queen Imea throwing the dragon heartstone into the crevasse, and her heart leaped again.

"It should be here!" She stumbled to her feet, her woozy head making her sway. The female Aquinder put a paw out to steady Silver, and the shock of the touch zapped through her limbs.

Silver snatched her arm away. "Don't hold me back!"

Ssun giggled. *Look at her ferocity. She is a friend to our kind.*

Dortaal's voice cut in. *She is afraid because she shall die, too. They're bonded.*

Silver never imagined she could dislike an Aquinder, but Dortaal was testing her limits.

"I am not. I don't care about me. Only Hiyyan."

Both things can be true: a fear for herself, a fear for the Aquinder. Care for the Aquinder and care for herself can also both be true. Must be true. The Padahu paced, her expression a gentle rebuke. *I don't like her understanding things she shouldn't know. On the other hand, she should see what world she has become a part of.*

She is not part of my world, Ge, the ancient Aquinder said.

Peace, Dortaal. Her gift makes her more part of our world than almost any other, the younger Aquinder countered.

Ssun nodded. *Kyan is right. The girl possesses a dangerous gift. A challenging one. A rich one.*

Dortaal grunted. *One she doesn't deserve.* He waved his claws dismissively. *A child. I'd rather communicate with one equal to my age, to my wisdom.*

You'd rather none of them be able to communicate with us, Ge said.

If only that were an option!

"Who are you?" Silver said again, crouching. She paid only half attention to the foursome, her eyes scanning the ground, her fingers grappling beneath stones. Queen Imea had thrown the dragon heartstone here. Where had it gone?

We are water dragons; that is all, Kyan, the female Aquinder, said. *Child, get up.*

With a graceful movement, Kyan held her paw out, palm up. In the center, the dragon heartstone glowed with a weak but steady violet light.

Silver gasped. "Please," she whispered. "Please. That's what I need."

She asks so sweetly, Ssun said, nodding with approval.

Desperately, Dortaal corrected.

Both things can be true at the same time, Ge repeated.

If I give this to you, Kyan said, *what will you do with it? Will you use it to heal the Aquinder to whom you are bonded?*

"Yes! That's the reason I want the heartstone."

The lovely water dragon's eyes went flat. She moved closer, bent down, obscuring the other figures in the room. Her scales shimmered like a valley river in the summer sun. Despite definitely being younger than the other Aquinder, there was still something about her that made Silver think she had been alive for a very long time. Silver thought of the ancient goddesses of the old mythology. It was said they had buried gems and precious metals under the desert for humans to find. Had they also buried dragon heartstones?

Kyan's mouth twitched in a barely concealed smile. *Your understanding of the world outside your own is small, I'm afraid.* Her talons curled around the heartstone, and she righted herself again. *And that is what gives me pause.*

Yes, said Dortaal. He stroked his mane. It was decorated with glass beads that made a discordant tune as he moved. *She doesn't understand the purpose of the heartstones. She is not worthy.*

Have any of them ever been? asked Ge. *I suppose it depends on how you look at the situation.*

Dortaal moved closer, so Silver scooted back. Those teeth were so near her.

What will you do with the heartstone? Will you race with it, using the water dragon like some kind of herd animal in your quest for glory? Will you go to war with it, using the strength and power it gives to overtake your royals and claim the world for yourself? Will you allow Hiyyan to subjugate other water dragons and make claim to his world as well?

Silver shook her head. She would never use Hiyyan in her quest for racing glory. But the rest? Overthrowing monarchies and owning many more water dragons? Were those things possible with the strength of the heartstone? What was the heartstone capable of, after all?

Silver licked her lips. A strange pull seemed to come from the stone.

She considers all angles, Ge said.

Ssun nodded. *There is much for her to think about. Much to learn. Much to discover about what the heartstones will and won't do. She will learn well. And do well.*

Yes. Silver's future came with clarity. She certainly would do well. But for now?

"I just want to heal Hiyyan. I just want us both to be free."

And all other water dragons? Dortaal asked.

"Of course!"

Do not lead her into promises she doesn't understand! They're not predictable, these humans. The female Aquinder pressed her lips together, thinking. *But bonds were created, and bonds exist, and they cannot be fully taken from this world, it appears. We must work with what we have and hope for the best.*

Silver got to her feet, sensing that some decision had been made. Her blood slowed in anticipation. "Please," she said again.

Sapphires gleamed as the female Aquinder held out the dragon heartstone and dropped it into Silver's outstretched hand. Then she shook her head, settling her cloak around her shoulders.

I don't know if choosing your Hiyyan above all others is the right choice, but it pleases the majority of the council. And so you have earned the heartstone. You'll do with it what you will, and we'll react as we must should we disapprove of your actions.

"Thank you for the chance to show you how much Hiyyan means to me."

The Aquinder smiled and, for the first time, looked as old as Silver thought she might be. Her weary eyes crinkled at the edges, and her nostrils flared, but there was a warmth in her expression, too.

I hope to discover the truth of your words, she said. *And I hope you are not disappointed in the truth of the heartstone.*

The Glithern immediately dipped into the stream and swam away, while the three larger dragons walked into the darkness before Silver heard them, too, take to the water and leave.

Her brain and body ached; she was full of questions and confusion, but only one thing mattered. Silver held the dragon heartstone high. She had no time to shout his name before Hiyyan had tackled her to the ground.

Silver laughed so hard it hurt her belly.

He was real. Real! She and her Aquinder wrestled together, frantic in their joy of being beside each other once more. And when they paused to take a breath, Silver felt a warmth pulsing in her palm. She opened her hand to admire it again.

Her dragon heartstone.

"We found it," she breathed. "I can heal you."

Silver pressed herself against Hiyyan's flank, and he pressed back. They rested for a moment, breathing in the crystallized silence of the burrow, their hearts swelling with gratitude, though for what they weren't yet sure.

Although questions still swam through Silver's mind, instinct told her to press the dragon heartstone against the wound on Hiyyan's wing.

Everything glowed: the stone, her arm, his wing. Warmth flowed through both of them. Silver had forgotten what it felt like to be healthy. She closed her eyes and prepared to soak it in, just as she used to soak in the sun in the vast desert. Suddenly, a thousand decibels of sound battled for space in her brain—some sounds were low and slow, others high and snappy. Silver pushed them away, her breath quickening.

When she opened her eyes again, the scales that she'd pressed the stone against remained gold, like a softly polished pendant from her father's workshop.

"Look, Hiyyan," Silver said softly.

Hiyyan craned his neck to inspect the new mark on his skin. Then he caught Silver's eye. It had worked! Finally, they would get out of the burrow and off the mountain. They would *fly* again. And then they would go to the Island Nations and procure their freedom.

Together, they grinned. Together, they lifted their arms high.

Together, they fell to the ground and bellowed in agony.

Silver's pulse hammered the space behind her eyes as the sounds, once again, built up to a roar in her brain. A tear rolled down Hiyyan's snout.

Soil rained down, the sound hitting the mucky floor like laughter.

No, Hiyyan said.

"This—this can't . . . be happening," Silver stammered. She tried to move her arm once more, cringing at the bitter pain in her muscles and bones. Frowning at her limb's refusal to move, she tried wiggling her frostbitten toes and stretching her aching neck. Nothing had changed.

They weren't healed.

The dragon heartstone didn't work.

FIFTEEN

Silver considered chucking the heartstone into the dark shadows of the burrow, hoping it would find and roll into a crack in the earth that funneled all the way to the core, where the useless bit of rock would melt and never taunt her again.

Instead, she tucked the heartstone carefully into her bag with trembling fingers and closed her eyes. Nausea rose in her throat as the noises in her mind continued chattering away.

"I failed," Silver whispered. "Finding an antidote is our only hope now. We have to get back to the Keep. Look, there's a way to climb out of here."

The duo moved slowly up the hand- and footholds in the walls, Silver and Hiyyan both crying out in pain with their efforts. She cradled her bad arm and curled her broken-nerve fingers on her good hand into a claw. Their breathing came heavy and deep. When they finally reached the forest trail once more, Silver doubled over, her head pounding with the racket.

Hiyyan stretched out beside her, his limbs trembling. *I hear* them, too. *Hundreds, maybe thousands, of water dragon voices. Words and song. Why are they talking so much?*

Silver's eyebrows shot up her forehead, and she blinked at Hiyyan. That was the most advanced sentence Hiyyan had ever bond-said to her. Somehow she knew he was singing the words, but as they reached Silver's mind, they were transformed into the language she knew best.

"Why are they talking so much? Why are *you* talking so clearly?" Surprise jolted Silver again. Her own words sounded mostly normal in her head, but something around the edges made them feel unfamiliar. They flowed differently. It was almost like when she held Nebekker's heartstone, but amplified a hundred times over.

She realized she was singing instead of simply speaking.

A burst of steam rose from Hiyyan's nostrils. His breathing was more labored than ever. Silver snuggled in next to him. She wasn't sure they could go on without a longer rest.

You speak dragon, Hiyyan said. *I haven't taught you those songs before.*

"No, that's impossible." From her mouth and into the painfully damp air, her words were the same as she'd always spoken, but there it was again: that feeling she wasn't quite thinking the words she meant to think. And yet, their meaning *was* the same.

"I'm speaking my own language," Silver protested. "And you're speaking yours."

I hear dragon.

"*I* hear human. Say something else. What are you thinking about?"

I'm sick and so cold, and I want to see my mother and—

"All right, fair enough!"

Hiyyan batted his long-lashed eyes at Silver, and she allowed herself a tiny laugh. She pressed her face into his mane, searching for some semblance of warmth. The voices continued to race through her head, but Silver let them. The noise made her dizzy, and that, in a strange way, took her mind off all her other bodily aches and pains.

I can speak your language, Silver thought with wonder. *Fully. Not just a word here or there, not only a single song.* "And you can speak mine. This would have been so useful in Calidia. But now . . . it feels like it's come too late for us. Too late and too useless, like a broken heartstone."

Hiyyan sighed, and the bonded pair wrapped themselves around each other.

"We must keep walking," Silver murmured.

A little more rest, Hiyyan replied.

Silver closed her eyes and waited for the next darkness.

◊ ◊ ◊

They woke in the Dragon Den, nested under so many furs and blankets that Silver wasn't sure if it was the layers making it difficult to breathe or the poison swirling so close to her lungs. It took too much effort to decide, what with all the noise in her mind.

"There's so many voices," Silver whispered. "I can't turn them off."

"You're awake, then." Nebekker sat on the edge of the pallet, book in her lap. Her hand drifted to Silver's forehead and paused there, as though checking her temperature. The old woman frowned and the wrinkles around the corners of her eyes deepened. "I wondered if you ever would, after Lers found you wandering around outside and dragged you back in, caked in mud and incoherent."

"Think yous'n can eat?" Lers, perched at the base of the blanket pile, nodded kindly at Silver and Hiyyan.

"I do actually feel hungry," Silver said, and Lers immediately went off in search of food. Silver was elated to see Nebekker and Lers, but then the disappointment over the dragon heartstone crashed in again.

As she pondered her failure, the voices started up again. Talking, talking. So many voices: . . . *warm meat . . . I am in charge . . . race you downriver! . . . where is . . . not enough for winter . . . the humans come closer . . . new ice cave . . .*

"Heartstone," Silver gasped to Nebekker. "Broken."

"What do you mean?" Nebekker asked, folding the book closed, setting it on the floor, and leaning forward with concern.

Lers came back into the Dragon Den with Mele just as Silver was pulling the heartstone from her bag. It emitted a weak light that made Mele gasp, but Lers set down his tray without a second glance at the object. Silver let Nebekker inspect the heartstone while she focused on the food.

"Broth. For yous both. Get that down, and there's summat bread, too. G'awn, show me yous can eat."

This time, it was more than the poison weakening Silver's ability to lift a spoon to her mouth.

"Here, I'll help you." Mele came over. She took up the spoon and teasingly said, "Open the burrow, the desert fox wants to go home!"

Parents would say that to desert babies when feeding them spoonfuls of yogurt, but it was the exact wrong thing to say to Silver. Her throat closed around the sip she was trying to swallow. Even Mele realized what she'd said once it was spoken aloud. She tipped the spoon into the bowl and set everything aside, her cheeks as red as garnets.

"Sorry, Silver," she said as she ducked her head. "Your heartstone is beautiful. I'm so happy you got one! How'd you find it, anyway?"

Silver squirmed and glanced at Hiyyan. She remembered some things about the trials: seeing her family bound, the dangerous tug in the depths of her belly when she considered the power the stone could give her. Fog shrouded other things. There were dragons—four of them?—exuding quiet strength and purpose. And two were Aquinder. That alone made her trial seem impossible.

"It's hard to remember everything that happened. And some of the things I'd rather forget."

"Like what?" Mele said, her eyes shining with curiosity.

"There were challenges. Queen Imea was there."

"What?"

"She wasn't really there. At least I don't think really." Silver rubbed her eyes. The more she spoke about the trials, the more confused she became. Nothing in that dark forest had been real. It couldn't have been. And yet it seemed real. She'd been exhausted and in pain. She'd touched real skin, made real decisions. Hadn't she?

"There were lots of choices I had to make. Once I even—" Silver swallowed. Her action was too uncomfortably close to what Nebekker had scolded her for earlier: sacrificing everyone and everything in the pursuit of her own dreams.

Silver's voice went low and husky. "I chose freedom for water dragons over saving the people I love the most."

Mele went quiet for a moment, contemplating. "That's not the decision I would have made, I think," she said finally.

"I know," Silver said miserably.

"But it's a decision someone would have to make," Nebekker spoke up.

Mele nodded slowly. "And that's what makes you different from anyone else. You're willing to make the harder choices, take the unwritten path, struggle against a wind that wants to bury you in shifting sand dunes."

Silver's pulse slowed to a crawl. Mele's words warmed her heart.

"Thank you, Mele," she said.

Mele took up the spoon again. "Someone has to be that person. To think of the bigger picture, of the world beyond our hearts. I can't do it, but I'll always help you when you have to."

Nebekker passed the heartstone back to Silver. "It looks perfectly fine to me."

"When I tried to use the dragon heartstone to heal Hiyyan, it didn't work. I'm doing something wrong."

Mele and Lers shared a troubled look.

"You can't even heal Hiyyan?" Mele asked.

Silver shook her head. "I failed."

"No, you passed." Nebekker rubbed a gnarled hand over her face. "You have a heartstone, don't you?"

"Yes, but what am I doing wrong? How did you learn to use yours?" The old woman was the only other person in the world who Silver knew possessed a dragon heartstone.

"It wasn't like putting a key in a lock to open a door," Nebekker said. "I continued healing and my abilities were enhanced over time."

"I need to study healing first?" Silver turned the stone over in her palm. "What's the point of a magical stone if I have to do all the work? Maybe I need the wisdom of the Watchers to decipher it."

Nebekker's nostrils flared. "What makes you think they know anything about heartstones? What have they revealed to you thus far?"

Silver let her gaze fall on her Calidian friend, knowing Mele's face showed all the hope and despair that clouded her own thoughts when it came to healing Hiyyan.

A log in the fireplace sent a flurry of rainbow sparks into the air, and the light ricocheted off the heartstone, dazzling the room.

Nebekker was right. The two of them were the only ones with any real knowledge about heartstones . . . and that wasn't good enough.

Silver let a flood of voices penetrate her thoughts before pushing them away again. *Something* had happened—changed—when she received her heartstone, but nothing that was useful to Hiyyan.

Mele sighed. "We'll figure this out. Just tell us everything you remember."

Now Silver's expression changed, and she turned away, unable to face her friends. She'd abandoned them during the trial. She'd turned her back on her entire family.

"I can't speak of it. Not yet."

"You don't ever have to," Nebekker said, pacing the room with her slow, stuttered step. "Even if a hundred annoying girls ask you a thousand times about your experience."

Silver swallowed back some guilt. She'd certainly peppered Nebekker with enough personal questions to make the old woman want to toss Silver into a glacier's crevasse for good. But now wasn't the time to stop probing.

"Nebekker, can't you tell me anything? Please. Some clue to help me understand why my heartstone doesn't work?"

Nebekker seemed to drift away from Silver, her face going slack and her eyes glazing over. She rounded the room once, twice, her breath deepening and taking on a noisy, rattling quality.

"You ask again and again about how I found my dragon heartstone. I imagine my story is much like yours. Strange figures demanding us to make difficult choices. I will never ask about your trials, Silver, because they are personal to you. They are private, yes, but also they are things I cannot understand because they have not been my experience. You could defend your choices with passion, but an outsider could never grasp your reasons. Not unless they could see deep into your heart."

"*I'm* not an outsider," Silver whispered. "Not anymore."

"Hughn," Nebekker grunted.

A look of understanding passed between Mele and Lers and, without a word, the two rose and left the den.

Nebekker nodded. "No, I do not believe you could understand my decisions during my trials, Silver Batal. And you also cannot understand what I've carried with me since. I am going to tell you two things, and after I tell you, I want you to never ask me about my trials again."

Silver swallowed hard and nodded. Nebekker's face looked older and more tired than ever before. The coolness between them was melting away. Nebekker's face was heavy with memory, with pain, and with guilt.

"The minutiae of the trials are inconsequential. I was asked to make choices, and all you need to know is that I chose Kirja over all. Over *all*, Silver Batal. I don't know if it was the correct answer, but it earned me a dragon heartstone. Now I think my choice was naive, for it also tested my heart. Have you ever heard of a little town called Deir-aa?"

Silver's fingertip traced the edge of a fur. "No."

"You wouldn't, because it hasn't existed for many decades. You see, the moment I chose Kirja over all, a great tsunami rose up and swallowed the town and all its inhabitants. It's the town I was from. Where my family still lived. I chose Kirja over all, and my choice was immediately challenged. I know those water dragons who'd bestowed the heartstone on me were watching carefully. I'd told them my family didn't matter to me. My past didn't matter. So they wanted to see how I would react when they took both away from me."

"How did you?" Silver whispered. Scenes flickered at the edges of her vision: Jaspaton destroyed by a great sandstorm, her family gone, her heritage swept away in a wind. Her chest clenched as if she'd swallowed gemstones. *No.*

"I moved on. Shut everything out and kept going . . . wandering . . . until I found a place so different from my home that I could stop for a bit. Where no one knew my past or how I was responsible for the murder of hundreds of people."

Silver shook her head, a fire racing into her cheeks. "No. You're not! You didn't raise the tsunami."

"I just know. Somehow I chose right, but I also chose wrong. I have wondered my whole life what I was supposed to choose. You seem to have done better than I, and I am grateful for that."

"But, Nebekker, it can't—" Silver shook her head, her voice

filled with fire. "I won't believe it. And to blame yourself all these years?"

Nebekker waved off the protest. "That was the first thing I promised to tell you. The second is that there is nothing in my history, my knowledge, or my heart that can help you fix your heartstone. I simply do not know what is wrong with it. But then, as I've shown you, I don't understand dragon heartstones much at all."

Silver glanced down and brought the heartstone closer to her face. It looked like any old bit of polished rock cradled in her palm. And maybe that's all it was.

Maybe she'd hallucinated in the burrow, picked up a rock, and somehow convinced herself it was the thing she was searching for. Silver let out a bitter laugh and drew back her good arm, prepared to throw the stone into the fire. Nebekker held her breath. Silver's hand paused above her head.

Pop! The fire rained sparks again, as though challenging her. Silver took a slow breath and set the heartstone on the food tray instead.

"It's not quite done with you yet," Nebekker huffed. "I've also done a poor job of understanding this poison. I have looked for days for a way to counter it. The answer simply might not be here."

No antivenom and a broken heartstone—what then? Silver shook her head, refusing to put words to that terrible thought.

Right then, Lers and Mele appeared with another dinner tray. When Lers lifted the lid from the pot, the incredible aroma brought tears to Silver's eyes.

"Clay-roasted lamb with rice," Mele said. "It smells as good as . . . I mean *almost as good as* what we'd tasted in the palace of Calidia."

"But you han't finished the broth." Lers frowned as he picked up the old tray and swept away.

"Try to eat," Nebekker chided. "Who knows when you'll get food like this again?"

Silver shook her head. "I'm not hungry."

She stretched her limbs, noting that she'd once again lost all feeling in her left arm, and nestled her cheek into a fur blanket. "Mele, did you find anything in the library that could help me understand why I failed?"

Mele scrunched her face, thinking hard. "Nothing I can think of." Then, she reached out and patted Silver's foot comfortingly. "But I'll never stop searching, Silver. I've read . . . so much! I will say that Gulad Nakim was some kind of kid. Brajon would have loved him. They taught his story all wrong at school. Wars and water dragons this and that. Boring."

Mele helped herself to Silver's lamb, stuffing bite after noisy bite into her mouth so that Silver had to listen hard to hear Mele's words around the racket.

"When he was a kid, he used to bet the other kids that he could predict what would happen. Gulad won so much that he amassed a small fortune. Well, enough to buy all the sweets he wanted, but that's wealth to me!"

Silver's eyebrows rose. "Like what kind of predictions?"

"He could guess specific things that would happen each day."

"Kind of like how he predicted the killing of the Aquinder and buried all those . . . eggs . . ." Slowly, Silver rose to a seated position, her eyes widening, her voice becoming thick with wonder and awe. "In the desert. He *knew*." Quick as a whipping desert wind, Silver gasped. "Nebekker! Can you talk to Kirja?"

Nebekker responded calmly, as used to Silver's outbursts as she was. "We communicate, yes. We can sense things, understand emotions on a certain level. We've known each other long enough to—"

"Yes, yes." Silver waved her hand impatiently. "But can you *talk*? Full sentences, full water dragon songs, all translated perfectly? Complex ideas and also . . . can you talk with *other* water dragons?"

"No." Nebekker shook her head, confusion pushing through the calm. "No human can."

"And when you found Kirja, you *nursed* her back to health, didn't you?"

"Yes."

"Because you were good at healing all along. And Gulad was good at predicting the future or maybe reading people and guessing events to come . . . something like that. Yes, that's it! I've figured out the secret to the dragon heartstones. Mine's not broken." Silver laughed. "It's just made for *me*, enhancing the thing I'm already good at—communication—the way it did with your talent of healing."

"Oh!" Mele exclaimed.

"And that means even though I can't heal, I can go back out there and talk to the water dragons who inhabit the mountains. Snuckers and Snowfluff dragons . . . whoever I can find. One of them will surely know about a Screw-Claw antidote, having lived among them so long!"

Silver was leaning over to hug Nebekker and Mele when a shout followed by a sound like metal clanging against stone on the other side of the Dragon Den door made them all pause.

"Lers?" Mele said.

Silver jumped as Lers shouted: *"Come back here!"*

Mele flung the door open. Even from her nest, Silver could see a figure dressed in fitted all-black dart across the snow.

"No!" Silver recognized that dark, flowing hair. "Mele! Nebekker! She's here. Sagittaria Wonder!"

Quickly, Silver reached for her dragon heartstone.

But the tray she'd set it on was gone. Cleared by Lers.

Sixteen

"S he has my heartstone!"

Silver threw off her blankets, got to her feet, and limped outside. Mele grabbed her before she could topple sideways into the snow as darkness descended over Silver's vision.

"I'm sorry, Silver. I didn't realize yer stone was on the tray." Lers, too, helped Silver into the great hall of the Keep.

"You just let Sagittaria in? Without warning us? As if . . ." Silver gasped. "How could . . . you? You know she and I . . . that she wants . . ."

"We are Watchers," Gavi said, coming over once he noticed the commotion. "Neutral. We care not for your little tiff."

Tiff! As though her history with Sagittaria Wonder were no more important than arguing with Brajon over who got Aunt Yidla's last nut pastry.

Silver sputtered. "Don't you understand what this means for Aquinder?"

Gavi glared at Silver before the cranky old Watcher slowly

made his way up the stairs. "We cannot deny her entry to the Keep."

Silver's eyes blazed with fury. It hardly mattered what a cranky old ghoul thought. Silver knew that if he could deny anyone entry, it would have been her.

She forced herself to calm down and focus on Hiyyan back in the Dragon Den. *The heartstone is gone. Sagittaria Wonder stole it.*

Hiyyan came to life, dashing away his building pain. Silver immediately understood his plan—he would try to intercept Sagittaria Wonder before she made it to her Dwakka. He rose, sniffing so that the scent of the two-headed water dragon reached Silver, too.

Silver moved toward the stairs, Mele on her heels. "Hurry! She's already too far ahead."

"There's a shortcut to the river." Silver heard a voice call out.

Silver turned to see Dasia, the Watcher whose cooking could nearly rival that of Aunt Yidla, observing her from the top of the staircase. She nodded at one wall, where a tapestry of a child queen wearing an old-fashioned headdress moved, as though a draft was blowing through the room.

"They each lead to a different part of the river. Will Sagittaria Wonder have gone south to Herd Valley, north to discover the far side of these mountains, or east to the sea?"

"Thank you, Dasia." Silver paused as a rushing clatter came from the hallway behind the door next to one fireplace.

Hiyyan skidded to a stop in the great room and announced himself with a furious roar. *"gggrrrUUUUNNNNGGGHHH!"*

"Hiyyan!" Silver ran to the Aquinder. "Did you see her?"

Not. See.

Silver drew her eyebrows together. Hiyyan's communication had slipped into the simple words they had used before the dragon heartstone. She closed her eyes and tried to speak with the more melodic dragon tongue that had come so naturally to her. But all she could manage was a note or two of a song of frustration.

"Ugh!" Silver pointed to the tapestry of the child queen. "Dasia says this is a shortcut. I'm going in."

Hiyyan stepped forward importantly, breathing in deeply at the entrance. Silver received wisps of scents: grasses and herd-animal manure from one, sharp metals and pine from another, and, finally, the saltiness of green and brown seaweed, plus something else: water dragon.

"Get a candle," Silver said to Mele.

"We're not going down there?" Mele squeaked.

"I have to!" Silver took the candle from Mele and stepped forward to peer down a dark set of stone steps, followed closely by Hiyyan. It would be a tight squeeze, but the tunnel was just wide enough for the Aquinder. Silver was glad of it. She wanted Hiyyan by her side.

Silver had a good sense of where the steps led. Hiyyan's heightened senses relayed the thick smell of dampness.

"Not another underground river," Silver moaned. "This explains how Sagittaria got in and out of the Keep, most likely on her Dwakka's back." Again, Hiyyan's heightened senses picked up useful scents: the oily leather smell of Sagittaria's close-fitted clothing, a pack filled with crackers and dried meats.

"You two aren't going alone." Mele's voice shook.

"Mele, you and Luap should stay here." Luap's small frame and tiny appendages weren't built for battle, and Mele wasn't exactly the fighting kind, either. Silver wasn't sure she could protect Mele *and* chase after Sagittaria. She thought of Ferdi's letter and wished that the reinforcements he promised would walk through the Keep door!

"But Silver . . . ," Mele began, but fell silent as Nebekker carefully hobbled toward them. She leaned on her walking stick, and Silver's old friend seemed, in that moment, as ancient as the stones of the Keep.

"Stay," Silver said again, then added, "Take care of Nebekker." The two shared a solemn look, and Mele nodded. Silver knew the former cleaning girl would be a capable and kind tender to Nebekker. Not like all the trouble Silver caused.

Watchers gathered in the hall, nervous and tittering. Silver had one more request of Mele: "And Mele . . . take care of Hiyyan."

No. I go.

"There isn't time to discuss this. You're sick."

But Hiyyan was more stubborn than a herd animal. He blocked Silver's way to the stairs.

"Stop joking around!" Silver shoved at a water dragon who wouldn't budge. "I need to hurry!"

Hiyyan turned his side to Silver so that his newly golden scale was flashing. *Together. Always. Bonded.*

"Yes, I know! But not right now . . ." Silver's frustration burned in her cheeks. Didn't Hiyyan understand? He wasn't well and the traveling would make him worse. She didn't have time to argue that point with him. Sagittaria was getting away, and Silver's most important duty was to protect him. If he insisted on blocking her path, she had no choice but to fight dirty. "I don't want you to come. You'll hold me back. Right now, our bond doesn't matter to me!"

Hiyyan inhaled sharply and drew back. Was it his heart breaking that Silver felt or her own?

"Hiyyan, I . . ." Silver wanted to say a hundred things to Hiyyan to wipe that crushed expression from his face, but Nebekker cut in:

"You can't chase Sagittaria alone. Kirja will go. She waits for you outside."

Fly. The single, resolute word came to her. And Silver was glad of it. She would travel faster in the air, rather than underground like Sagittaria.

"Take this." Lers presented Silver with salted meat, crackers, cheese, and cookies in a cloth napkin that she stuffed into her bag. "Goin' east, there's a section about a hundred miles along that comes aboveground 'afore dipping back under. I'd head there if I was chasing someone."

Silver nodded.

Hiyyan tipped his head back. *"HWUUUWWRRNNN!"*

The Keep wall trembled. He was angry to be left behind. He was angry at Silver. She was sorry about that, but somehow his fierceness met Silver's own, and she raised her chin.

Silver held Hiyyan's face in her good hand, both of their mouths drawn in tight, determined lines. "I will be back for you soon. Heartstone in hand, healing in sight."

She was Desert Fox; she was Silver Batal. She had earned a dragon heartstone. She was bonded to an Aquinder, and it was her responsibility to protect him, even if it made him angry.

Silver knew that, in time, Hiyyan would understand. There was no one who could drive a stake between her and Hiyyan, and no challenge they would leave untested in their pursuit of the things that were theirs.

This time, the roar that shook the foundations of the Keep came from Kirja. Silver clenched her jaw, threw open the front door of the Keep, and stepped out into the icy, dark world beyond.

SEVENTEEN

Silver's heart fluttered as Kirja's wings flapped. They took to the air, and even though icicles formed on her lips, Silver gasped with delight at being in the sky once more. It had been too long! Kirja's body was longer and slimmer than Hiyyan's, and her flying style was smoother and more practiced than her young son's. There was no thick mane to hold, so Silver leaned forward and wrapped her arm around Kirja's slick neck. Joy and determination blended uneasily, like oil and vinegar from one of Aunt Yidla's salad dressings. Even with Silver well cloaked, with only her face peeking out, her eyes stung as they watched the landscape below for any sign of Sagittaria and her Dwakka. The sky ahead offered the very first of the day's light in sharp silver, with a violet streak across the bottom of the horizon.

They skimmed just beneath the low clouds and circled until even the horizon behind them began to greet a new day, then they landed on a craggy cliff to rest and assess their surroundings. How far had they flown? Pain and exhaustion left a groggy heaviness behind Silver's eyes, but she shook it off, peeling back layers of fur until the bitterness of cold cleared her head completely. Silver stood on the edge of the cliff, facing the way they'd come, and her thoughts went to Hiyyan. Could she communicate with him from this far away?

We are well, she tried. *No sign of Sagittaria yet.*

No sign here.

Silver jerked so hard with shock that she almost lost her balance and went tumbling over the cliff. *Hiyyan! Where are you?*

No know. Dark.

His essence flowed closer than expected . . . somewhere in the mountains . . . in the river caves.

You came anyway! she shouted in her mind. Her fear for Hiyyan's safety made her angry. Why had Mele and Nebekker let him go? *You're injured!*

You. Too. Careful. Dwakka smell in tunnel. Far ahead.

Silver narrowed her eyes and scanned the landscape again, as though expecting Sagittaria Wonder and her Dwakka to pop out from underground at any moment.

"Did you raise him to be so stubborn?" Silver looked at Kirja, who shrugged.

Can't stop him. Loves you. Needs to help.

"Injured, he'll be as useless as a jelly pickax."

`Still, Silver replaced the furs over her face. Anger, fear . . . and relief, she had to admit to herself. She was glad Hiyyan was close. If there had been time, she would have flushed him out of the cave and sent him back to the Keep, but Sagittaria had too much of a head start.

We're moving on, Silver thought, emphasizing her disapproval. *Looking for the river opening Lers told us about. See you there. Please be careful.*

Far on the eastern horizon, the light was turning a moody

gold. They flew toward it, noticing that the air was becoming thicker and slightly warmer as they left the central mountain range behind and approached the sea. Not warm enough to throw off the furs, but enough that Silver could expose her face without her lips freezing to her teeth. A tiny hope that Sagittaria was stuck in the caves because of a frozen river was erased with the relative warmth. The river flowed unceasingly right into the sea.

"Look." Silver pointed to the blue line suddenly running through a light-softened valley. "I don't see Sagittaria or her Dwakka. Are they behind or ahead of us?"

"*Kkkrrreerrlll,*" Kirja growled her discontent. No swimming Dwakka was faster than *her.*

Silver patted Kirja's neck and watched the river snake its way toward the ocean. Kirja opened her wingspan, and they rode the airways in a wide circle, searching the ground below. The valley was low elevation enough to be green with grasses and shrubbery. It reminded Silver of Herd Valley.

"Looks like home," she said softly.

A gentle purr rumbled through Kirja's belly, and Silver was glad to have her on this journey. Silver was happy Hiyyan had his mother, but she ached for her own. Her sadness was dashed away at a flicker of movement below.

"Look!" A drum pounded in Silver's chest. There, just emerging from the shadow of a cliff wall, was an outline of a large water dragon in the river. "Dive, Kirja!"

Kirja pulled her lips back in a snarl and dipped her head toward the earth. She tucked her wings close to her body, and at the same time, Silver clenched her leg muscles and pressed flat against Kirja's back in preparation for the drop.

They cut through the air smoothly, slicing across the blue as a blur. As they flew closer, only a Jaspatonian dunes–breadth away, one of the Dwakka's heads looked up and sounded an alarm. Sagittaria Wonder didn't bother to check over her shoulder, instead imitating Silver, pressing closer to her water dragon and yelling for it to turn back the way it came.

Silver realized with panic that Sagittaria and the Dwakka were headed right toward her Aquinder.

Hiyyan, watch out!

"Land near the cliff. Cut off the opening," Silver urged Kirja. "Protect Hiyyan!"

They landed in the river smoothly, grazing the top of the cold water before Kirja pulled her wings close to her body. Where Sagittaria and her Dwakka had been, there was now only a scattering of bubbles. They swam to the spot, the cave opening dousing them with shadows. Instinctively, Silver lifted her feet, recalling the last time Sagittaria Wonder had reached up and pulled her off a water dragon, back into the waters beneath Calidia.

But this time, Sagittaria Wonder was more interested in getting away from Silver than in teaching her a lesson. Silver squinted into the darkness of the cave. There was a brief, strange thrill in being the hunter, rather than the hunted.

We saw her, Silver messaged to Hiyyan. *Cut her off at the river rising. Be careful!*

But before Hiyyan could respond, the thin mountain air was rent by a shrill scream, followed by a deathly silence. A single Snucker fled out of the river-cave opening and past Silver.

"What did you do?" Silver asked, keeping her legs safely tucked away.

The Snucker didn't answer but seemed to laugh at Silver as it passed by with its teeth bared and its malevolent little red eyes flashing. She tightened her grip on Kirja. She knew that whatever made Sagittaria scream like that was not a pesky little Snucker.

"Kirja, we have to go in. Hiyyan's stuck in there with whatever it is."

Silver's heart battered her chest as she realized what kind of monstrous creature could challenge someone as fierce as Sagittaria Wonder: There was another Screw-Claw awaiting Silver.

And her beloved Aquinder.

With Silver's dagger in one hand and the other useless at her side, the duo crept carefully into the opening. Kirja paused, allowing Silver's eyes to adjust to the low light. The scent of rotting flesh was strong. Something else was in the cave. Something that liked meat. When a warning growl filled the air, Kirja paused.

Silver said, "The Dwakka?"

Kirja nodded, brought her body low, and skulked forward, testing each step with a sniff of the air and a twitch of her ears. It wasn't long before Silver spied the tip of the Dwakka's tail in the distance. The water dragon's muscles were stiff and its heads swayed side to side protectively, letting loose a steady stream of warning growls to something Silver couldn't see.

Behind the Dwakka, sprawled on the ground and clutching her chest, was Sagittaria Wonder. As Silver and Kirja approached, the great dragon racer opened her eyes and curled her lip.

"I shouldn't have turned back," she snarled. "From a whelp like you? What could you do to me that . . . that . . ."

Sagittaria ended on a breathless note, pulling her arm back to reveal a glistening red slash across her torso. Silver gasped.

"No!" She slid from Kirja's back and into the shallow river's edge, crouching before Sagittaria. "We have to get you help."

"You? You can't even help your own water dragon."

Silver sensed Hiyyan very close by. He dragged himself forward. Silver had trouble seeing, a green glow taking over her vision. All of Hiyyan's movement had ramped up the spread of the poison, which must have been filling his lungs. He should have stayed at the Keep!

"I'm going to cure him. And you, too." Silver tipped forward, then back, her words slurring.

"Even with her last breath . . ." The water dragon racing champion coughed out a laugh. "You really can't decide if you hate me or not, can you, Desert Fox? Leave me here to d—"

"SCREEEEEE!" Two Dwakka heads let loose spine-tingling cries before lunging at something in the cave. Silver forced herself to her feet and ran forward blindly, hand gripping her dagger. Kirja flashed her fangs and marched forward. A silvery, furred beast glowed eerily on the other side of the Dwakka. It was smaller than the Screw-Claw Silver had faced beneath the glacier, but her breath still caught in her throat.

She swallowed hard and shuffled forward.

"Don't let that thing bite you!" Silver shouted at the Dwakka.

Silver didn't know why she was helping the Dwakka, just that she had to. She summoned her remaining strength, ran, and slid across gravel, slamming her dagger into one of the Screw-Claw's legs before another leg kicked her in the side and into a wall.

"Guuunnnnggghh," she moaned in pain.

But her move had given the Dwakka and Kirja enough time to home in on the ice dragon together, and while Silver was still struggling to her feet, they moved as one. Both Dwakka heads clamped onto two Screw-Claw front legs, and Kirja snapped her jaws onto its back legs. Kirja's paws trembled as her broken talons tried to grip the cave floor. The Screw-Claw gnashed its teeth. It tried to slow them down with its hind legs. The two water dragons dragged the monster toward the cave entrance, out of Silver's sight. She breathed heavily as she awaited their return.

Kirja's words reached Silver before she saw the Aquinder. *Screw-Claw smart. It run. Away.*

And then, another Aquinder's voice: *Silver.*

"Hiyyan!" Silver rose, then fell, then rose again, determined to rush to Hiyyan as he emerged from the shadows. His breath came as grunts, and his feet dragged, making the tops of his paws muddy.

"Oh good, a full reunion." Sagittaria tried to stand but stumbled and fell back into the mud, clutching her chest wound. "Are you hiding an island prince in here, too?"

"They're poisonous," Silver said.

"Yes, island princes can have that quality."

"The *Screw-Claw*."

"How opportune for you, then," Sagittaria said with a dark grin.

"I won't let you die. I won't let any of us die. There has to be a medicine out there, an antivenom. With help from my heartstone, I'm going to find it. So give it back!"

"In time?" Sagittaria said. "Your Aquinder has only moments left, girl."

Silver crawled to Hiyyan, running her palms over his scales. She refused to believe Sagittaria. "I told you, I—"

"Will be the hero to save us all. Yes, I know. Desert Fox.

Racing champion. Finder of rare antidotes. Saver of Sagittaria Wonder? Ha! I'd rather decompose slowly in this vile cave than give you the satisfaction."

Silver frowned. "Return the heartstone before you wither, at least."

Sagittaria laughed. "I don't have it."

Silver froze. "What do you mean you don't have it? You took it from the tray!"

"And then I gave it away."

Silver recalled the grinning Snucker, the way the water dragon's teeth had flashed violet. No, not teeth. A dragon heartstone.

"Convinced our little friend to take it to the coast." Sagittaria smirked. "With the promise of much food, once I found my way there and met up with it. Snuckers are easily persuaded."

Silver hadn't found them to be, but what did that matter now? They had to chase down the heartstone *again*. She looked at Kirja.

Then at Hiyyan.

Then at Sagittaria Wonder. Silver couldn't leave her to die in this cave.

The decision tore her in half. Even her legs couldn't make up their minds; they were spread, with one foot pointing to the cave entrance and one to Sagittaria.

"Grruuugghhh!" Silver growled, slapping her hand against her thigh. "We can't leave you here."

Hiyyan sighed.

I mean, if you think that's the right thing to do. Silver ducked her head, searching for the warm sensation that would tell her Hiyyan agreed with her or the cold that revealed he didn't.

Her ankles tingled, her working palm slowly heated as though she was approaching a fire after a long day in the snow.

"Go, Desert Fox. I would."

"I won't!" Silver spun on Sagittaria, lost her balance, and fell to the ground. "I refuse to be like you."

"Being merciful won't get you very far in this world, or the racing world, girl. Go. Get your heartstone."

Sagittaria Wonder's Dwakka, normally a nasty thing, lay low to the ground, both of its heads sporting worried expressions. Turned out, even the nastiest creatures might have a heart.

Silver rifled through her bag, pulling out a few meat pastries, which she offered to Kirja. "I know you're tired, but can you please fly back to the Keep? Bring Lers, if you can."

Kirja munched the treats, nuzzled Silver once, and retreated from the cave. Silver watched the beautiful Aquinder check left and right for danger, spread her wings gracefully, and take to the sky.

Now . . . what? Hiyyan bond-said.

"Nothing to do but wait." Silver tore her underlayer into strips to use as bandages. She worked over Sagittaria Wonder, who was too weak to protest, although she still gave Silver a reproachful look. Silver ignored her and wrapped the cloth around Sagittaria's chest tightly, hoping the pressure would stall the bleeding.

The Dwakka hovered over Silver, both heads assessing Silver's every move. It felt like dune beetles crawling up the back of her neck.

"Can't you find something else to do?" Silver finally snapped.

The Dwakka sat back on its haunches. The smiling face

swiveled toward Silver and reached out in pleasant tones: *Poison. Not. Bad.*

"Yes, the poison is *very* bad," Silver said.

This time, it was the angry face that swerved close.

No. Its voice in her head was gravelly. *Poison. Not . . . problem.*

Now Hiyyan's voice filled her mind. *Dumb Dwakka.*

Both Dwakka heads snarled.

"Not a problem? Look at her!"

By the time Silver finished, Sagittaria seemed to be in a trance, her eyes facing up but unfocused, her breathing slow and rattling. Silver loosened Sagittaria's collar, then sat back against Hiyyan and watched her warily. The Dwakka snaked around Sagittaria.

"How did you know I was at the Keep?" Silver whispered.

The racing champion's words slurred. "I had a dream . . . saw you . . . near Keep."

Silver frowned. Sagittaria Wonder had never seemed the type to give any importance to things like dreams. Too practical, too driven to live in the real world.

Hiyyan nudged the back of Silver's arm until she lifted it and let his head sneak through to rest in her lap. He didn't fit, his jaw hanging over Silver's legs, but she simply rubbed his forehead and tipped her head against his mane.

"Try to rest, Hiyyan," she said faintly. Her head was spinning as Hiyyan grew weaker.

With a last surge of energy, Hiyyan grinned at his human. His teeth glowed green, then he went limp.

As the poison greedily ate its way through their veins, Silver slumped over, too.

EIGHTEEN

Silver's sleep was brief and disturbed.

In her dreams, she was surrounded by darkness. The shadows moved, shimmering like water at night. Silver squinted, and the darkness cracked. Tiny fissures all over, each one filled with a menacing orange glow. Somehow the darkness screamed, and the air became too hot to bear, blowing on her face until she thought she would burn to ashes.

Desperation and hopelessness overwhelmed her. All joy had gone from the world. She closed her eyes, but her eyelids seared with fire. So she opened them again, just to a squint, but that was enough to see that, very far away, a thin ring of light was sluicing through the darkness. When she blinked, she realized creatures were in the light. Hundreds and hundreds of them, swimming and flying and swooping, creating rainbows of color beyond the bitter darkness close by.

Water dragons!

"Help me!" she called to the dragons.

But they didn't hear her. She opened her eyes wide. There was more than dragons. There were people, too. Dragon riders. And fire. Everywhere the dragons went, slashing their claws or ripping their fangs at the blackness surrounding Silver, flames followed, erupting from the horrible darkness, engulfing the beautiful creatures of light. She reached her hands out and caught a palmful of ash.

"Stop! Stop fighting!"

But on and on the darkness and flames went. In and out the water dragons swooped, some surviving their attacks, others falling into nothingness. Silver threw her own arms and legs out, battling the darkness. Her body fell through space and kept falling and falling and falling.

"Help me!" she screamed. The rainbow of dragons was now completely gone.

A single great beast reared over her. It was as black as starless night, with those strange orange cracks in its hide. When it opened its mouth to finish her off, Silver could see a vast chasm of nothingness inside.

"No!"

Silver, wake!

Silver jolted up. The serene Dwakka head stared down at her. Possibly . . . worried? The moment Silver thought she saw any emotion on the Dwakka's face, it turned away.

Silver eased back and reached down to touch Hiyyan, pressing her palm to his face. He didn't move, but still the connection was electric, stirring her heart to race even faster than before. Silver took a slow breath.

"I didn't mean what I said before. I will always want to be bonded to you. It's the most precious thing to me."

She would do anything for that wonderful Aquinder, even if it meant going to the molten depths of the earth.

Even if it meant following him into the grave.

Silver stood and took a short stroll to loosen her stiff joints as they waited for Kirja to return with Lers. Each step was painful and forced, and she winced each time she bent her knees or wound her ankles in slow circles. A pale light met her at the entrance to the cave, and she silhouetted herself there, surprised. Had they slept a half day and whole night?

When she'd retraced her steps, Silver knelt next to Sagittaria Wonder, whose breathing had settled in the night. Silver lifted a bit of bandage, then a bit more. Her mouth fell open.

At some point in the night, the wound had scabbed over and new skin had grown. There was no sign of poison or lingering infection.

"Looked your fill yet?" Sagittaria Wonder's voice was cranky but strong. She coughed once, then sat halfway up and looked down.

"Do you always heal so quickly?" Silver asked.

"Impressed?" Sagittaria gave a smug half smile. "Still can't get those stars out of your eyes."

Silver's cheeks heated, but her retort was interrupted by the sound of heavy footsteps.

"Kirja," Silver cried out as the water dragon ducked her head and entered the cave, Lers on her back. She shook off a thin layer of frozen rain.

The healer dismounted and strode right over to Sagittaria Wonder. "She don't look too bad," he said.

"She was worse last night." Silver paused to catch her breath. "I didn't think she would live."

"Huh," he said, probing with his hand.

"Keep your hands off me," Sagittaria snapped as Lers took a piece of bandage, brown with dried blood, in his fingers. "Who are you?"

"Lers. Keeper of the Keep." His beard rose on both sides as he surveyed Silver. "I never got to say that to you, girl, but I always like saying it." Lers turned his back on Sagittaria and went to Hiyyan, inspecting his wing thoughtfully. "I know something about medicine. You grew antibodies, and quick-like, too. That's odd. Generally a thing what happens o'er generations, between breeds evolvin' together. But it's awful useful now."

"I'm not interested in being useful." Sagittaria climbed onto the back of her Dwakka, its two heads back to being one gentle and one surly, and slipped into the river. "I have a meeting with a Snucker."

"*Xxxxssshhhh,*" Kirja hissed, splashing into the river and blocking Sagittaria's way out of the tunnel. *Useful woman not leave.*

"Stay!" Silver cried out. She tried to stop Sagittaria but collapsed at the riverbank with exhaustion.

"He looks real bad," Silver heard Lers say as he hauled her up by her arms, helping her to a seated position. "And so do you."

Silver's lashes fluttered, her eyes threatening to close. She willed them to stay open, to search for Hiyyan. He was an unmoving heap propped against a wall, just a few steps from Silver. She tried to move a foot toward him, but couldn't. Her lungs seized with every breath. Silver noticed that Lers was looking peculiarly at Sagittaria, and she tried to figure out what the keeper was thinking. When it hit her, she threw herself prostrate in front of the Dwakka.

"Dwakka have poison!" she said.

"Venom in sacs to disburse at will. A useful tool in many circumstances," Sagittaria snarled as both Dwakka heads reared back.

"How long . . . did it take you . . . to build up . . .

immunity?" Every word felt like a lifetime, but she *would* push through. For Hiyyan!

The Dwakka heads swayed left to right as Sagittaria contemplated Silver. "Almost a decade. One drop, and then two, and then three, every recovery taking less time and effort than the one before. Do you know how many Dwakka riders have died of bites from their own dragons? Pathetic."

"But not . . . you. You . . . are strong."

"And smart." Sagittaria patted her Dwakka's neck, her eyes glinting in the low light. "No other could have compelled a Dwakka to give up some of their precious poison stores."

Silver remembered from her careful research that Dwakka produced venom in their first year only, and after that stored the liquid in glands in their mouths. Once it was used up, it was gone forever.

"Yes, smart. Which is why . . . you can't leave!"

"You can't stop me. Not from leaving, and not from getting your heartstone from that Snucker."

Silver narrowed her eyes and curled one fist. "You made an antivenom and . . . *You. Owe. Me.*"

"*Urour?*" Kirja laid her wings over Hiyyan protectively.

Lers nodded. "It's in 'er blood. The cure."

Kirja made a clicking noise. *Villain. Bad blood.*

"We need your blood," Silver and Lers said at the same time. Sagittaria barked a laugh.

"Wouldn't hurt much." Lers brandished a small vial and a knife. "If we can transfer summat antibody-rich blood from her to Hiyyan—"

"You are not cutting me, keeper," Sagittaria snapped.

"Oh." Silver crawled one inch toward Sagittaria. "He." Silver crawled more. *"Is."*

Silver gathered her strength and lurched upward, grabbing on to a dangling Dwakka rein and yanking down a Dwakka head as hard as she could.

She was glad to discover it was the sinister head, which snapped its jaw at her. Silver's glare was fierier than anything the water dragon could produce. The green that had taken over the whites of her eyes reflected back at her. She delighted in looking like an evil goddess from the old tales. This was for Hiyyan.

To the molten depths of the earth and back.

Or, failing that, a drop of blood.

Silver's lip curled. "We could have . . . left you in this cave . . . to die."

"Which wouldn't have happened." Sagittaria's amused tone infuriated Silver.

"None of us . . . knew that! You've said before . . . you don't want harm to come . . . to any Aquinder. Now prove . . . we need . . . vial-ful. Give . . . or . . . else."

Through her blurring vision, Silver saw three heads tip back and fill the cave with laughter. Kirja growled, sending vibrations into her boots.

With one last laugh, Sagittaria put her boot to Silver's chest and pushed Silver aside, knocking her unceremoniously onto the gravel. The Dwakka crouched to face Kirja in a fighting stance.

"You said." Silver stayed on the ground, her limbs too heavy and swollen to continue. Not just poison and pain, but something more than that. She was tired of fighting all the time. "You said you . . . loved . . . water dragons . . . remember that." Silver raised her eyes to the woman she once called hero as her words and last bit of energy faded. "Please . . . Sagi . . . ttaria Won . . . der."

But all Sagittaria Wonder did was flash Silver a disgusted look. "I'll make you a deal. Show me how to get a dragon heartstone—my own, not yours—and I'll donate a drop of my precious blood."

"Deal. Blood . . . first." Never mind that Silver hardly understood how she'd gotten her own. The heartstone found Silver on its own terms.

Sagittaria pondered Silver's terms for a moment. Then, she slid from her Dwakka, pulled out her own blade, crouched, and tucked it under Silver's chin. "If you're lying, I destroy you, once and for all."

"Hey!" Lers yelled.

"No . . . let her," Silver whispered.

"Fine." Sagittaria presented her arm to Lers. "If it hurts, I hurt you back."

Lers was a head shorter than Sagittaria but about twice as wide. Silver wondered how they would match up in hand-to-hand combat. Lers's beard bristled as he carefully tucked the tip of his knife under Sagittaria's skin until a bead of blood appeared, then he pressed the vial close and filled it. When he was done, he gently blotted the spot and readied a small bandage, but Sagittaria swatted him away.

"I am not a child." She spun on Silver. "There, it is done. Now tell me where you found the dragon heartstone."

"I didn't . . . find . . . found me." The words were said baldly, with little room for question. Sagittaria Wonder realized that, her face tightening with anger.

"How did it find you?" she said through gritted teeth.

"Dragons . . . four." Over Sagittaria's shoulder, Lers was making an opening in Hiyyan's skin. Silver winced at the sight. Her body felt light, ready to float away. She dug her fingertips into the gravel to keep herself grounded to this world. *Stay, Hiyyan.*

Silver's eyes flickered from Lers and Hiyyan to Sagittaria and back. Hiyyan didn't move as Lers injected Sagittaria's antibody-rich blood into his veins, then applied pressure for a moment before bandaging the wound.

Sagittaria, too, was quiet, one hand playing over her chin. "Tell me more, girl."

"Powerful . . . leaders . . ." Silver rasped.

Sagittaria's knife glinted in Silver's peripheral vision. "Yes, and? How did you find them? What did they say to you?"

Silver shook her head. "They found me. Gave me . . . choices."

"Found you! How is that supposed to help me?" Sagittaria frowned thoughtfully. "Do you know how many water drag-ons are on their council? Ah, I see in your eyes that you do. Yes, four. And I have some idea where to find them. Being close to the queen through all her years of political work is good for that, at least. Now tell me what kinds of choices? Come on, speak up!"

Silver's lips were too heavy to say anything more than "Trial."

"They set you a trial," Sagittaria said. "Let me guess: a per-sonal one? Different for everyone. Hmm. I believe you. But just in case you're lying to me, I'll be on my way to a meeting with a Snucker at the coast."

With one cry of fury, Sagittaria and her Dwakka burst through Kirja's barrier and raced out of the cave. Kirja turned to give chase.

"No!" Silver mumbled. "Let . . . go."

Let go?

Silver rubbed her face on the cool ground. Sleep would be so nice. Long, long sleep. "Yes." She didn't have the strength to explain further. The dragon heartstone could wait. All that mattered was Hiyyan and making sure the antibody worked.

Lers tucked his materials into his bag and scooped Silver up off the ground, depositing her next to Hiyyan. Then he reached over to pat Kirja. The two shared a hopeful glance.

"Different . . . breeds," Silver said to Lers. "Do you think . . . will still work?"

Lers crouched next to Silver and said, softly: "Sometimes, nature is kind to us. And sometimes, it ain't."

Silver closed her eyes, slowly scanning Hiyyan's body from tail to mane. Already, things seemed to be happening. A lessening of the pain in their shoulders, an opening in the spaces around their lungs, a comfortable reduction in how hard their hearts were beating.

A kindness.

It's working, isn't it? Silver smiled, tears gathering under her lids.

Soon.

Hiyyan's use of the word Silver had oft repeated to him as a promise made the tears slide down her cheeks. She reached up to wipe them away.

"Rest . . . a bit."

Her body slumped heavily; her brain seemed to swim in green goo. She let it all happen. No fighting, no clinging to life, freedom, the future. A true movement-free, thoughtless rest. Time passed, but she couldn't count how long. The light at the entrance to the cave grew brighter and less green. White noise took on a new clarity. When Kirja shifted to get comfortable at one point, Silver found she could turn her head to look at the mother dragon and it didn't feel like stones were crunching in her spine.

Silver bent her knees and placed her palms against the ground. Timid, but hopeful, she pressed her weight off the gravel. And rose to her feet.

"Hhhhrruuhhh," Hiyyan breathed, rolling his sounds against the roof of his mouth like a purr. The Aquinder blinked his eyes open and looked at Silver.

"You're awake," she breathed.

Kirja pranced, waking a napping Lers with her excitement. *Lives!*

"Look at this," Lers said.

Silver peered at the original tear in Hiyyan's wing. Slowly, but surely, scabs were growing. A stinking green ooze dribbled down Hiyyan's side, soaking into the gravel beneath them.

"It's so fast," Silver said.

"A good find. This'll save lives," Lers said.

"Good? It's the most amazing find in the whole world!" She was a new Silver, hopeful once again.

Get her. Hiyyan cranked his head around to meet Silver's eyes with fierce determination.

Yes. Silver sent her shoulders back. *We'll race her to the heartstone and get back what's ours. But first, you have to get better.*

When the healing had progressed to the scabbing over of Hiyyan's scales, Silver gave him a pat, then walked with Lers and Kirja to the entrance of the cave. She showed Lers her fingers, still an unsettling gray.

"What about these?" Silver said. "Do you think they'll ever heal?"

"Frostbite gone an' nipp'd ya real hard, eh?" Lers kindly took Silver's hands in his and scrutinized the skin, then he shook his head sadly. "I'm not one to say a thing's true if it ain't. Your nerves were damaged, and there's no going back from that. Be glad it's just the tips. You won't lose anything else."

Silver hugged Kirja before sending them back to the Keep. At her sides, her fingers curled and uncurled. The brisk air blew at her short hair. The sky was sharply blue, painfully bright when Silver looked at it too long.

She wondered what her father was doing that very moment. If he was toiling over Queen Imea's scepter. If he was searching every traveling trader's wares, desperate to find the most perfect gemstones buried under the desert, if he was sending messages with those traders to pass far and wide: riches for anyone who brought him flawless stones. Riches and favors from the queen.

Silver had chosen something different, and it was the best and right thing for her. Her fingers curled once more as she clasped her hands behind her back. Still, every time the world created a new gap between her and her father's dream for her—the legacy of her family—her heart broke a little.

Even if she'd wanted to become a famous Batal jeweler, dead fingertips wouldn't allow it. She could never become the daughter her father wanted her to be.

Silver sighed.

Hiyyan sighed.

"I hadn't even heard you come close," Silver said. "Or felt you."

Silver sad. Hiyyan padded his big paws a few steps forward and settled in next to Silver, letting the winter wind blow his thick mane across his face.

Silver peeked at Hiyyan, marveling at how big and majestic he was now that he was well enough to stand tall again, his blue scales framed by the dark-stone cave, the green valley, the entire snowcapped mountain.

"No, not really sad. Just thinking about things. How I don't feel much like a Batal anymore."

Silver. Desert Fox. My human.

"Those are good things to be." Silver pulled her arm out again and inspected the scar she'd received in her father's workshop. A pop of molten metal had scalded her, leaving a dark shape on her wrist that looked undeniably like a curled-up water dragon. Her thumb played over the skin. This is where she was meant to be.

Like dragon. Hiyyan raised a paw and flashed his talons, then looked meaningfully at Silver's gray-tipped fingers.

"They do look a bit like claws, don't they?" Silver turned and inspected Hiyyan's golden scale. A scar for her, a scar for him. Then, she rubbed her hand over his wing. "This, though, makes me happier than I've been in a long time. Hiyyan, I can't believe that just yesterday the poison was pushing at our lungs, at our hearts. Now it's gone."

Better. Hiyyan flashed his double row of razor teeth. *Fly!*

"Fly," Silver said, stretching out and savoring the word as though it was the first time she'd said it. A stupid grin lit up her face. "Do you think you can?"

Hiyyan puffed out his chest and gave Silver a side-eye.

Watch me.

Hiyyan took several steps into the valley, his paws crunching through a thin top layer of frozen dew, his breath blanketing him in a misty cloud. Even the sun seemed interested, peeking through two low, ragged-edged clouds to send a beam of soft brass light across Hiyyan's body.

Hiyyan shook out his mane, rolled his shoulders back

slowly, and sent his wings out, ruffling the very tips of them. Their span was as wide as the river that flowed from the cave.

He took two more steps forward, and then two more at a run, and launched himself into the air.

The first hard push of Hiyyan's wings against the air was lopsided, and Silver gasped as he struggled to regain balance. Then muscle memory took over, and Hiyyan soared like a water dragon who'd never touched ground.

"It worked," Silver breathed, watching her Aquinder become a sapphire dot against the violet sky. She pressed her hands together, entwining her fingers, lightning bolts zipping over her skin.

"*Gaaaauuuuuhhhhnnn!*" Hiyyan roared, triumphantly.

The Aquinder took another loop, disappearing behind a nearby mountain peak, before returning to the valley and landing with an earthshaking impact. Silver ran to Hiyyan and threw herself around his neck.

"You did it!" Hiyyan's eyes were shining, and Silver laughed, her words breathless. "How'd it feel?"

Strong. Grand! And after a beat: *cold.* Hiyyan shivered, and Silver giggled again. She felt so light and happy that her own feet threatened to carry her off the ground and float her over the mountains.

Now we chase. Hiyyan's eyes darkened into pools of volcanic stone. *Sagittaria.*

"Our heartstone," Silver said. "Are you sure you're ready?"

The waves of warmth Hiyyan sent Silver made her skin sweat under her layers of clothing.

The race was on.

NINETEEN

Silver ducked into the cave for the last time and collected her things. An extra bag sat next to hers. "Lers left us food!"

She devoured flatbreads crusted with black and white seeds, fed Hiyyan some dried fish and berry patties, then climbed onto his back. Her emotions were wild: Delight and thrill at finally being healed combined with the pulse-pounding drive to take back what was hers. If they didn't hurry, Sagittaria Wonder would reach the coastline before they did, even with their flying advantage. And once in the sea? She could go anywhere.

"To the skies once more," she said, and Hiyyan spread his wings, smoothly lifting them away from the river.

Silver relished the sharp wind through her short hair and the two-handed grip she had on Hiyyan. It wasn't long before she saw the north seas with their big, bobbing ice floes and icebergs dotting the stern gray surface of the water. Her heartbeat sped up.

"We're almost to the coast. Sagittaria has to come out near here."

She strained her eyes, searching for movement below. A dark splotch could have been a Dwakka, but upon closer inspection was some other species of water dragon Silver wasn't familiar with. Another spot wasn't even a water dragon; it was a whale spouting a fountain of water into the sky. There were boulders to search—or those dark blobs could be a resting dragon, curled up in a ball—and shore caves that begged further exploration.

"Too many places to hide," Silver said. "She can't have gotten here ahead of us, though. Keep your eyes out for a Snucker."

"Haur," Hiyyan grunted his reply, his big head swaying left to right as he scanned the shoreline.

They flew past the coastline and over the sea itself. The fleeting morning changed the gray water to sweet pale blue. Silver saw islands just off the shore, some no larger than a fingerprint on a page of writing, while others were large enough to support life. There were flat islands, but also towering karsts, their bottoms narrower than their tops as the water ate away at stone, hiding tunnels and lagoon sanctuaries. Noisy seabirds created a chaotic din, and colonies of small water dragons, plus a few larger breeds who seemed to live solitary lives or in small pods, lounged on land or swam in search of a meal. But no Snuckers.

One island even had what looked to be a smattering of stone buildings. If Sagittaria had come out ahead of them, she might have headed for an island like this, sheltered and with dozens of places to lay low and rest for a while.

"There." Silver pointed. "Land for a moment, Hiyyan."

Hiyyan dipped his head toward the island, and Silver's stomach rose to her throat as the Aquinder dove for the smooth, expansive sand beach. He landed softly, a much-improved maneuver from the first time he'd ever landed. Back then, he'd crashed into the desert on the outskirts of Calidia. Silver slid off his back smoothly and surveyed the island. Higher up in the center, snow lay over the land thickly, like the powdered sugar Aunt Yidla dusted over her honey-and-nut pastries. But lower, where Silver stood, the beach was only damp. A path cut through a stand of evergreen trees whose roots fought, and won, a battle with the rocky ground.

"Through here," Silver said.

The duo trudged down the path, which quickly opened into a semicircular clearing. There, a single stone structure dominated the center of the space, while a dozen more smaller buildings with rustic roofs surrounded it.

"Sagittaria might be in one of these. Let's start with the big building."

Silver took two steps but froze when there was a rustling in the treetops. Suddenly, figures dropped from the branches to surround them. They each sported fierce expressions with bared teeth and flashing eyes, and their short hair was spiked up like the spines on a desert lizard. Their tunics, colored in various shades of green and gray to provide camouflage, were close-fitted over athletic bodies. Boots, which seemed to be dipped in some kind of rubber sap to keep them dry and likely able to cling to tree trunks, laced up to their knees.

"Yaw!" cried one, brandishing a long dagger at Silver. The tip wavered right under her nose.

Hiyyan roared and stepped toward the man with the dagger.

"I don't have a weapon," Silver cried.

"Call off your beast," the woman next to the dagger-wielding man growled. "He's more weapon than we have."

"No need," came another voice, this one startlingly familiar. "Hiyyan, old friend! Come say hello!"

Silver and Hiyyan whipped around as one.

"Ferdi?" Silver exclaimed.

"The one and only."

The desert prince looked exactly the same as the last time Silver had seen him, deep underground in the outskirts of Calidia. Same infuriatingly smug expression, same overconfident bearing, even the same dark-blue uniform.

"What are you doing here?" Silver said.

"I'm an islander, and this is an island," Ferdi shot back with a grin. "A training island. One I picked specifically for its location."

Silver looked at the dagger the man still held aloft warily. "Training for what?"

"Only for resiliency," Ferdi said, wiggling his eyebrows to make Silver giggle. "We come here in the roughest season to toughen ourselves up like true island warriors. We can't always lounge on the beaches of my home island. No, we warriors live in the cold, in the wake of an unforgiving wind, off a stingy land, blah blah."

Ferdi dug his fists into his hips and looked into the distance over the seas, striking the pose of a weather-hardened warrior.

Silver bit back a laugh. "And have you become a warrior yet?"

"Not yet, unfortunately. We only got here a couple of days ago. Still living off the oh-so-delicious rations of dried fish and grain biscuits. They're tough enough to break your teeth"—Ferdi grimaced—"but specially formulated for optimal nutrition, or so my father constantly tells me when I complain. Now that we're settled, though, there will be fishing ex—"

Ferdi's eyes sparkled as he took in Silver's impatient expression. "I'm rambling."

"I'm on a mission."

"Just you two? Where are the trackers?" Ferdi looked over Silver's head and past his warriors, as though expecting more faces.

Silver turned around, too, surveying the figures half-hidden in the trees until the words from that hasty note dawned on her. *I've sent help . . . stay put.* Now, Silver understood why the mercenaries were confused when she kept assuming they were chasing her down on Queen Imea's orders. Because that wasn't who'd hired them. Spinning back, she pointed at Ferdi. "You sent the trackers after us! Why were you having us followed by those buffoons?"

"If by buffoons you mean one of the best tracking teams in the world, specifically instructed to get you to me safely before anyone else could get their hands on you, then . . . yes. I sent them. I couldn't keep waiting for my father to decide whether or not he was going to offer you safety at the Island Nations, so I took matters into my own hands."

"I thought they were mercenaries sent by Queen Imea. They never told us differently!"

"Sorry about that." Ferdi looked sheepish. "I sent word to the trackers through an emissary, instructed them to keep all details shrouded. For safety! Yours and theirs. The less they knew, the less trouble they'd run into. I guess I didn't account for *your* kind of trouble."

Silver scratched the back of her neck guiltily. "They should be somewhere at the base of the mountain right now. Hopefully in not too terrible shape?"

Ferdi laughed.

"But why did you only send for us? They left Mele and Luap behind, and they almost did the same for Nebekker. Brajon said—there was one called Brajon," Silver clarified so Ferdi wouldn't think of her cousin, "that I was the only one they wanted."

"I never told them to do that!" Ferdi glared left to right at the warriors as though searching for a specific one. His eyes narrowed as they landed on a particular shadow. "I should have gone to the trackers myself."

Silver thought back to the argument between Omelda and Horrible Brajon. "I think some secrecy and greed were involved on their part, too."

"That little . . ." Ferdi shook his head, then flashed her an expression of unmasked admiration. Silver's neck went warm. "But they were no match for you. So what brings you here?"

The elation of seeing an old friend disappeared as Silver's fury came back. "We're chasing Sagittaria Wonder. She stole something of mine."

"Chasing her *here*?" Ferdi repeated. Ferdi's confusion was palpable—his training island was truly remote—but Silver had little time to explain.

"We were at the Watchers' Keep. I had my dragon heartstone—"

"A heartstone?" Ferdi breathed. "How did—?"

Silver waved off his attempt to detour the conversation. "Sagittaria stole it. We caught up with her at one point, but she got away again."

"And you're sure she came this way?"

"We know she came to the coast. When I saw the buildings, we came down. She's somewhere in these north seas, and it's likely she came ashore here to hide and rest."

Ferdi tipped his face to the sky, raised his arms, and made several complicated signs with his hands and fingers. Silver looked up to just catch a glimpse of another warrior, still in the trees, face to the north and making another series of hand signals.

"One moment," Ferdi said. They stood silently, gazing up, for the span of ten heartbeats. Silver kept trying to glimpse the person in the tree, but they were well hidden. Almost as good as camouin. Ferdi obviously knew how to look, though, because he spoke up again. "Ah, they saw a blue dragon and a girl arrive, a pod of Padahu swim past, some seabirds—I don't need a report on seabirds!" Ferdi shouted that last bit at the person in the tree before facing Silver once more. "No Sagittaria, and no Dwakka."

"Impressive communication system," Silver said. "I assume they're positioned across the entire island?"

"Yes. They should have seen anything come ashore, but just in case . . ."

With a flick of Ferdi's fingers, several warriors slunk even farther into the trees, off on a mission. "If she's here, they'll find her. We know every inch of this place. We swept the island first thing on arrival and then again every morning. It wouldn't be the first time a water dragon colony has overwintered and tried to claim the buildings, then got angry when Islanders landed ashore. There was one year that . . ." Ferdi shivered. "We don't need to talk about what happened to those warriors."

Silver winced. Considering her run-ins with Screw-Claws, she could imagine what those ill-fated islanders had to face. "I'm sure your sentries would have seen her or her Dwakka if she were here. It must mean she's still in the caves. I need to get back to the mainland shores or I'll miss her."

Ferdi didn't hesitate. "Let's go get her."

Silver's jaw dropped. "Don't you have royal duties?"

"I know these seas better than anyone. Well, better than you, at least. And Hoonazoor is with me. We can scour the ocean and shore while you search from the sky. The two of us will find her in no time. And it'll be much easier for two to apprehend her than one."

"Can you leave your warriors?"

"My second is capable," Ferdi said. He lowered his voice, ducking his face close to Silver's with a wink. "I can't say no to an adventure, same as you."

Silver nibbled her lip, worried. "You can't risk coming with me, Ferdi. You have other responsibilities."

Silver turned and began walking back to the shore, where Hiyyan would have enough room to take to the skies again.

Ferdi chased after her. "I'm coming with you, whether you agree or not. You can't tell me where I can or can't go. This is my island." Ferdi caught up and, without warning, took Silver's hands in his. "My islanders are good and capable and just as loyal to me as Hiyyan is to you. They're sweeping the island again as we speak and will hold any captive until my return.

Nothing Sagittaria Wonder could say to them would turn them from me or my father."

Silver sighed. "Fine, come along, then." There was no time to argue, and she had the feeling Ferdi would be helpful in ways she couldn't yet imagine.

She watched as he shouted out more orders, his suddenly masterly voice surprising Silver. This was a new side to the maverick Ferdi she knew. Once Ferdi was satisfied, they marched back to the beach, where Hiyyan ran ahead to greet Hoonazoor, whose iridescent head was peeking above the water, looking out for them. The water dragons sang a song of greeting, a sweetly melodic tune, and then Ferdi waded into the polar water to meet Hoonazoor.

Silver shivered just watching him in the sea. "I think I prefer the warmer oceans near Calidia," she called out.

"I do, too." Ferdi laughed between his chattering teeth. "But this is part of the toughening up. Nearly frozen water will turn me into a real man, according to my father." Ferdi rolled his eyes. "Whatever that means. I think I'd be happy remaining a boy."

Ferdi resolutely mounted Hoonazoor and took up her reins. He pointed. "We'll work up the coast from the south, starting about a mile down."

Silver nodded. "We'll head north. I'll fly inland a bit to see if she's still coming east along the river." Silver patted Hiyyan's flank, then dug her fists into his mane. "Hiyyan will send Hoonazoor a song if we see her."

"Bring home the trophy." Ferdi flashed her a grin.

Silver pressed her lips together as she watched Hoonazoor dip under the surface of the sea so that only Ferdi was exposed to the frigid air. She knew Glitherns, Hoonazoor's breed of water dragon, were the only ones that could spend their entire lives underwater—their big, strong gills supporting their breathing—and that preferred swimming completely underwater, too.

Let's go, Silver said to Hiyyan. She clamped her leg muscles as Hiyyan ran, then took to flight, lowering his head so that they could cut through the air dynamically, gaining a level of speed Hiyyan hadn't dared attempt when they were searching the mountain valleys for Sagittaria.

As they returned to land, Silver did a quick rundown of their health, sending her thoughts to her toes all the way up to her head. As she did so, she was also scanning Hiyyan, tip of his tail to his elongated nose. She was elated to discover no lingering effects of the Screw-Claw poison.

They reached the coastline, and Silver pointed at a dark fleck below. "There!"

She pulled Hiyyan to the left to turn him around. He spun so sharply that Silver had to tense her whole body to keep from sliding off into the mountains far below. When he righted again and flew closer, Silver leaned in and saw the dark fleck become bigger, take on a familiar form.

It was Sagittaria Wonder emerging from the mouth of the river on the back of her Dwakka, the dragon heartstone dangling from her fist.

TWENTY

Sagittaria looked up and spotted Silver the same moment Silver saw her.

"Send a song, Hiyyan!" Silver cried.

Hiyyan opened his huge jaw wide and bellowed a tune to the sky.

One of the Dwakka's heads looked up at Hiyyan, while the other head peered down the coastline and hissed. Sagittaria yelled something that was lost on the wind, and both heads snapped forward again. The Dwakka sped up, churning white froth as it left fresh water and entered the salty north seas.

"Fall in behind her until Ferdi gets here." Silver tightened her grip on Hiyyan's mane and pressed low against his scales. Her furs flew behind her as they turned and picked up speed.

"*Gggeerrrrgh,*" Hiyyan growled, his snout pointed at the Dwakka, the air moving aside as he smoothly cut through it. Silver glanced to the south and squinted.

They're almost here.

Ferdi's blue riding suit wasn't easy to spot against the lapis sea and sapphire sky. Hoonazoor raised her head, the sun glittering off her scales, and sent a song to Hiyyan. Silver's Aquinder responded, and the air was filled with a strange melody. Hoonazoor banked away from the shoreline. Silver realized they were communicating their strategy through song.

She couldn't keep a triumphant smile off her face. "We have her n—"

But when she looked down again at Sagittaria Wonder, the breath was stolen from her lungs. The champion water dragon racer was gone.

"No." Silver leaned left to right, her heart as frantic as a wild bird in a cage. "Where did she go?"

Hiyyan let loose a howl of frustration and turned in a wide circle, searching the waves below them.

Under, Hiyyan bond-said.

Silver nodded. "They must be. Dove down, hoping we would lose sight of them. Hoonazoor won't miss, though, once she gets here. Keep circling. Sagittaria, at least, can hold her breath for only so long."

But after a few more minutes of circling, the Dwakka still hadn't emerged.

"Where is she?" Ferdi yelled to Silver when they'd caught up.

She shook her head, feeling as if she had herd dung for brains for losing her target. "She disappeared."

"It's not your fault. These karsts offer all sorts of places to hide. But if she gets out to open ocean, she's in for a shock. That's my dominion," Ferdi said with a determined look.

"I will follow her wherever she goes," Silver said. "The open seas, your Island Nations, even back to Calidia."

"Wouldn't they love that," Ferdi said. "Sagittaria leading you right into Queen Imea's hands."

Silver set her jaw determinedly. "She has something that belongs to me. And me? I have a duty. To Hiyyan. To . . ." She thought for a moment about what the four water dragons on the council had said: She didn't fully understand heartstones . . . Her gift was rich, but challenging . . . She had to prove her loyalty to Hiyyan and also to . . .

"A duty to all water dragons."

Ferdi raised his eyebrows. "That sounds intense."

"Maybe it is. I'm not sure. I need the heartstone to help me figure it all out."

Land, please, Silver said to Hiyyan.

The Aquinder pulled his majestic wings forward to slow their pace, swooped low, and landed on the surface of the sea with hardly a splash. As Ferdi fought back a shiver, Silver was glad Hiyyan was tall enough that she could keep fully out of the water.

They both turned toward the open seas and urged their water dragons forward. As they searched, every jumping fish, loping whale, and bobbing seabird made Silver's breath catch in her throat and her hands urge Hiyyan to sprint ahead.

It was exhausting.

They were so far into the open sea, now, that they couldn't see the coastline behind them or the island chain where Ferdi's warriors waited in the distance. There was only an endless blue, a shade darker than the horizon itself, dotted with a series of dark triangular shapes in the distance.

"Flying desert dust! I can't believe she got so far ahead of us." Silver slammed her fist into her palm, anger just barely keeping her tears at bay. "I can't believe I let her get away in the first place."

"Stop that," Ferdi scolded. "We'll find her, and we'll get your dragon heartstone back." Ferdi pointed to the triangular shapes. "There's an island ring not too far from here. Her Dwakka will need a rest after all this swimming, and that's the only possible place."

Ferdi trailed off, not voicing the condition they were both thinking: *if she went this way.* Silver frowned and shifted in her seat. Sagittaria Wonder could be halfway to Calidia by now, if she'd chosen a different direction. Silver shaded her face from the winter sun, which glared at her.

Steady, cold waves rolled on in their various shades of blue and silver as far as she could see. The enormousness of the seas thrilled her and reminded her of the expansiveness of the desert, but it was also unfamiliar to her. This was Ferdi's home, and he understood the dangers of the waters: the creatures it contained, the way it could wear a person or a water dragon down until they found themselves stranded with no relief in sight.

Focus, Hiyyan bond-said.

Silver nodded. "Let's go."

Ferdi pointed Hoonazoor in the direction of the island ring. Hiyyan took to the skies once more. The morning sun skirted the eastern horizon low until early afternoon. Distances in the ocean were deceptive. What Silver thought would have taken only an hour or less took closer to three.

Finally, they reached the first island and circled it, searching for signs of life beyond sun-napping seals and raucous bird colonies. Skirting around the tip of an isthmus, Silver's eyes narrowed and urged Hiyyan forward.

They reached a huge lagoon, ringed by more of the

black-tipped islands, where Sagittaria Wonder floated, studiously looking from a piece of parchment to the island chain and back.

"Sagittaria Wonder!" Silver felt a rush of energy from her toes to her scalp as she yelled. "The dragon heartstone is mine!"

Sagittaria turned her Dwakka to face them, smirking. "You don't deserve it."

"It was entrusted to me. You don't get to decide what to do with it." Silver nudged Hiyyan forward again. *Slowly. Carefully. We don't know what tricks she's hiding.*

Sagittaria waited for Silver to approach. "Do you know how long I had to track Nebekker to find her stone? Years and years. And you lost your stone after one day. So careless." Sagittaria opened her palm and tossed the heartstone lightly in the air, catching it again. "But I could have taught you to be responsible. In different circumstances, Silver Batal, you would have been a fantastic squire. Your single-minded drive to race water dragons sets you apart. Properly honed, you would have been a champion to rival, well, even me. It takes a certain temperament to care about nothing more than the race."

"I care about more than racing," Silver said.

"Do you?" Sagittaria raised an eyebrow. "Then you won't care if I destroy the heartstone. You won't understand or believe me, but it's for the good of all water dragons."

Confusion rippled through Silver like a gentle wave. The dragon heartstones helped water dragons. Nebekker's helped heal Kirja. Silver's allowed her and Hiyyan to communicate seamlessly. That meant humans and water dragons were one step closer to bridging the gap between their species.

How could something that could do such wonderful things be bad?

"We'll never let you destroy it," Ferdi said. To Silver, he said, "She can never take away all the things you've worked so hard for. She knows you will outclass her someday. She fears it. Wants to keep you from achieving the greatness you were meant for."

Silver felt a delicate fluttering in her rib cage at Ferdi's words. Sagittaria Wonder curled her lip.

"There are so many things children like you cannot understand," she said. "But you should know this: Water dragons forever and always come first with me."

"You always put yourself first," Ferdi said. "In and out of the races."

Sagittaria wrapped her fingers around the heartstone, while her other hand tucked the parchment away. She shrugged. "Believe what you want. I'm not in the business of changing your mind, little prince. I have bigger problems to solve. Four dragons' worth." With a whip of the Dwakka's tail and a magnificent splash, Sagittaria and her water dragon disappeared under the surface once again.

"No!" Silver clutched Hiyyan. "After her!"

Just as smoothly as Sagittaria had, Hiyyan dove into the water. Silver held her breath as they sped toward a strange orange glow deep in the blackness of the volcanic island system. Bubbles raced for the surface as they zoomed to the bottom. Within seconds, Ferdi was beside her, Hoonazoor cutting through the water even more smoothly than Hiyyan.

Silver paid no attention to her lungs as they ached for air. She would catch Sagittaria, and she would get her heartstone back. But it was when Ferdi passed her, coming almost close enough to the Dwakka to grab its tail, that Silver realized that what rushed against her cheeks wasn't water, but air.

It was pulling her down into the vacuum of the deep sea. Bright, panic-laced dots burst in the corners of Silver's vision. If she went much farther, the pull would be too strong for even Hiyyan to battle back to the surface.

But under the panic, there was something else, a feeling deep in her chest, behind her lungs, that ached in a completely different way. It made her think of home.

Silver wanted to go home.

Home, Hiyyan said, his thoughts clouded over with images of molten earth and volcanoes. His chest ached with a familiar longing.

This was Hiyyan's home.

Before Silver could suss out the thoughts crowding her mind, the pressure increased until her temples throbbed and she couldn't think of anything at all. Just as suddenly, they were thrust out of the water and onto dry land. Silver sucked in a wild breath. There was oxygen here. But the air smelled funny, like when the Jaspaton miners got too deep under the earth.

"Gases," Silver said. She looked around. Ferdi and Hoonazoor were to her left, and Sagittaria was directly in front of them, staring out over some kind of precipice, a hot wind blasting her wet black hair away from her face.

The water dragon racer looked back over her shoulder one time, raised her arm, and threw the dragon heartstone over the edge.

"No!" Silver screamed. The heartstone skimmed the tip of the water, a sea that strangely flowed above their heads, and as it did, a shimmering creature—a huge fish—gobbled it up and swam off.

"What—" Ferdi sputtered.

"You have got to be kidding!" Sagittaria Wonder balled up her fists and sent her Dwakka into a run. They leaped as high as they could to catch the ocean and swam up, disappearing into darkness.

"I'll go after her," Ferdi began, but Silver threw her arm out. "Look."

The fish, realizing the heartstone wasn't a delectable ocean morsel, returned and spit the dragon heartstone back. It bounced once, then twice, then rolled over the precipice.

Silver dashed to the edge and looked over. Black rock went down hundreds of feet to where rivers of lava swirled and splashed angrily. The dragon heartstone had landed on a small jutting of rock about halfway down.

Hiyyan came up beside Silver and looked over.

"Do you think we can get it?" Silver asked. "Safely?"

Hiyyan cocked his head to the side, his lush white mane blowing back with the force of the hot air rising swiftly. *Go. Get.*

Ferdi came up beside Silver, followed by Hoonazoor, who slithered over awkwardly. Like most water dragons, the Glithern struggled on land.

"We won't be able to get down," Ferdi said. He turned to Hoonazoor and opened his mouth to speak, but he paused when he spotted a dark shadow in the water above them.

Silver squinted as the backlit figure came closer.

"Sagittaria's back." Silver swung herself up onto Hiyyan. "Climb on, Ferdi. We're out of time."

The island prince got seated behind Silver and waved Hoonazoor in the opposite direction to delay the approach of the racer. She nodded and threw herself into the water.

Then, Hiyyan spread his wings and dove into the hot, stinking mouth of the volcano.

It was impossible to breathe. Poisonous vapors burned Silver's throat, and the rate and angle of their descent frightened her. If she fell off Hiyyan, she'd fall into a pool of scorching lava, not a cool sea. She gritted her teeth and buried her face in Hiyyan's mane, letting her watering eyes drain into his fur. Seated behind her, Ferdi gasped at air and tightened his grip on her waist.

It felt like hours, but the drop to the perch took only seconds of free fall, plus one grand swoop on approach. Hiyyan landed gently, and Silver opened her eyes. Just in time to see a dark, ratlike creature emerge.

"What in the world are you?" Silver cried out. She watched in horror as it lapped the dragon heartstone into its mouth with a long, sticky tongue and dashed into a tunnel.

"By all the dunes!" Silver yelled after the horrible little creature. She gave chase. "Come here. Give me that back!"

With Hiyyan and Ferdi on her heels, Silver swooped and swerved through the dark tunnel. As the orange lava glow behind her faded, she bumped into walls with her shoulders and toes, bruising herself all over. Around another bend, and then one more, where the light grew again. Silver threw her arms out and skidded to a stop in a room that was entirely missing its floor. A handful of pebbles flew over a cliff, dropping into the lava below.

"Argh!"

Hiyyan froze, but Ferdi couldn't stop, barreling into Hiyyan before knocking into Silver just enough that she teetered on the edge of the precipice for one heart-stopping moment before, finally, going over.

"Silver!" Ferdi screamed. He threw out an arm and caught Silver's wrist.

"Ungh," Silver groaned as her shoulder was wrenched out of its socket. Even as she swung wildly, she realized she recognized her surroundings. The heat, the orange glow, falling into the depths of the molten earth. She had just dreamed about this place!

"Hold on, Silver." Ferdi carefully stepped closer to the edge and held out another hand. Hiyyan whimpered. "Stay back, Hiyyan. There isn't enough room for you to maneuver without singeing your wings."

As if on cue, the hot earth popped and sent a shower of sparks and lava toward Silver. One caught on the bottom of her boot. The acrid smell of burnt leather took her breath away. She peered over her shoulder, then wished she hadn't. The lava was so close it stung her eyes.

Still, Silver ground her teeth together. "Where's that rat?"

Ferdi grunted. "Honestly . . ." He wiggled his empty hand, reminding Silver it was there. "It's the last thing we should be worrying about."

Silver heaved her dangling arm up, but it was several inches from meeting Ferdi's.

"Scramble!" Ferdi said. "Isn't that what desert foxes do?"

Sweat poured down Silver's face. Ferdi, too, glistened with heat and effort, his eyebrows drawn but his eyes frantic, tears spilling over from the sulfurous air. His dark hair blew back from his face, and he clamped his teeth together, too.

"*Please*, Silver," he whispered. "I can't . . . guhn." Ferdi's boot kicked gravel into Silver's face as her weight pulled him closer to the edge.

They would both have kept flailing if Hiyyan hadn't started sending rolling waves of calm to Silver.

Live. My Silver, my human, my friend.

Silver pressed her lips into a thin line and caught Ferdi's eye, holding him in her gaze until his expression softened.

"Okay," he whispered. "Slow and steady, Silver. Swing left and right, left and right, just like that, almost got it . . ."

The toes of Silver's boots dragged across the volcano wall, leather sizzling, as she swung back and forth, and then with a rush of energy, she threw her arm high. Ferdi caught her forearm with a snap, holding on with everything he had. He fell onto his belly, and Hiyyan immediately wrapped the end of his tail around Ferdi's ankles to drag them back from the edge.

Ferdi stood, pulling Silver up with him, and hugged her tightly.

"Thank you," Silver gasped.

"I'll never let you fall," Ferdi murmured into her singed cloak.

Together, they turned and looked at the small ledge that ran around the opening to the tunnel on the other side. The rat could have gone only that way.

"Is there enough room to get you across?" Silver asked Hiyyan. While she and Ferdi could possibly scrape along the wall ledge, it would be impossible for Hiyyan to follow them on foot. But Silver would not leave him behind.

As if reading her thoughts, Ferdi said, "He's going to have to try."

"Go first, Hiyyan, fly, then we'll follow along the ledge. Leap, then flap, *hard*," Silver said.

Hiyyan nodded, let loose an echoing roar, and launched. There was a half-second of drop, then Hiyyan's wings thrust against the air. He sailed over the opening with more ease than Silver expected.

Satisfied, Silver and Ferdi pressed their backs against the wall and scruffed their way along the ledge. The gases made Silver light-headed, but she turned her toes out and kept going. On the other side, Hiyyan used a wing to pull her all the way to him.

"It can't be that easy," Silver said wryly as she hugged her Aquinder with relief.

"Or maybe we earned a break," Ferdi said, countering Silver with his optimism.

With a snort, Silver peered into the darkness of the new tunnel. One good thing, she decided, was that the rat had nowhere to go but ahead. But how to get the heartstone back from the critter?

Hiyyan was reading her thoughts. In reply, he grinned mischievously, his double row of razor teeth glinting in the low light. Silver laughed, shaking her head. "Come on."

But before they could enter the tunnel, a voice soared across the noxious air. "Desert Fox!"

On the other side of the room, Sagittaria Wonder snarled her frustration. Her hair was a mess, singed in places, and her riding suit was torn from the effort of scaling the volcano to follow them.

"The crossing's impossible for her," Ferdi said.

"For her dragon." Silver shook her head. "But never underestimate Sagittaria Wonder. Hurry."

They pursued the rodent until they came to a wall. Nowhere to go, left or right. Silver hardly cared, because standing defiantly on two legs up against the wall was the rat. That feeling of home flushed her veins thoroughly again.

"You're caught now," she said. Silver unwrapped her scarf and scooped up the rat in one quick movement. Her hands danced to avoid the creature's nipping teeth. "Stop that. All I want is my heartstone back."

"You're going to wait for it to, you know . . ." Ferdi said. "*Dispel* it?"

The island prince was so squicked out that Silver couldn't help but giggle.

"You're very princely right now," she said. She stuck her nose in the air and lifted the register of her voice. "Oh ho, I'm much too grand to speak of bodily functions."

Hiyyan snorted until Ferdi was pink with embarrassment.

"Have your fun, Silver Batal, but I'm not the one who'll be combing through that creature's excrement when the time comes."

"Hiyyan offered to make a snack of it, so we might get the stone back quicker than—"

As though the rodent could understand Silver's words, it squeaked and leaped from Silver's arms, huddling against the wall, shaking. Silver lurched for it, bumping her shoulder hard against the rock.

Without a sound, the solid rock face gave way.

TWENTY-ONE

Silver toppled over in a heap, almost snagging the rat before it scurried away into the new space revealed to the trio.

"*Mrow?*" Hiyyan blinked his big, dark eyes.

Ferdi pushed the opening wider, like a set of doors. But it was Hiyyan who bustled through first, stepping with a noble brilliance that Silver had never seen from him before. His head was held high, his wings pulled tight and straight against the sides of his body, his tail curled off the ground. With a grace that would put even Prince Ferdi to shame, Hiyyan bowed his head low for a moment, then stood upright once more, his gaze focused and unwavering.

Silver came around to see what had caused this change to come over Hiyyan.

The room that had opened before them was vast and gleamed with obsidian laced with precious stones. Around the edges of the room, water dragons of all sizes, colors, and breeds lounged on cushions or against glimmering black walls.

Despite her exhaustion, Silver's heart leaped with joy at

the sight of them all, the same as it had the first time she'd seen real water dragons. Adorable Abruqs, despite not being under the queen's command, couldn't keep themselves from perking up at her entrance, their noses raising to the ceiling. A Dwakka with two pleasant faces instead of the usual one kind, one angry, scratched its back against a rock. Through the center, a hot spring flowed, clouding the space with steam, and inside the stream, Silver could just make out the spine of a Glithern. There was even a Droller in the back, its huge size no match for the cavernous room. It was the first time Silver had seen one without all the transport trappings that weighed down the Calidia Drollers.

And then, on the opposite side of the room, just visible through the mist, Silver made out a stone dais inlaid with four smooth gemstone circles, each with an elaborate geometric pattern.

And on those circles, four water dragons perched.

Ferdi couldn't keep back his shout. "Are those more *Aquinder*?"

Laughter rippled around the room.

"They are. And I know them." Silver faced the female Aquinder. "You gifted me the dragon heartstone."

And already you have lost it, said Dortaal, the old Aquinder, his song full of grit and judgment.

Not lost. The female Aquinder, Kyan, rolled her eyes, rose from her circle, and tracked her nose along the floor. With satisfaction, she reached into a small opening in one wall and pulled forth the ratlike creature that had swallowed the stone.

This will only hurt for a moment, Kyan said. Suddenly, she squeezed the rat's belly. With a strangled hacking sound, the creature spat the dragon heartstone out and across the floor.

Silver ran to retrieve it, wiping the gunk off it with her scarf and tucking the stone as deep into her pocket as she could. No one was taking it from her again. Not Sagittaria, nor these dragons.

We want you to have it, the Glithern named Ssun said exasperatedly. *That's why we gave it to you in the first place.*

"Just making sure," Silver said. No, *sang.* Once more, she was capable of speaking in the water dragons' own language.

Ferdi gave her a look of surprise and admiration. "You . . . ? How . . . ?"

"I can fully communicate with water dragons. My heartstone gift."

"What are they saying? Who are they? What are their names?"

"They are the water dragon council. Kyan, Ssun, Ge, and Dortaal." Silver pointed to each in turn. Three water dragons nodded a greeting, while Dortaal simply twitched his nose in disgust.

Silver shoved her hand in her pocket and rolled the heartstone around in her palm, where it grew warm. "You say you want me to have the heartstone. But what is a dragon heartstone really?"

Intruder. Ge, the Padahu, narrowed her eyes at the space behind Silver.

Silver and Hiyyan spun around. Sagittaria Wonder, her temples dripping with sweat, entered the room.

"You found us," Ferdi said. Hiyyan growled.

Immediately, four Abruq circled Sagittaria, forcing her to stay near the entrance.

"Not easily," Sagittaria growled. Her breath came quickly as she assessed the room.

You brought her here, Dortaal roared, glaring at Silver. Everyone flinched at his anger.

"I didn't!" Silver protested.

You led her here, Dortaal amended.

"I didn't . . ." Silver clenched her fists. It *was* her fault Sagittaria was in the chamber. Hers, and that horrid rat's. "I didn't mean to."

The girl does not control who follows her, countered Ge.

We should never have given her the heartstone. She should never have bonded with a water dragon!

But she did, Kyan said smoothly. *And we weren't the ones who made these laws. We only do our best to understand and enforce them.*

The other one was a better choice, Dortaal growled. *She went into hiding like a smart human.*

Silver knew they meant Nebekker. "But even she couldn't stay hidden forever."

Thanks to you, Dortaal said.

Hiyyan's muscles tightened. Silver probed his emotions, realizing that he wanted to please the council, but he bristled at the way they spoke about Silver. Eventually, he moved ever so slightly closer to Silver, and she felt a protective energy surround her.

They made different *choices,* Kyan countered. *And I think you forget that Nebekker went into hiding as much to live quietly with her heartstone as to protect her heartstone. What use is that to us? Besides, I think the timing is right for this young one. The hidden world of the water dragons can't stay that way forever. Even now, the core trembles. How long until that tremble becomes a quake? Trials and tragedies are brought to us by many forces, all older than we are. And so it just might be this youthful one on which pivots the fate of our lives.*

"What are they saying?" Sagittaria Wonder pointed at Silver. "I know you understand them."

"I don't know what you're talking about," Silver lied.

There is no need to hide our words, Silver Batal, Kyan said. *Nor to hide the gifts the dragon heartstones bestow upon their bonded pairs. For too long we have dealt in mystery. Too long have we hidden from the world. Peace between our kinds shouldn't be so difficult.*

Ferdi edged into the space between Silver and Sagittaria, as though readying himself to defend Silver.

"They said they want us—humans—to understand the dragon heartstones," Silver explained.

Kyan smiled, her patient eyes contrasting with her double row of sharp teeth. *You understand them better than any other, don't you?*

Silver slipped a glance at Sagittaria and rubbed her tongue against the back of her teeth.

"At first, I thought all the heartstones were healing stones. But then I realized it's not that. Mine didn't work that way, after all. But Nebekker always had talent with healing. Long ago, Gulad Nakim knew the Land and Sea Wars were coming—he could foresee things even as a kid. And I had a natural talent for communicating with water dragons. Which means . . ." Silver swallowed, her feet shifting against the ground. It felt wrong to reveal the secret she'd discovered. "The heartstones enhance our natural gifts. And that's different for everyone. At least I guess it'd be. I only know about the three heartstones."

"Interesting," Ferdi breathed.

And what else? Ge nodded encouragement.

"Gifts can be enhanced by any heartstone, I think. Nebekker's helped me communicate, but it's just not as strong as when I'm using my own heartstone. And the same goes for bonded dragons: The gift is stronger between a human and dragon who are bonded, which is why Nebekker couldn't heal Hiyyan even though she could heal Kirja. The poison was too powerful. And it's why I can talk to any water dragon but can actually tap into Hiyyan's senses."

Sagittaria looked from Silver to the dragon council. "What about bonds? Must they exist for the heartstones to work at all?"

Silver squirmed. She knew what the legendary water dragon racer was really asking: Could *she* use one? "I don't know. I think there is more to the heartstones than I have discovered yet."

Kyan nodded. She seemed ready to speak again, but Sagittaria Wonder stepped forward.

"Give me one," the water dragon racer demanded. "I'll test the question right now. If you won't let me destroy them, I must have one."

"Why do you want to destroy them?" Silver clenched her fists, exasperated.

Sagittaria snarled and looked from dragon to dragon. "You have all forgotten where we came from. Where *you* came from."

When the water dragons glanced at her, Silver rushed to translate.

"Hhhrrmmm," Kyan growled her dissent, standing regally, her tail sweeping around her paws.

"If you remember so clearly, then you know that the past must remain buried," Sagittaria said. "The good and the bad."

"What is she talking about?" Silver whispered to Hiyyan. He shrugged, his own thoughts reaching Silver as a jumble of songs that made no sense.

You think we have more power than we do. Ssun shook his head sadly. *We can no more stop the future than you can.*

Sagittaria's jaw clenched and unclenched. "Bury the heart-stones. Destroy bonds for good!"

Silver looked at each face in the room.

"You'll never take our bond away. It's not a dangerous thing!" She buried her nose in Hiyyan's mane for a moment, steadying herself. "We just want to be free, to live, and to race," she said under her breath.

"This is more important than races, girl." Sagittaria's eyes glittered dangerously.

Silver opened her mouth to snap back, but just then she caught a glance of another dragon lingering in the shadows behind Sagittaria. Before Silver could speak. Sagittaria's Dwakka burst into the room, heads swiveling and growling, and swept the Abruq away from Sagittaria.

"Get behind me!" Ferdi yelled.

But Silver was already reaching for Hiyyan. Before she could climb on his back, the water dragons against the walls mobilized to secure the Dwakka while Sagittaria, in a flash of black riding suit and hair, somersaulted between Silver and Ferdi. More water dragons got underfoot, knocking Ferdi to the ground and causing Hiyyan to rear up with a frustrated growl.

Shlink. In all the chaos, Sagittaria leaped onto Ssun's back while, at the same time, pulling a long dagger from her belt and pressing it against the water dragon's throat.

Hiyyan's skin went as cold as a glacier. He snarled and crouched low, prepared to pounce.

"Don't do it!" Silver cried.

"Give me a heartstone. Either destroy them all, or give me one!"

Every dragon and human in the room froze, the only motion the up and down heaving of chests, the only sound the echo of bubbling hot springs. The hairs on the back of Silver's neck rose.

It doesn't work that way, Kyan said calmly. *We don't have a supply at our disposal. They appear from the depths of the volcano, very rarely, and we follow to call to the human who is under trial for one. That is all.*

Silver's hands shook. She tried to clear her throat, but a stubborn lump remained. How was she supposed to translate when Sagittaria Wonder threatened the life of a water dragon?

"They can't . . . they don't have . . ." Silver croaked.

Sagittaria caught on. She nodded at the ornamental clasp around the Glithern's neck. "What about yours?"

It was only then that Silver noticed that each of the four regal water dragons wore their own stones, the individual colors blending seamlessly into their scales.

The same, Ssun choked as Sagittaria pressed her forearm more tightly around his neck. *They appear . . . we are called . . . to the council . . .*

Dortaal moved slowly toward Sagittaria. *It is thought they can be transferred through blood.*

"Transferred through blood?" Silver repeated. Kyan hissed.

Go on, the ancient Aquinder continued, as if Sagittaria Wonder could understand him. *Spill this water dragon's blood. See if the heartstone then becomes yours. Test the theory.*

"She cannot!" Silver cried.

Sagittaria Wonder hesitated as she looked from the water dragons to Silver, her hold on Ssun beginning to loosen, and Silver knew he'd called her bluff. But then, in a moment she would replay in her mind a thousand times, never certain what really happened, Dortaal moved quickly, grabbing some part of Sagittaria Wonder—her hair? her shoulder? the knife itself?—and thrusting her back so that the dagger nicked the side of Ssun's throat.

No! The furious cries of the water dragons engulfed Silver. She pressed her hands over her ears, but they were in her mind, their shock and anger and outrage. The room filled with their echoes, the sound a rising choir of despair. With a roar, Kyan and Ge encircled Ssun, teeth flashing at Sagittaria and Dortaal. The old Aquinder stared them down.

Abruqs danced around, their feet in a frenzy, uncertain whom they should protect, whom they should restrain. Ignoring them, Dortaal ripped the dragon heartstone from Ssun, smeared it through the small vein of blood dribbling down his neck, and presented it to Sagittaria.

You shed this water dragon's blood, and I am called to give this to you.

You cannot! Kyan said. But she didn't stop him. The theory had been tested and found sound.

The dagger clattered as Sagittaria dropped it and backed away. "No."

"What have you done?" Silver said. Her voice shook. Her hands went cold. The very room seemed to become a vacuum of impossibility. She didn't know if she was screaming at Sagittaria or at Dortaal. "Why did you do this?"

Water dragons murmured and shuffled. Ferdi put a hand on Silver's elbow, not to stop her anger from rising up, but to show support.

Do you think humans are the only ones driven by individual motivations? That we water dragons are all of one mind? Simple girl. Dortaal draped the bloodied heartstone around Sagittaria's neck. *I have waited an age for this.*

Sagittaria Wonder put one fingertip to the heartstone, stunned at first, but then her eyes began to sharpen. Calculating.

"Give it back," Silver said. Always, always, she wanted Sagittaria Wonder to be the hero of her younger days. "It's not yours."

It's hers, Dortaal corrected Silver. *And what wondrous things might she do with it? What is her great talent, Silver Batal? How will it be enhanced?*

With one great snarl, Kyan silenced the chaos in the room. Her eyes blazed with fury. She took two steps forward, planting herself directly in front of Dortaal, her paws wide on the ground. Tension crackled, every water dragon's back raised in expectation of something Silver didn't understand. Slowly, never taking her eyes from Dortaal, Kyan lifted and tapped her talons, one at a time, beginning from the outside and working her way in.

Tap, tap, tap, tap, tap.

Ge gasped.

"What's happening?" Silver asked Hiyyan. His mane brushed her face as he shook his head.

I don't know. I don't understand this.

No, Ssun moaned. *Do not do this on account of me.*

This, too, Kyan said, *has been a long time coming.*

Dortaal pulled himself to his full height. He was a massive, majestic water dragon. He laid his paws out before him, flat to the ground, just as dedicated to keeping his gaze locked with Kyan's.

Ge shook her multicolored head, distressed. *This is how water dragons formally challenge one another to battle. It is an honorable thing but . . . girl, I have never spent time among humans, but I've heard rumors of how terrible you can be to one another. So you probably don't understand this, but water dragon familial bonds are very important. Kyan challenging her own father is shocking!*

Hiyyan made a distressed sound in the back of his throat.

"That's her *father*?" Silver asked. But there wasn't time to explain, because even more slowly than Kyan's talons, Dortaal's claws tapped. One, then two. Three.

No! Ssun rose quickly to stop them, but just then, Dortaal pressed his final talon to the stone.

The battle began immediately. Teeth gnashing, claws slashing, colors blurring, fur flying. All other water dragons stood down and watched. The mineral scent of blood reached Silver. This couldn't be happening.

"Stop!" she screamed.

Ferdi grabbed Silver just as she'd decided to dash into the melee. The ground suddenly jerked under her, and she fell hard on one hip, Ferdi following to land awkwardly across her ankles. The fighting paused as the water dragons felt the tremor. Cracks opened in the stone walls. Aquinder and Glitherns breathed heavily, circling warily.

The tremblings, Ge said, and, as though calling up a force from the very center of the earth, the ground beneath Silver began to shake even more. A few bits of ceiling came crumbling down, and Silver shuffled closer to Hiyyan, pressing her shoulder against him. But the rattle lasted mere moments before settling.

"What's happening?" Ferdi got to his feet, then threw his arms out to maintain balance as the ground rolled once more.

There have always been tremblings, Dortaal said. *They mean nothing! Resume the battle or admit defeat and be dismissed from the council!*

"Don't fight!" Silver yelled.

This is the dragon way, Ge said.

Hiyyan growled. *I don't like it.*

The woman caused it, Ge said.

At this, several voices in the room rose up with a singular demand: *Throw the woman into the volcano!*

"I'll do it!" Silver snarled, reaching for Sagittaria.

No, this is deeper than the woman. Deeper than any human and not for them. Dismiss them. Spit them out! Kyan screamed at the walls.

A strange sensation came over Silver, turning her brain in circles and lifting nausea in her belly. Now the walls were shaking, too. She swayed as the room went fuzzy and then faded from her vision completely.

TWENTY-TWO

Silver rolled onto her side with a groan. Her back ached, and a fierce pounding in her head refused to be ignored. Was it too much to ask that she and Hiyyan would get *one* whole day of feeling good?

She opened her eyes to slits, the pale, northern morning light stinging her pupils. Ferdi stood over her.

"Please, Silver. Eat some breakfast today."

He asked so gently, a wobble of worry in his voice, that for the first time in three days, Silver took the bowl of porridge he offered her. In different circumstances, she would have enjoyed the richness of the coconut cream the grains were cooked in, but now they scraped painfully down her throat.

Ferdi sat at the bottom of Silver's cot. On the ground next to her, Hiyyan raised his head and rested his chin on Silver's leg, blinking his big, dark eyes at her.

An image of the Dragon Council room, and the four water dragons in power, filled Silver's mind.

Yes, she told Hiyyan. *We need to understand what happened there.*

And what happens next, Hiyyan replied.

Silver nodded.

They were on Ferdi's training island. Before that, the last she could remember, she was deep underground, trading a puzzling conversation with the council of water dragons. There was blood . . . Sagittaria with a heartstone in her hand . . . a terrible battle between father and daughter . . . the very core of the earth shaking. After that, the water dragons danced or swayed—or maybe it was the room that moved—and everything went dark. Silver bit her bottom lip. Somehow they'd punted her and Hiyyan and Ferdi out of their council room and across the seas.

She hadn't belonged there. They'd made that clear. Deeper than any human and not for them.

Silver pressed her fingers over the small lump in the chest pocket of her tunic. With shaking hands, she reached in and pulled out the dragon heartstone, her eyes filling with tears.

"And now there are three in the world," Silver said.

"What do you think Sagittaria will be able to do with hers?" Ferdi asked.

"I don't know. She's full of talents. What I don't understand is why she accepted it when she seems to want bonds and heartstones destroyed completely."

Hiyyan let loose a low growl. *She is wrong.*

Silver's thumb rubbed the heartstone slowly. *Is she? Without bonds and heartstones, the things in the council wouldn't have happened. I brought that chaos. I . . .*

Hiyyan growled again, this time flashing his teeth at Silver. *No! Sagittaria brought chaos. Your heart is true and loyal.*

Ferdi cleared his throat and gave them a sheepish look. "Uh, don't mean to interrupt, but I know you're talking and I'm feeling a little left out, here."

"Sorry, Ferdi. We're just trying to understand, well . . . everything."

"Sagittaria? The council? The battle?"

Silver winced.

Not for you, human, Hiyyan reminded her, gently.

Silver gazed at the Aquinder for a few beats of time. Maybe he was right and Silver had to keep her nose out of water dragon business. On the other hand, her bond connected her to the water dragon world in ways few other humans were. So . . . what was her place, then?

"What about the tremblings?" Silver asked. "Dortaal said they'd always been there, but the other dragons were alarmed."

Ferdi took Silver's empty bowl and stared at it, but he couldn't hide the troubled way his eyebrows drew together.

"In our stories, the Great Tremblings created the Island Nations. But they were created out of a darkness that we'd never want to see again." Ferdi shook his head. "They're just stories."

"There are a lot of things I used to think were just stories," Silver said, quietly. "But the more the world shows me, the more I find truth in the tales. We need to learn more." Silver counted on her fingers. "And we need to find out what Sagittaria and her new heartstone are up to. And we need to—"

"Find safety," Ferdi said firmly. "Because nothing will get done if you're always hiding. Come with me. My father hasn't wanted to get involved with you and Hiyyan any more than he already has. But things are changing . . . are happening. The time for political apathy is over. Stand before him with me, Silver, and together we'll demand action."

"And if he refuses to help?"

"Whatever you need, I'll help you. Wherever you go, I'll come. And if my father can't make a promise of protection to you . . ." Ferdi's eyes went mischievous, but there was a determined strength behind them, too. A prince on the verge of becoming a king. "Then he'll see what kind of son he's raised."

"*HHHHHuuurrrrrgh!*" Hiyyan roared his approval.

Silver's smile was tiny, but it was sincere.

She kneaded the back of her neck for a moment.

Ferdi is right. And his offer is noble. But we're close to the Watchers' Keep. We should check on Kirja and Nebekker and Mele before we go to the Island Nations. They need safety, too. Silver felt Hiyyan's pang of longing to see his mother. Felt it not only through their bond but also as an echo of her own longing to see her family. The pull to go south to Jaspaton was stronger than it had ever been. She couldn't even guess when she'd step foot in the deserts again.

"Tomorrow," Silver said. "Today, I regain my strength. Tomorrow, we return to the Keep. After that, to your home, Ferdi."

Ferdi reached a hand out, squeezed Silver's fingers once, and nodded.

◊ ◊ ◊

AN IMPOSSIBLY WARM breeze ruffled Silver's hair. It was growing back, tickling the base of her neck now.

"The Calidian Stream," Ferdi said, his approach across the island beach nearly soundless. "It's a warm current that flows north for a week or two every winter. An anomaly of weather."

"It will make our passage to your home island a little less brutal." Silver gazed over the seas. Ferdi had mapped out a route for her and Hiyyan to take. It cut through the Iceberg Seas as far north as possible. There would be warriors along the way to ensure her safety.

"I hope to . . ." Ferdi trailed off, his cheeks flushing pink.

. . . *make everything less brutal for you,* Silver finished in her own mind. Was that what Ferdi was going to say, or just what she hoped would happen?

To her left, Hiyyan and Hoonazoor lay on the sandy beach, singing to each other. Their notes unraveled into words for Silver. A conversation about what the Island Nations were like. Hoonazoor changed the direction by asking about the water dragon council. Hiyyan raised his head and caught Silver watching them. He hesitated and Silver felt a pang of curiosity. Was Hiyyan avoiding Hoonazoor's question because he didn't know the answer, or because Silver would overhear?

Sensing her turmoil, Hiyyan sent Silver a blanket of warm emotions. Yes, there was a lot for them to figure out, existing between the water dragon and the human worlds as they did, but they would do it together.

Ferdi gave Silver a sidelong glance and a smile. "I wish I could understand them."

Silver didn't reply. She watched Ferdi step lightly across a series of rocks, his arm disappearing into the tide pools several times. There was something special about seeing him in his natural habitat—the ocean—that reminded her of seeing water dragons on the sea for the first time. They all belonged somewhere. They all drew their strength from a place, from home. Silver wondered how much her life would change once they'd convinced King A-Malusni to protect them. Once they'd figured out how to make Hiyyan free and would spend fewer and fewer moments in her desert home as they raced across the globe. Could she ever be as strong in the ocean as she was in the desert? Would she ever gain that way that Ferdi had—that way of interacting with the environment so naturally, so full of wisdom and confidence?

Or would she always feel like an outsider?

"What are you hunting for?" Silver asked. Ferdi leaped, his feet sure on the slippery rocks, and drove his hand into the water again.

"Whatever the sea provides." He straightened up and grinned, holding his arm high. The weak winter sky backlit him, so he looked like a magnificent granite statue of a warrior. A wiggling, multilegged creature dangled from his hand. "Octopus. Delicious. And there's loads of laver here. Sea greens," he amended, seeing Silver's confusion.

Ferdi came back to the beach and pulled out a knife. With swift expertise, he cleaned the octopus, sliced it into pieces, and wrapped it in the sea greens. He passed several little packages to Silver. "Breakfast. For strength."

She sniffed the food, forcing her expression to remain neutral even though the briny scent was heavy enough to make her stomach flip-flop. It was just different, she reminded herself. An entire civilization thrived on this kind of food.

She popped one package into her mouth and chewed. The taste was sharp, the texture chewy at first, then tender.

"It's good," she said.

Ferdi laughed. "Don't sound so surprised. I'm actually a pretty decent cook. It's either learn how to make delicious things from what the seas provide or live off those horrible hard crackers I'm always sent on my journeys with."

Silver thought about what Brajon would make of the octopus packages. It would probably tear him apart, his love of food warring with his dislike of everything about the ocean. Despite her exhaustion, Silver laughed.

"What?"

"I'm imagining Brajon doing what you just did. He'd fall in before he'd ever catch anything, and then if he did catch something, he'd probably refuse to eat it, whining about not knowing if it was poisonous and wishing he'd brought his mom along to cook for him."

"He has it good. Desert food is wonderful," Ferdi said.

"Islander food is pretty great, too." Silver shared a smile with Ferdi, then dropped her lashes, her cheeks flushing with warmth.

"Good enough to make you hurry to the islands, once you're done at the Keep?"

"I don't need good food for that," Silver said.

Silver looked at her hands, chapped from salt water and callused from where she gripped Hiyyan's mane as she rode the water dragon. Her fingertips would always be that sickly shade of gray. The water dragon–shaped burn scar would always pucker at her wrist.

"What's wrong?" Ferdi said, brushing his hands of the last of their meal.

"Nothing. Thinking about home."

Ferdi looked thoughtful. "You'll be a hero to them, you know."

"Not to my father." Silver shook her head and looked down again.

Ferdi leaned forward, twisting his head upside down so that Silver had to look at him. A laugh burst from her without warning.

Ferdi sat back on his heels, pleased. "I get it. I know all about complicated fathers."

"Better than most, I suppose." Silver curled a strand of hair around her finger as she pondered. "Ferdi, what do you think the gift will be? The one the heartstone will enhance?"

Instead of answering, Ferdi asked a question of his own. "When Sagittaria says she cares only about water dragons, and nothing more, do you believe her?"

Before seeing Kyan and Dortaal face off, Silver would have answered with an emphatic *no*. But maybe Sagittaria Wonder knew things Silver didn't. Things about underground rumblings and council members who did—and certainly did *not*—want to have any involvement whatsoever with humans.

Was her bond with Hiyyan wrong? Even if it was, would it change anything? Silver could never want to sever her bond with Hiyyan. He didn't seem to want that, either, even when he was faced with the water dragon council. With his kind, with his home.

Home is beside you. Always.

That was the most important truth, wasn't it?

Still, she wished someone she trusted could answer her questions. Nebekker's life of hiding away meant the old woman knew little. And Sagittaria Wonder's villainous behavior meant Silver couldn't safely turn to her.

A face flashed in her mind: a shaven head tattooed with the constellations, layers of cloaks and belts concealing all manner of herbal tinctures and mystic paraphernalia.

Arkilah.

Silver shuddered and pushed the image from her brain. Perhaps the threat of the unknown was more terrifying than what Silver did know.

"I don't know." Silver stood. "I don't know a lot of things. But I do know that Hiyyan's healed. I have my dragon heart-stone. What comes next . . . ? I think . . . I fear . . . it will be a lot. I'm going to need your father's help. I have so many questions, but there have to be answers out there somewhere. And I have to go—now—to begin finding them."

"You know you have help, Silver. His, mine, all my people's." As if to seal the promise, Ferdi placed his hand over his heart and grinned.

TWENTY-THREE

Under the soft light of winter's midmorning, Hiyyan lowered his body for Silver to climb on. He waited a moment, even after she'd settled astride and one of her hands was wrapped in his mane, to allow Silver to squeeze the dragon heartstone in her other palm and send her thoughts to Kirja.

Silver blinked at a starry sky that seemed close enough to swim in and waited. How far could she send her communications with the assistance of the heartstone?

Is it safe back at the Keep? she tried.

It is safe. We are the only guests here.

Silver smiled to herself, looking down at the heartstone. Very far, then.

"Let's go." Hiyyan inhaled two deep breaths, then made two running leaps, and they took to the skies.

It was night when they reached the mighty stone Keep at the summit of the mountain. Hiyyan landed heavily in front of the entrance, sending Silver rolling into the fresh, powdery snow. Silver remained on her back, staring narrow-eyed up at the Aquinder. Hiyyan snorted a few laughs.

"One of these days I'll trade you for a less troublesome water dragon," Silver said. "A sweet little Snowfluff dragon, maybe?"

Hiyyan blew a cloud of steam into her face and chuckled again.

Silver stood and pounded on the massive wooden Keep door. Mele opened the door, just like the last time Silver had come to the Keep. She and Hiyyan entered, letting the heavy tapestry fall behind them.

"You've come back," Mele said. There was uncertainty in her voice.

"You wondered if we ever would?" Silver said.

Mele bit her lip, wanting to say more, but a sound across the great room changed her mind. Both girls looked to where Nebekker stood at the top of the staircase, appearing far healthier than the last time Silver had seen her. The old woman still leaned heavily on her walking stick, but her face was full of color once more and her eyes shined with depth of curiosity.

"And so the two of you have returned in one piece," Nebekker said. She descended, her walking stick punctuating every stair and step she took. "I am glad you weren't lost."

Silver rubbed the back of her glove across her mouth. Yes, she and Hiyyan were there, and they hadn't lost each other. They were more strongly bonded than ever before.

But Silver had lost other things, though it was hard to really put her finger on what. She felt tired and a bit older, sadder and more fearful than she ever had in her life.

But there was, as there always was, hope.

"You look healthy," Silver said.

"I feel hale as a great racer. Ready to take on an army of water dragons."

Silver raised an eyebrow at the mention of an army of dragons. *What did the old yarnslady actually know?* Before she could ask, Mele piped up.

"*You* look like you could use some food."

"I'm desperate for a hot meal or three," Silver admitted. There would be time to question Nebekker later.

"Come on, then." Mele headed across the room.

"She's made herself useful here," Nebekker said.

"My talent for hospitality, you mean?" Mele shared a meaningful smirk with Nebekker.

"It's amazing what one can get away with when they make themselves agreeable. A certain desert fox could learn something about patience, about the delicate art of fading into the background instead of always being front and center. This one's a listener of the finest sort." Nebekker cocked her head to one side. "A bit of a Watcher, as well."

Silver dropped her gaze to the ground. She couldn't help who she was . . . but maybe she could learn to be *more* things.

"What has she been seeing?" Silver said.

A cloud fell over Nebekker's face. "We'll discuss that after you've had a meal and a rest."

A sharp pain like a desert scorpion bite burrowed into Silver's chest, but she bit her tongue. If Nebekker thought it best she waited to hear the news, then she would wait. Be patient.

Silver joined Mele and Nebekker at the dining table for

flatbreads topped with meat in a garlicky eggplant and yogurt sauce.

"Tell me, did you recover your heartstone?" Nebekker added a pinch of sumac and a drizzle of pomegranate molasses to her bowl.

"Yes," Silver said.

Mele leaned forward, her food untouched. "Was it a great battle between you and Sagittaria?"

"The biggest battle was against a volcano rat." Silver wiped her mouth with a napkin and sat back. Thinking about what had happened in the dragon council lair dashed away her appetite.

Silver told them about getting to the coast, finding Ferdi, following Sagittaria into the underwater volcano, and the chase through tunnels and across lava pits.

"And then we went through a kind of hidden door and were in the council's den."

"What was it like?" Mele asked.

Silver told her about the various dragons, including the four leaders.

"More Aquinder," Mele breathed.

"One of the things that stood out the most to me was how independent they were, how they lead and ruled without input from humans."

"Different than our racing-obsessed lifestyles," Mele said.

"Right." Silver nodded and looked at Nebekker. "Two things are troubling me. One, Sagittaria got her hands on a heartstone." Silver ignored Mele's *meep!* "And two, the council talked about trembles starting up again. Do you know what that all means?"

Nebekker pushed her bowl away and shook her head. "No,

quakes aren't uncommon, but the fact that the dragons are noticing more seems to mean something, doesn't it?"

"Stay for a while and let's search the library for clues," Mele said.

"What I really want is to go home." A vision of her parents made Silver's eyes mist up. She blinked it away. "But I can't. Not yet. Ferdi's mapped out a covert path to the Island Nations, with his warriors stationed along the way. He assures me we'll get to King A-Malusni safely, and we might be able to discover some clues about the tremblings in his culture's old stories. But we have to leave tonight, under cover of darkness."

Out the window, the twilight sky was streaked with rose-jelly pinks. It was a lazy, olden-days sky, the kind Silver would have appreciated without a care in the world back in her Jaspatonian life. But now, it just meant it was time to be on the move again. Silver looked from Nebekker to Mele, ready to see their nods and hear their agreements with Silver's plan. Except . . .

"I'm staying," Mele declared, avoiding Silver's searching look. "Something is keeping me here, and I'm not sure what it is. A feeling. I'm going to stay until I sort that out."

Silver set her spoon gently on the table. Dinner was turning into a rock in her belly.

"But Mele—"

"I'm better off here, searching that library for clues. Jaspaton isn't *my* home, and I don't need King A-Malusni's help with anything. In fact . . ."

"You have his water dragon."

"Silver Batal." Mele wagged her spoon at Silver. "Aren't you the one always telling me that water dragons don't belong to any human? That Luap and I, bonded as we are, are meant to be together?"

Silver's laugh was a little sad. She appraised her friend in the low golden candlelight. She had dragged Mele through more than the girl had ever bargained for already. Could she really blame her for wanting to remain somewhere safe, warm, and full of the kind of knowledge Mele was most interested in? The race for Aquinder freedom—and Silver's, too—wasn't Mele's, it was Silver's alone.

"It's true. You don't have his dragon. Luap is her own dragon. And you're your own person. Which means . . ." Silver sighed. "I'll miss you."

"Same."

Silver nodded and sat tall once more. "Nebekker? Will you be ready soon?"

The old woman sipped a hot chocolate complacently. "Kirja and I are going west."

"West?" Silver's spoon rattled against the table as her knee bumped the wood with shock. "What in the deserts for?"

"In search of information that will help shed light on what you saw in the dragon council den. Perhaps in search of legend and lore. And, above all, in search of an old friend, Silver." Nebekker set her mug down. "It's time Arkilah and I had our reckoning. Mele saw her returning to the deep deserts in the Ever."

"What will you do when you find her?" Silver said.

Nebekker stood and pulled her hood over her head. "I only look wise, Silver Batal. Even an old woman like me acts on half-formed plans sometimes. The hope that they'll work out in the end never truly fades away. We become more wary, true, but we also believe harder that things will work out for the best, whatever that might be. Arkilah knows things that I need to know, too."

"And that *I* need to know! What else are the heartstones capable of? What can Sagittaria Wonder do with hers? What's the queen planning next? And the rumbles the dragon council mentioned?" Silver's mind swirled with all the things she needed to know. "I'm coming with you. The Island Nations can wait."

Nebekker came around the table to stand next to Silver's chair. The old yarnslady looked down on Silver, and there it was: that warm, grandmotherly expression. Maybe Silver was still Nebekker's favorite scrappy young person, after all.

"Your safety in the Island Nations *can't* wait." Nebekker's hand rested on Silver's shoulder. "It's time, Silver, for you to learn something. Your desires are not at the center of our journeys. We are your loyal friends. We love you deeply. We will help when we can. But we are all on our own paths. You and me and Mele. Even Hiyyan, Kirja, Luap. Let us help when we can, when we offer. And let us go when we don't. I'm going to the deep deserts alone."

From any other person, said in any other way, Silver would feel reprimanded. But Nebekker's words put into the air something Silver had been coming to understand on her own, and instead of feeling shameful, she felt stronger than ever. Proud and understanding.

Her dream of water dragon racing still danced at the edges of her future, but it didn't have anything to do with anyone else, and that was okay. Her goals and plans were shifting into bigger things, like freedom and the bonds between humans and water dragons, and that was okay, too.

She nodded at Nebekker. A part of her wanted to ask when

she'd see Nebekker again or to make plans to meet up in a particular place and a particular time, but something told her that they would find each other again when the time was right, simple as that.

It's time to leave, Silver sent to Hiyyan, down in the Dragon Den. And then he, too, needed to be asked a certain question: *Are you coming with me?*

Hiyyan's delight was brief, but Silver felt it as a delicious warmth in her arms and legs.

I am coming with you. You are my human.

Silver rose and hugged Nebekker, even though the old woman straightened her back like a prickly desert shrub and mumbled something about disliking good-byes.

"Keep watching," Silver said to Mele.

And then she was off, gathering her things, bounding down the stairs to the great room, and dashing out the side door, where Hiyyan waited. She climbed on, relishing their connection as they moved as one. Silver pulled out the rough map Ferdi had sketched her and sent a vision of it to Hiyyan. The grand Aquinder spread his wings.

"To the sky, to the sea, to the islands, where we'll be free," Silver said against the frosty night sky.

Hiyyan roared at the stars.

A new race had begun.

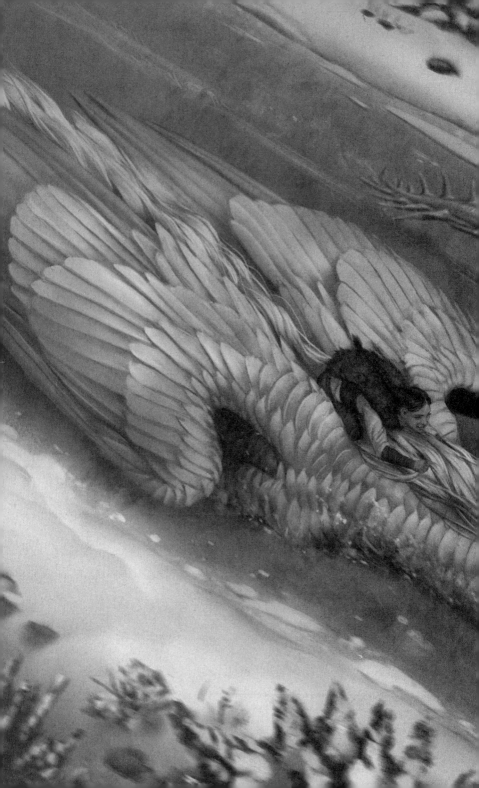

SNUCKER

Acknowledgments

I brim over with gratitude when I think about all the hard work and heart that goes into putting Silver Batal's adventures into book form.

To my editor, Tiffany Liao: Your strengths and talents counterbalance my weaknesses. I am becoming a better writer, thanks to you. I deeply appreciate your vision for these books and this series, your thoughtfulness and insight, and your in-house advocacy for our project.

The Holt/Macmillan team is a powerhouse that I'm so grateful to have in my corner. Thanks to all, and most especially to Christian Trimmer, editorial director; Mark Podesta, assistant editor; Lindsay Wagner, production editor; Jie Yang, production manager; Brittany Pearlman, senior publicist; Mariel Dawson, executive director of ad/promo; Lucy Del Priore, school and library marketing director; and Jen Edwards, head of sales.

I am also grateful to all the book stores, small and large alike, who have stocked my books on their shelves. Thanks to Jess Brigman for so passionately getting SILVER out there!

The cover and interior illustrations, and the book design, take my breath away. Sincerest thank-yous to artist Ilse Gort and designer Liz Dresner, who probably have holes in their tongues for how often they must bite them when someone says, "You can't judge a book by its cover." (You know better, and it shows in the best way possible.)

Agent Brent Taylor is the best human in the business. Thank you for your boundless energy, your endless enthusiasm, your relentless strategizing and negotiation, and for being an advocate of the highest order. I'm so glad we get to work together. Thank you also to Uwe Stender and the entire TriadaUS team.

My family means everything to me. I am so grateful for their patience, cheerleading, pride, and generosity. Thank you for keeping me grounded, when required, and letting me soar, when needed. I love you.